THE WATCHERS IN THE SHADOWS

Gordon MacLeish's hideous painting materialized before Robin's eyes again. The Watcher, fanged mouth gaping, stared at the children picking flowers, white eyes on fire with a hatred that yearned to destroy them.

"Dear Jesus..." Robin put a hand to her mouth.

With a hunger that sought to devour them.

That was the real horror in MacLeish's painting. The obscenity. The thing in the shadows wanted more than death, more than mere destruction.

But this is no painting, Robin's mind screamed. This is a photograph, and I know it's real because I took it!

The Feeding

Leigh Clark

LEISURE BOOKS NEW YORK CITY

A LEISURE BOOK®

July 1992

Published by

Dorchester Publishing Co., Inc.
276 Fifth Avenue
New York, NY 10001

Printed in the United States of America.

The Feeding

PROLOGUE
The Portrait

It was an ordinary family portrait.

The kind you put on top of the piano, or give to the grandparents for Christmas.

The last one had been taken more than three years ago. Katie was almost seven now, Joshua ten. Photographers' families are seldom photographed. Robin the professional took this one like any amateur, tripping the time-release shutter on her Hasselblad before running over to the sofa to pose with her arms around the rest of them, smiling at the camera.

She came out looking ten years younger, as usual, with dark blond hair falling in loose curls to her shoulders and a bright smile reflecting none of the tension that lay coiled beneath the surface of her marriage. The tension showed on Matt, her husband. His face was tight with intensity and concern as he sat there on the sofa, right arm hugging Katie, left arm around Joshua. Katie looked like a mischievous blond elf, blue eyes sparkling with the brilliance of sunlight on clear water. Joshua, his reddish brown hair more or less combed, displayed the slight belligerence of a normal boy. A make-believe toughness, tempered by an easy smile and honest brown eyes, seemed to conceal nothing.

It was only later, after the horror had come upon them all, that you could detect something else—something deep within those honest eyes.

A darkness, cold and distant.

Waiting, patiently, for the appointed time.

I: The Calling

1

The Bone Pile

It began with the accident.

But there were other warnings.

Earlier in the day, out in the desert northeast of Los Angeles, they had pulled into one of those gas stations with a few dusty palm trees and a faded billboard advising motorists that this was their last chance for the next 100 miles.

Robin Brenner stood beside their silver-gray Mercedes-Benz 500 SEL in the white heat, wishing she had worn shorts and halter top instead of the jeans and sweater intended for the car's air-conditioning and the cooler temperatures of the High Sierras. Her right hand shaded her eyes as she looked at the dirty stucco station and the peeling GAS-FOOD-ICE sign above its door.

Katie pulled at her left hand. "Mommy, I'm hot."

"Hundred and six right now." The attendant pumping gas into the Mercedes was a withered man with gray stubble on his head and chin. "Get up to maybe a hundred and nine, hundred and twelve before the day's out."

"That sure is hot," Matt Brenner agreed, stretching next to the gas pump.

"It'll be cool in the mountains, Katie," Robin said.

"We'll never get there." Katie kicked at gravel with her new white Reeboks. "We been drivin' all day."

"Not much farther to go." Robin put an affectionate arm around her daughter. "Just hang in there, baby."

The attendant squinted at Robin. "Where you folks from?"

"L.A." Robin smiled at him. "Pacific Palisades."

"What part of them mountains you headed for?"

"Black Cavern," Robin said. "It's in the Sierras, not far from—"

"I know where it's at." The attendant picked up a rag and started to wipe dead bugs off the windshield.

"You know more than I do," Matt Brenner said. "I never heard of the place until she dug it up somewhere."

"It was in the *Times* travel section," Robin said.

"Friend o'mine used to live up thataway." The attendant rubbed hard at a petrified bug. "Don't live there no more."

"Moved?" Matt asked.

"Dead." The attendant looked up from the windshield. "Died in them mountains. Had people somewheres in Indiana. Hauled the body back there for burial. Least they said it was his body. Wasn't nobody wanted to take a real close look."

Joshua put down his *Alien Attack!* video game and climbed out of the back seat to come stand beside his father. "What'd the guy die from?" Joshua asked.

"Never said." The attendant grinned down at the boy. Some of the old man's teeth were missing, the rest stained or rotted. "Maybe curiosity. They say curiosity killed the cat."

"We got a cat back home," Joshua said, "but he's not curious. His name's Superman. He's fat and he sleeps all the time. He'll probably die from a heart attack."

The attendant started to squeegee down the windshield. "Black Cavern even made the local paper th'other day. Somethin' about all them bones they found up thataway."

"Bones?" Joshua moved forward, the dry desert wind ruffling his reddish brown hair.

"Big pile of 'em." The attendant used the squeegee to mark the height of the bone pile. "Two old boys on this gov'ment money, up there to check out which way them caves—"

"The complete cavern network's never been fully explored," Robin interrupted.

"That's right, ma'am." The attendant nodded at her. "Big old dark hole in the ground. Ain't nobody knows how long she runs or just where she ends up."

He paused. The silence of the white heat was broken only by the distant hum of traffic from the desert highway and the sharp squeak of the attendant's squeegee as it scraped across the windshield.

"So," he continued, "these two old gov'ment cave boys, they head on up thataway, and find this big heap o' bones, like I say. They get all shook up over it, so they call in the state troopers. And some boys from the local paper shows up along with 'em."

"What did it turn out to be?" Matt asked. "An Indian burial ground?"

The attendant grinned. "Well, now, if it was Indians, they musta been on the warpath not too far back, 'cause some of them bones still had pieces o'fresh meat stickin' to 'em."

"Oh, yucch!" Katie closed her eyes and grimaced. "Gross!"

Robin took her by the arm. "We're going to go get something to drink. Joshua?"

"Were they human bones?" Joshua asked, awestruck.

Robin walked over and gripped her son's wrist hard. "I said we're going to get something to drink, Joshua."

"Coke machine over by the far wall, ma'am," the attendant offered. "Have to hit it a few times to make it work."

"Thanks a lot," Robin said.

Joshua looked back longingly over his shoulder, all the way to the door.

After they were gone, Matt Brenner asked, "Were they human bones?"

"Well, now . . ." The attendant squinted up into the sun. "They were chopped up, messed around some, but it ain't hard to tell human ones. Not if you ever seen 'em before."

"Did the two speleologists finish their work?"

"That's the real funny part." The attendant moved over to the side windows. "Newsboys come back the next day with a TV crew, and damned if them bones ain't all gone. And them two old gov'ment cave boys along with 'em. Clean vanished."

"What happened?"

"Now that's real hard to say." The attendant ran a hand over the stubble on the side of his face, the hand trembling slightly. "It's a awful big sink hole they got themselves up there. Mighty easy to lose your way in the dark or fall down some steep shaft. Never hit bottom."

Matt stared at the old man. "How do you know about this?"

The attendant's face turned pale. "Maybe I read the local paper now and then."

"Did you see those bones yourself?"

The pale face flinched. "Maybe I got another friend left that place 'bout the same time as th'other. But maybe this one was a mite luckier and didn't leave in no closed box."

Maybe he's pumping gas now at some dried-up station in the middle of the desert, Matt thought, but he asked, "When did all this happen?"

"Maybe two months back. Maybe three, four." The attendant squinted at the highway in the distance.

And at something beyond the highway.

"Time runs all together out here. Hard to keep track of where you're at." His voice dropped to a murmur. "All's you know for sure's you ain't there." He turned suddenly to Matt Brenner, asking in a loud voice, "Need your oil checked, mister?"

"No," Matt said. "The oil's all right."

Later, back on the road, Katie was busy preparing her Princess Leia doll for marriage to her Han Solo doll. The Luke Skywalker doll would be best man. She was humming a version of the Wedding March to herself.

Joshua stopped pretending to play *Alien Attack!* "Dad," he said, looking up, "where did those bones come from?"

"Joshua." Robin shot him a warning glance. "We're not going to get started on that again."

"Bones!" Katie made a face. "Gross!"

Joshua ignored his sister. "I saw you talkin' to him, Dad. What'd he say? Where'd they come from?"

"Joshua . . ." Robin began.

"Turns out they were only cow bones, scout." Matt glanced at his son in the rearview mirror. "Some crooks stole a rancher's cows, then took the meat and dumped the bones in the cave."

"What were the cows doin' up there in the mountains?"

Matt hesitated. "The cows were farther down near the valley. The crooks just dumped the bones in the cave because I guess they thought no one would ever look there."

Joshua slumped back into the seat, his face long with disappointment. "Cow bones!"

"Cow bones!" Katie grimaced again. "Gross!"

2

Accident

By nightfall they were in the mountains.

Headlights caught flashes of pine trees, guard-rail, boulders, steep rock face; heating replaced air-conditoning to ward off the chill night air. Katie lay curled up asleep with Han Solo and Princess Leia safe in her arms, dreaming of their wedding. Joshua slumped against the back seat door, hands in his lap, holding *Alien Attack!*, head back, eyes closed and mouth open, as if he had fallen asleep counting stars.

Robin looked at her husband for several minutes, his face dimly outlined by dash lights, before she asked in a low voice, almost a whisper, "Were they really cow bones?"

He glanced over at her. "You too, huh?"

She frowned. "Be serious. If they found something like that near Black Cavern . . ." She let the sentence hang. "Maybe we should go to Yosemite instead."

"Black Cavern's less crowded. Just you, me, the kids—and the bone monster."

"Okay! Make a joke out of it." Robin turned away from him and stared out the window at the dark landscape rushing past.

"Hey." Matt touched her shoulder. "Robin?"

She continued staring out the window.

Matt cleared his throat. "Okay, the old fart at the gas station said he thought they were human bones. Whatever they were, nothing's there now."

Robin turned from the window. "What happened?"

"Just disappeared. According to him."

She put a hand to her throat. "My God, who took 'em?"

"No one." Matt laughed. "He probably made the whole damn thing up. A little tale of terror along with your gas, compliments of the management."

Robin shivered, shifting closer to her husband. "But what if it's true?"

"You can take a picture of it. Call it 'Troll's Den.' "

"Very funny."

Matt smiled at her. "You know, babe, you're taking it just a bit too seriously. Forget it, okay?"

Robin wrinkled her forehead. "Maybe we shouldn't go there, Matt."

He raised an eyebrow. "Hey, whose idea was this fun vacation, anyway?"

"I didn't mean—" Robin started.

"*Vista Encantada* is only the biggest project of my entire career, and right now it's getting bitched up six different ways to Sunday by Ed Jackson and his Z-Team shitheads."

Robin let out a long sigh and suddenly felt very old and tired. She was sorry they ever made him head of *Vista Encantada.* He had accused her, more than once, of feeling that way, but she had always denied it, always claiming she was so happy for him because she knew how much it meant . . . but it was all bullshit. She hated the goddamn *Vista Encantada.* I don't use my work as an excuse to ignore my family, she thought resentfully. She remembered all the photographic assignments she had turned down—including one that would have paid her expenses to New Zealand—because she had to do something for the kids or Matt. If Ed Jackson really did screw up *Vista Encantada* beyond repair, it might just turn out to be the best thing for everybody. God forgive me, she thought, reverting unconsciously to the habits of her Catholic childhood—although she no longer believed in God and had no real wish to be forgiven.

Vista Encantada was a sprawling shopping center-office building-amusement park-condominium development south of Los Angeles on the Orange County coast. The ad campaign had started months before initial bidding even opened. LIVE! WORK! SHOP! PLAY! IN THE MAXI-ENVIRONMENT OF THE FUTURE. *VISTA ENCANTADA.* THE ENCHANTED VISION OF YOUR CALIFORNIA DREAMS. Matt Brenner's company, CalForm, Inc., won the contract and made Matt head architect in charge of concept design. It was the kind of chance he had dreamed of for years. He was delighted, and so was top management.

No one was delighted about his request for two weeks off right in the middle of the project, but CalForm liked to see its key people keep their marriages together, and the Brenners' family counselor, Dr. Sidney Greenberg, had recommended some kind of vacation. Immediately. A recuperative recess, Dr. Greenberg had called it. Career suicide was Matt's description. But he wanted to keep the marriage together, too, and things were getting bad.

"We've been through all this before, Matt," Robin said evenly. "We both know how important *Vista Encantada* is and how busy you are, but—"

"Don't sweat it. I'll have lots of free time after *Vista Encantada* goes down the tubes."

"But," Robin ignored him, "we also know that our family is more important than anybody's work—yours or mine—and we both decided that what we need right now, all of us, is some real time together."

"Some time, sure, but two whole weeks? One week's more than enough for Jackson and the Z-team to put *Vista Encantada* right down the toilet."

Robin tried to smile. "Darling, you're a workaholic. We'll need at least two weeks to detox you. Besides, we both agreed."

"You agreed. Then you made me agree."

"Poor baby." Robin reached over and pinched his cheek sharply.

"Hey! No touching the driver while he's on duty!"

Robin snuggled close to him. "You sure about that?"

"Well, I guess it all depends on just where you

want to touch him."

She clapped a hand over his mouth. "There are children sleeping in this car," she whispered in his ear.

"Them?" Matt glanced over his shoulder at the back seat. "They're dead to the world. When we get there, we'll have to throw cold water—"

"Matt!"

Robin's scream burst inside his ear. The children started from sleep with cries and whimpers. Matt jerked around and saw a blazing wreck sprawled across the end of a long, blind curve, rushing up into the headlights. The front end was shattered where the car had crashed head-on against the rock face, flames leaping up from the burning engine.

Matt jumped on the brakes. They grabbed hard and locked, throwing the Mercedes into a wild spin. He steered with it, his body responding automatically as he tried desperately to figure out what they could be skidding on. No ice this low in summer. No recent rains. No . . .

Gasoline—flooding from the burning wreck out across the asphalt, waiting for a stray spark to flash into a river of fire.

Matt accelerated and turned hard right, away from the drop-off. Sliding out of the spin sideways, with tires squealing, the car hit the inside guardrail, smashed through it, past a wall of pine trees, and jolted to a stop, loose rocks grinding and thumping beneath the belly of the Mercedes.

Clouds of dust swirled in front of the headlights. Katie was screaming uncontrollably, while Joshua tried to shut her up, his own voice shaking.

Robin sat tensed, both arms braced rigidly against the dashboard. "Dear God . . ." She closed her eyes and shuddered. "Christ!"

Matt opened his door.

Joshua reached for the back door handle. "I'm goin' with you, Dad."

Matt turned on him. "You're staying right there with your sister until I tell you to move. Understand?"

Joshua shrank back into the seat. "Yes, sir."

Robin grabbed her husband's arm. "Matt, that thing's on fire. It could explode."

He got out of the car and locked the door behind him.

Matt could smell it now, the slightly sweet, gut-wrenching smell of roasting human flesh. He started breathing through his mouth. He got out two flares from the Mercedes' trunk and placed them down the road to warn approaching traffic, then he moved in on the burning wreck.

It had been a Toyota Corolla, '77 or '78, bright yellow. Matt approached it from the driver's side, the point of initial impact. It had crumpled in on the driver. They would need the Jaws of Life to get him out, but there was not much time. A few more minutes and the gas tank would go.

As Matt moved in closer he could feel the heat of the flames. He bent down to look through what remained of the driver's shattered side window, and saw that they could forget the Jaws of Life. The driver was young, barely out of his teens. The steering column had crushed his chest to a dark red pulp, pinning him against the crumpled front seat like an insect on a display board. Flying glass from the shattered window had shredded his face; loose flaps of skin stirred in the sharp mountain wind. Thick smoke rose from the front seat where a small but intense fire burned in the cushion, feeding itself on fat from the driver's thigh.

Matt drew back, inhaling a lungful of acrid grease smoke.

He heard it then.

High-pitched, piercing, like the whine of an engine pushed to breaking point, it came from a girl huddled in a corner of the cramped back seat. Her left leg was slashed and bleeding, the right one missing from mid-thigh down. Blood spurted from the ragged stump, forming a thick puddle. The girl screamed like a wounded animal, eyes rolling back until only the whites showed.

Matt moved fast around the burning front end of the passenger door, skidding on the slick, oil-covered pavement.

The passenger seat was frozen solid. He pushed on the release catch, but nothing happened. He could feel the heat on his back and taste greasy smoke from the burning corpse in the driver's seat. He grabbed hold of the passenger seat and pulled on it until flashes of pain shot up his arms. It gave, but as he started to lift out the injured girl, she struck at him blindly. Blood gushed from the stump. Matt felt it running down his forearms, warm and viscous.

He carried her over to the shoulder across from the wreck. Robin was out of the Mercedes by now, running toward him as he lowered the girl onto the cold gravel shoulder.

"Oh, my God," Robin whispered, tears gathering in her eyes. "Matt, she's dying!"

He tore off his jacket and tied it around the bleeding stump. The jacket turned dark red in seconds, almost black in the flickering light of the burning wreck. He twisted the arms of the jacket to form a makeshift tourniquet.

"Stay with her." He got awkwardly to his feet, turning back to the wreck.

Robin took the girl's right hand gently in her own. The girl gripped Robin's hand suddenly with both of hers, pressing into the bone so hard Robin winced. Then the girl began screaming again, a high, thin sound on the cold mountain wind.

"There now." Tears spilled down Robin's cheeks. "There, there."

A large section of the front seat cushion was on fire, and Matt's eyes stung fiercely as he stared into the thick, nauseating smoke. The girl and boy might have been traveling by themselves, each taking turns at the wheel while the other slept. But they were young, heartbreakingly young. At that age you usually carry as many friends as the car will hold.

Matt was still searching when he heard the cry.

At first he thought it was the gas tank finally catching fire. He jumped back from the car, heart pounding hard in his chest. Then he heard it again and knew what it was. He stuck his head back into the greasy smoke, groping around until he found the screamer. He was wedged upside down behind the driver's seat and as Matt pulled him loose, the scream became unbearable—loud, raw, angry, nothing like the dying whine of the girl with the severed leg. It was the scream of someone still living, still fighting hard to stay alive.

Matt dragged him out of the Toyota's smoke-filled interior just before his own lungs gave out. The boy's screams turned into deep, wracking coughs. Matt coughed with him as he moved away from the burning car, over to the shoulder where Robin knelt beside the girl with the severed leg. The girl's blonde hair lay soaking in the blood that pooled around her head like a black halo.

Robin looked up, her face wet with tears. "Matt," she whispered, "she's dead."

"This one's not." Matt coughed violently. "Not yet, anyway."

As Matt lowered the boy onto the gravel shoulder, he cried out again.

Robin leaned forward. "Matt, he's hurt bad."

"I think he'll make it."

"Is anyone else still inside?"

"The driver." Matt wiped grease from his face. "But there's no point bringing him out. He's on fire."

Robin stumbled to her feet. She ran off down the shoulder and was violently ill. Matt heard vomit splatter onto gravel as he untied his jacket from the dead girl's stump and wrapped it around the trembling boy, who was now in deep shock.

Inside the Mercedes, Katie sobbed loudly to herself, while Joshua was trying to see what his father and mother were doing with the two people on the other side of the road. He had climbed over into the front seat to get a better view, but he still could not tell what was going on.

Katie looked up at him, her eyes red, cheeks streaked with tears. "Joshua, you're s'posed to stay in the car!"

"I am in the car, airhead." Joshua pressed his nose against the driver's side window, cupping hands around his eyes to shield them from the glare of the burning Toyota.

"You're s'posed to stay in the back seat!" Katie screamed.

Joshua ignored his sister. He pressed his nose

flat against the glass.

There was a loud *whumpf!* The Toyota burst into a ball of fire. Katie squealed, covering her face with her hands. Pieces of flaming debris spun out into the night sky. Joshua saw his mother clap her hands to her ears and start screaming. His father stumbled to his feet and threw his arms around her, his eyes on the blazing wreck all the while.

Joshua turned and looked in that direction. Another explosion made the ball of fire bulge out brighter.

Joshua's eyes blinked against the glare, his mouth fell open. "God damn," he whispered to himself.

He looked away from the intense brightness, over to the right, where the darkness of the pine forest was fitfully illuminated by the flickering orange glare of the burning wreck and by shafts of pale moonlight falling from the cold night sky.

That was when he saw the other girl.

She lay sprawled face down inside the pine forest, about 60 feet back from the burning wreck, barely visible through the dark trees and the shadowy moonlight. Her light-colored T-shirt was stained with dark blotches. Blackness puddled on the ground beside her, glistening in the pale moonlight. Something else glistened too, something metallic on her right ankle. Joshua knew she had to be from the wreck, and had been thrown free when the car crashed into the rock face. She must have gotten to her feet somehow and staggered aimlessly into the forest, he thought. Joshua wondered if maybe she was dead.

And suddenly, he was afraid.

He did not want to look at a dead thing. He saw

a dead bird once in their backyard at Pacific Palisades. It was a seagull. Its stomach had been split open and two blue jays were pecking at its distended intestines. He had yelled at the jays to try and scare them off, but they only looked quizzically at him, then went back to work on the guts of the dead gull. Joshua did not want to see any more dead things.

The shadows moved then.

They moved slowly, emerging from the cold blackness of the forest like dark objects surfacing in dark waters. They moved in close around the girl, keeping low to the ground, black shadows encircling the still body.

At first Joshua thought they were coyotes.

Please let them be coyotes, he prayed.

He remembered how that coyote killed a little kid in Burbank last year. She was playing in her front yard and the coyote came right in and killed her and tried to eat her up. After Katie heard about that, she screamed every time she saw a dog.

Some of the shadows rose suddenly to stand on two legs. They stood hunched over, dark arms extended, fingers curled like claws, black against pale moonlight.

Joshua knew that they could not be coyotes.

His body turned cold. He tried to say "goddamn" again, but his voice wouldn't work. He started shaking like the time he had pneumonia and his Dad had driven him to the hospital at night when it was raining. He forced himself to move closer to the windshield, arms trembling, hot breath misting the cold glass.

The clouds lifted; the moonlight brightened.

He saw what the shadows were doing to the

injured girl.

"Dad!" Joshua croaked. "Dadeeeeeee!"

One of them, larger than the rest, moved apart from the others. It began to scent the air, turning around slowly, its claw-like hands reaching out into the night, searching for something. Its eyes seemed to burn white in the darkness.

Joshua gasped in terror. He fell back against the leather front seat, and tried to shut his eyes. They would not shut. He raised a hand in front of his face to ward off the evil, to make it vanish.

The inhuman eyes, burning white in the darkness, stared past the trees, past the pale moonlight and the horror of what was being done to the helpless girl on the forest floor. They stared fixedly at the silver gray Mercedes parked crossways at the edge of the forest.

Stared inside the car.

Stared at him.

3

The Fourth Body

The injured boy wrapped in Matt Brenner's blood-soaked jacket was comatose with shock by the time the Summit County Sheriff's patrol car arrived on the scene.

Several passing cars had slowed down earlier to stare at the smoldering wreck and the blood-spattered bodies, but no one stopped until a trucker pulled over and radioed the sheriff's station at Black Cavern.

The revolving red light on the patrol car's turret bounced rhythmically off what was left of the yellow Toyota. The man getting out was tall and heavy, with styled silver-gray hair and a deeply tanned, craggy face. He wore a white Stetson, black leather jacket, turquoise string tie and thick hand-tooled leather belt with BUCK engraved in ornate capitals on a large silver buckle. Sheriff

Buck Cody listened patiently to Matt Brenner's hurried account of what had happened.

When Matt finished, Cody shook his head slowly. "Hell of a thing." He knelt down and examined the unconscious boy, then the dead girl with the severed leg. He shifted the wad of chewing gum to one side of his mouth and looked up at Matt. "Find her other leg?"

"There wasn't much time to look for it," Matt said irritably. He was tired, cold, and more badly shaken than he would have admitted by the horrors of the accident.

Cody got to his feet with a soft grunt. "Anybody left inside the vehicle?"

"Just the driver," Matt answered. "He was dead before the gas tank blew."

Cody squinted at the smoking Toyota and the charred figure slumped over the steering wheel. "Have to put him in a body bag when he cools off a bit. Run him on down to the lab." Cody nodded at the dead girl with the severed leg. "Send her along to keep him company."

Matt pointed suddenly at the unconscious boy wrapped in the blood-soaked jacket. "He's in shock. Why don't you call an ambulance?"

Cody looked at him. "One's already on its way."

"Then what the hell's keeping them?"

"This ain't L.A., friend." Cody shifted his chewing gum. "My boys're volunteers. Takes 'em just a few minutes to wake up, get dressed, kiss their families good-bye. Not like they do in L.A. Get a little ol' fishbone stuck in your throat and a whole shitload of paramedics shows up on your front doorstep."

"Fuck that!" Matt said, his patience gone. "This

kid's in shock! If he doesn't get medical attention—''

Cody's face hardened. ''I told you once. They're on their way.''

Robin's stomach lurched. Her mouth was still sour with vomit, her legs were trembling, and now this—two men squaring off, snarling like unfriendly dogs on opposite sides of a fence.

''Excuse me, officer.'' Her voice sounded strained, unreal. ''Who's going to notify these poor kids' parents?''

Cody turned to look at her as if she had just arrived. ''That'll be took care of, ma'am. We can get positive I.D. on these two here right away. Have to wait for the lab to get one on that sorry son of a bitch there behind the wheel, pardon my French, ma'am.''

''Their poor parents . . .'' Robin's eyes filled with tears. ''It's so awful.''

''That it is, ma'am, that it is.'' Cody took out a notepad from his jacket. ''We'll get you folks' name and address here in just one minute. Right now all we want to make certain of is the occupants of that vehicle.'' He turned to Matt Brenner. ''You positive three's it? No more you might of missed?''

''I didn't check the trunk,'' Matt said testily.

Cody looked up slowly from his notepad, eyes narrowed. ''You got yourself one hell of a attitude problem, friend.''

''He went inside that car two separate times, officer,'' Robin added quickly. ''There was lots of smoke. It was ready to explode any minute.''

Cody shifted his wad of gum. ''So three's all she wrote. Two males. One female.'' He noted it down, slowly and carefully. ''We can always check the interior again after it's cooled—"

"There was another girl."

All three adults turned around to see Joshua standing there, his face pale with fright.

"I thought I told you to stay in the car," Matt snapped at him.

"Dad . . ." Joshua hesitated. "I gotta tell you . . . I saw her."

"Saw who?" Tension and exhaustion made Matt Brenner sound angrier than he actually felt toward his son. "What the hell are you talking about?"

He's always like that, Joshua thought. Always pissed off about something, or too busy to talk, like when he's working at home and you ask him about anything and he looks at you like he hates your guts.

"I saw this girl. Over there." Joshua pointed to the dark forest behind the smoldering wreck. "Laying down on the ground like she was hurt real bad."

Matt took a deep breath. "You better not be making this one up, Josh."

"I'm not!" His cheeks flushed with anger, and tears sprang to his eyes. "I told you I saw her. I did!"

Robin knelt down and put an arm around her son. "Josh, honey, where exactly was she?"

Now that his Mom was paying attention to him, Joshua began to sulk. His Dad never believed him. Never!

"I already told you," he said.

"Over there in the trees?" Robin pointed. "Where in the trees, honey?"

Joshua swallowed hard, blinking back tears. "In a clear space."

"Joshua." Robin took her son's face in her hands. "Did you see anything else? Or just the girl by herself?"

Joshua studied the three adults staring at him. His Dad looked pissed off, as usual. The tall guy with the cowboy hat looked bored, just like Porkbelly Peterson, his gym coach. He even chewed gum like old Porkbelly. His Mom looked real worried. She had been crying, and he hated it when she cried.

"I saw . . ." He stopped. He wanted to tell them about the shadows, about what they did to the girl, but if they didn't believe he even saw her, they'd never believe that. "Just the girl," he finished lamely.

Matt sighed heavily. "Guess we have to go look for her, then." He started across the road.

"Hold up there, friend." Cody stuffed the notepad back into his leather jacket. "I'm comin' with you."

But Matt was already across the road, at the edge of the forest.

"Dad," Joshua called out.

Matt stopped, turned around.

"Dad . . ." Joshua swallowed. "Be careful. Please."

An irritated frown crossed Matt's face as he entered the dark forest.

Once inside, he moved cautiously, picking his way through the trees, dark shapes against filtered moonlight. He had done some hiking back in his Boy Scout days but not much since then. Just last year he had taken Josh's Scout Troop out on an easy half-dayer in the San Gabriels northeast of Pasadena and had been surprised to discover how quickly the old skills returned.

It all comes back to you, he thought, moving through the dark forest. Orient yourself, let your eyes adjust to available light, and above all, don't rush it.

"Hey there!" Cody called out behind him. "Wait up just one goddamn minute, would ya?"

Matt kept moving at his own steady pace. A flashlight would have helped, but it was a little late to go back for one now. He squeezed through two pine trunks growing close together, sharp needles scratching at his arms and face, and found himself in the clearing where Joshua had seen the girl.

Matt looked around carefully, trying to identify shapes against the patchwork of moonlight and shadow. It was a fair-sized clearing, the kind that would make a good campsite. He saw nothing—no outstretched body of a girl or sign that a body had ever been lying there recently.

He was still looking things over, trying to understand why Josh would make up one like this, when he smelled it.

A sharp, rotten odor stung his nostrils and made his stomach go tight. Putrescence of decaying blood and flesh intermingled with the foul, musky smell of a dangerous predator on the hunt.

Something stirred in the undergrowth, snapping twigs, scraping over dirt and pine needles on the forest floor. It was something that knew how to be quiet when it wanted, something that now wanted to be heard.

Matt looked hard in that direction. He saw nothing, but heard labored breathing, quick and shallow. Whatever it was, it was moving toward him. The back of his neck turned cold.

Hot breath brushed his left ear.

Matt whirled around, blood pounding at his temples, fists raised to strike. He stood facing Sheriff Buck Cody. His first impulse was to smash that craggy face right out the back of Cody's silver-haired skull, but he fought hard for control.

"Somethin' sure stinks fuckin' awful out here." Cody looked over the clearing, chewing his gum with an even rhythm. "Somethin' good and dead and juicy."

"Some animal," Matt said, "just made a kill."

"No shit." Cody snapped his gum. "Then he let it ferment real good for extra special savory flavor."

"There's no girl's body out here," Matt said.

"Boy might of thought he saw one." Cody scratched the back of his neck reflectively. "Easy enough to do. All them shadows and moonlight and shit. I wouldn't go too hard . . ."

But Matt was already gone.

Robin let out a grateful sigh of relief when she saw her husband emerge from the dark forest. She hoped Cody didn't have any more questions. All she wanted now was to get into their nice, clean, safe car and get the hell out of there.

"What did you find?" she called out to him.

"Not one damn thing." He walked up to them, hands on his hips, looking down at his son. "That's just what you saw, wasn't it, Joshua? Nothing."

"I saw her, Dad!" The tears came again. He couldn't stop them now. But he kept looking up at his father. "I did! Honest."

"Where did she go then?" Matt was trying to sound calm, but there was a harsh edge to his voice. "If she was hurt bad as you say, she didn't just jog out of there."

Joshua wanted to tell him about the cold white eyes that had stared at him, evil white eyes burning in the darkness, burning into his heart and soul, making him sick and scared.

"She . . ." He faltered.

A piercing wail shattered the cold night air. It rose above the dark forest like a death cry.

Joshua clutched at his mother's arm. *Them! Coming out of the trees! Burning white eyes! Hunting him down!*

Matt Brenner turned toward the forest, a sudden and irrational fear gripping his heart.

But it was only the Summit County ambulance, coming at last for the injured boy and two corpses.

4

Kemmering House

No one said much the rest of the way in.

They stopped at a three-way fork in the road, and Robin checked the map.

"I hope that kid pulls through okay," Matt said to no one in particular as he lit an unfiltered Camel, cupping the lighter's flame with his left hand.

"We're not discussing it any more," Robin said, without looking up from the map.

"Please don't smoke, Daddy," Katie asked, her voice husky from crying.

Robin glanced up at him. "I thought you were quitting."

"I'm working on it." Matt crushed the cigarette in the Mercedes' ashtray, then slammed it shut.

"The map," Robin said leaning over it and squinting, "says there's three roads here."

"So which one do we take?"

"I'm trying to find out."

"Let's not make an all-nighter out of it, okay?"

Robin looked up angrily from the map. "I don't notice you volunteering to help."

At it again, Matt thought, and we haven't even unpacked the goddamn suitcases.

He forced a smile. "Sorry, babe. Take your time."

Robin turned back to the map. "The girl at the travel agency said take the one that goes into Black Cavern. We're on Eagle Rock Road right now. This one here's called High Street. It goes straight into town. But our place is outside of . . ." She stopped. "Okay, I get it. We take Black Cavern Road. That leads to Black Cavern the cavern instead of Black Cavern the town." Robin looked up triumphantly from the map.

"So which way do I turn?"

"Left."

Black Cavern Road was narrower than Eagle Rock Road, with even more twists and bumps to the mile. It seemed to be taking them straight into the black heart of nowhere.

"There!" Robin pointed excitedly. "That's what we're looking for."

A small, weatherbeaten wooden sign was partially obscured by brush and leaves. KEMMERING HOUSE. 2 mi. A crudely drawn arrow pointed right. They followed it onto a winding dirt road that was little more than a cowpath with pretensions. Low-hanging pine boughs scraped across the Mercedes' roof.

A sharp turn opened abruptly onto a grassy meadow ringed by an evergreen forest. A small mountain stream cut through the meadow, and a footbridge spanning the stream led out from the back of a large gabled house with tall, dark windows.

''Jesus Christ,'' Matt muttered. ''Looks like the Bates house from *Psycho.*''

''A haunted house!'' Joshua leaned forward. ''All right!''

''Mommy, it's creepy!'' Katie tugged at Robin's shoulder. ''Do we have to stay here?''

''Okay, everybody.'' Robin fished out a travel brochure from her purse. ''This is a lovely, historic old home with beautiful furnishings. Six bedrooms. A marble fireplace—''

''Historic?'' Matt parked the car in a circular gravel driveway. ''It's practically prehistoric. A real archaeological find.''

''—fully equipped country kitchen with pantry and chopping block and most modern—''

''Look, Katie!'' Joshua grabbed his sister's arm as they got out of the car. ''Up there. See?'' He pointed to the dark gables jutting out from the roof. ''See 'em? Flappin' around up there?''

''Birdy mice!'' Katie screamed, and covered her head, protecting her hair. ''Mommy! Birdy mice! I wanta go home!''

''—daytime maid and kitchen help with gardener pro—What are you talking about, Katie?''

''Birdy mice!'' Katie stomped her foot on the gravel driveway to emphasize the point.

''She thinks a word can only mean one thing,'' Joshua explained. ''So she won't call bats bats, 'cause she thinks that only means like a baseball bat. Okay? So she calls 'em birdy mice. A total airhead, huh?''

''There aren't any bats here, Katie,'' Matt told

her.

"Joshua said he saw 'em!"

"Your brother's just being a wise guy, honey. And if he doesn't clean up his act, he'll be a wise guy with the world's sorest rear end. Right, scout?"

Joshua sighed. "Dad, it's not my fault she's so dumb she'll believe anything you tell her."

"She's not dumb. She's just younger than—"

"Joshua, look!" Katie's voice was hushed with awe.

Joshua bounded up a long flight of stone steps to join his sister on the porch in front of two large double doors. She was staring, mouth open, at the door knockers. Two demon heads glared out at them, with pointed ears, long protruding tongues, fierce slitted eyes and a huge ring through each nose.

"Goddamn!" Joshua grinned with delight. "Monsters!"

"We don't use language like that, Joshua Brenner," Robin called from the car.

"Dad!" Joshua shouted over his shoulder. "Come look at the monster!"

"They're more like gargoyles, scout." Matt came up onto the porch carrying two suitcases and a wardrobe bag.

"Garghouls?" Joshua wrinkled his forehead.

"That's when you gargle with Listerine," Katie chimed in.

"Gar*goyles,*" Matt corrected him. "They were popular a long time ago, when people used to build churches big as Dodger Stadium." Matt turned to Robin, who had just stepped onto the porch carrying a flight bag and medicine case. "Way to go, babe. You picked a real winner.

Probably comes equipped with its own hunchbacked servant named Igor."

"Don't be a wiseacre, darling." She fitted a key to the lock below a demon's head.

The double doors opened inward. The house was not dank or musty, the way a summer rental is expected to smell. The warm scent of burning pine logs drifted out into the chill night air. One light was on at the top of the inside stairs, another in the kitchen. The living room, except for the fireplace, was dark.

Robin fumbled for a light switch and found it.

The grizzly reared up out of the darkness on its hind legs, jaws agape, clawed forefeet reaching out.

Robin screamed and dropped the bags she was carrying. Joshua shouted, "Goddamn," while Katie howled and hid behind her father's leg.

The stuffed grizzly bear glared down at them with implacable malice. By the flickering light of the fireplace he almost seemed to be slavering from his wide open jaws.

"Shit!" Robin bent over to pick up the dropped bags and keys, her arms trembling. "Goddamn stuffed bear!"

Joshua nudged her. "We don't use that kinda language around here, ma'am."

Robin whirled suddenly and grabbed him by the collar. "Watch your step, mister, if you know what's good for you."

"Just kiddin', Mom."

Matt threw back his head and laughed.

Robin glared at him. "It's not funny."

Katie stared wide-eyed at the towering stuffed grizzly. "Mommy, where'd he come from?"

"The same place all the others did," Robin

muttered, checking the bags for breakage.

The eagle was perched over the doorway, wings spread wide, beak open, head cocked slightly as though descending on prey. Moose heads stared down at them, and a wild boar, eyes narrowed, tusks gleaming, looked ready to charge from the wall. Over in a far corner, a Steinway grand piano sat in incongruous splendor.

"I don't like this place," Katie whimpered, still clutching her father's leg.

Matt ruffled her hair. "It's just an old hunting lodge, baby. Somebody shot the animals, then hung 'em up on the wall. They're all dead. They can't hurt you."

Joshua walked over to the huge marble fireplace, twice as tall as he was, and stopped. On either side of the fireplace, crouched, like guard dogs ready to attack were monsters, dragons with wings.

"Look Dad, more garghouls!"

"Those are griffins, scout." Matt walked over to the fireplace, dragging Katie by the hand.

Joshua turned around. "Huh?"

"Mythical animals. Part eagle, part lion and part dragon. Mythical means they're not real, but people thought they were a long time ago." Matt lifted Katie up so she could see one of the griffins eye to eye.

"Gross!" Katie grimaced. "Put me down, Daddy."

"Ugly, aren't they?" Matt turned and called across the room. "Where'd you say you found this place advertised, Robin? *Famous Monsters of Filmland?*"

"Give me a break." Robin walked across the gleaming hardwood floor to join the rest of her family in front of the fireplace. "Matt, look, that's real marble. Isn't it beautiful?"

He squinted critically at the fireplace. "Might be, if it fit with the rest of the house." He glanced around the large, high-ceilinged living room. "But this place is do-it-yourself Gothic gone bananas. Makes the Hearst Castle look like Danish Modern. Whoever designed it must have been out of his head."

"Not in the beginning," said the voice from the shadows.

Matt started at the sound.

An older woman with short gray hair curled tight to her head stepped out of the shadows. She wore cheap black polyester pants and a baggy purple cardigan over a pink print shirt. She was drying her hands on a dish towel.

"Sorry if I startled you. You folks must be the Brenners. I'm Mrs. Wilkens, the caretaker." She extended a rough, reddened hand. "I wanted to have the place all nice and ready for you. There's food in the refrigerator and fresh towels and soap in the bathroom. Just one, I'm afraid. Kemmering House was built back in the days when any kind of inside plumbing was quite the thing."

Matt took the offered hand. "Matt Brenner, Mrs. Wilkens. My wife, Robin. Our kids, Joshua and Katie."

Mrs. Wilkens beamed. "So nice to meet you all."

"Well," Matt said, "a guy named Kemmering is responsible for all this, huh?"

"Marius Kemmering." Mrs. Wilkens nodded. "Wealthiest man in town at the end of the last century. Never made any money here, of course. No one ever has." She chuckled. "Brought it all with him from Leadville, Colorado. Opened the first and only gold mine this part of the state's ever seen."

"Did he find lotsa gold?" Joshua asked.

"No, young man. As a matter of fact, he did not." She smiled at Joshua. "A lot more people look for gold than ever find it, and that's the truth."

"He must have really enjoyed this place," Robin said.

Mrs. Wilkens' cheerful red face grew somber. "Those last years, before the accident, weren't happy ones for Marius Kemmering. His two young children died here. His beautiful wife left Kemmering House one night and never returned."

Matt asked, "What kind of accident was it?"

Mrs. Wilkens shifted uncomfortably and looked down at her red hands clutching the dish towel. "Marius Kemmering kept pretty much to himself after his little ones died and his wife left him. Grew a bit . . . odd, if you know what I mean. That's when he bought those." She pointed to the griffins. "And those awful door knockers. And all these animals looking so vicious and awful. Not that I'm saying there was anything truly wrong with his mind." She recovered some of her cheerfulness. "I never knew Mr. Kemmering, you see. He died before my time. My mother, God rest her soul, she was the one who told me what she knew."

A silence descended over the room, broken only by the crackle of logs in the fireplace.

"Do you mind if I look at the kitchen, Mrs. Wilkens?" Robin asked.

"Oh, please do. I hope you'll find it to your liking, Mrs. Brenner." She turned back to Matt and smiled at him. "And what is it you do, Mr. Brenner? If you don't mind my asking."

"I'm an architect with a Los Angeles firm."

"My, my. No wonder you wanted to know so much about Kemmering House. An architect certainly would be interested in a fine old place like this."

"Uh . . . yes," Matt agreed. "Does that door over there lead to a basement?" He pointed to a heavy wooden door beside the stairs to the second floor. It was closed with a thick metal bar drawn across it.

"Yes." Mrs. Wilkens' anxiety returned suddenly. "Yes, that's the cellar door. Not much down there. An awfully large place, of course. Seems to go on for acres. But not much down there except . . ." She hesitated, as if deliberating whether or not to continue. "Marius Kemmering was an odd man, like I told you." She forced a smile. "And what he did, though no one knows why, is build a tunnel down in that basement there that connects this house to his old mine in the caverns."

Matt raised an eyebrow. "Some engineering project. What'd he do that for?"

"Oh, you know." Mrs. Wilkens raised her hands in a helpless gesture. "Wanted to be able to go visit his mine any old time he felt like it, I guess."

"And it goes all the way from here into the caverns?" Matt touched the heavy iron bar drawn across the basement door. "Anyone tried it out lately?"

"Oh, heavens no!" A frightened look came over Mrs. Wilkens' face. "No one's used it since Marius Kemmering . . . died."

"Don't open it, Daddy," Katie said fearfully, eyeing the basement door with obvious alarm. 'I don't like downstairses. They're gross!"

"That's right dear," Mrs. Wilkens nodded. "Cellars are no place to be. Especially after dark."

In the spacious country kitchen, Robin checked off the stove, refrigerator, disposal and microwave, all high quality units in good shape. The butcher's block was well situated and would come in handy. Some of the cabinets were a little high for her, but she wouldn't be doing much marketing for just two weeks. She was admiring the copper pots and pans hanging neatly from the ceiling in a square pattern over the butcher's block, just like a photo from the *L.A. Times* food section, when she heard the scratching at the window.

She turned. And saw the face.

The lips looked as if they had been cut away by a rusty chain saw, and a ghastly permanent smile exposed rotted teeth and infected gums. The face was scarred and withered, like a slashed apple left to rot in the sun. A ragged hole, ringed by gray flesh, gaped where the right eye should have been. The left eye stared madly at her through the windowpane.

Robin screamed, backing away from the nightmare face at the window, and bumped into the hanging copper pans. Three of them hit the tile floor with a ringing clatter.

Matt rushed into the room. "Robin! What . . ." He saw the face at the window.

"Matt!" Robin grabbed hold of him, burying her face in his chest. "God, don't let Josh or Katie see it. It's a . . . monster!"

"Yes." Mrs. Wilkens entered the kitchen and walked over to the window with deliberate steps, her face grim. "He's a monster, poor dear, but he's a gentle one. He won't hurt you."

The creature outside the window grew agitated at the sight of Mrs. Wilkens. He rubbed his hands across the glass frantically. Tears watered in his one bulging eye.

"Prather!" Mrs. Wilkens rapped on the glass. "Go home. Now." She spoke slowly, in a loud, clear voice, as if talking to a hearing-impaired child. "Go home. Mother will be along in a little while."

The creature retreated from the window, disappearing into the night.

Robin stepped away from Matt, her eyes red and swollen. "Mrs. Wilkens, I'm sorry. We didn't know."

Mrs. Wilkens shrugged, her lower lip trembling. "He's mine and I love him, but I know he's not pretty to look at. He can give people quite a scare when he comes up on them sudden like, but he's got such a kind heart." Mrs. Wilkens wiped at her eyes. The silence was heavy with the question that neither Matt nor Robin dared to ask. "He wasn't born like that," she said finally, "if that's what you're wondering. It was . . . an accident."

"A mining accident?" Matt asked quietly.

"It's something we don't talk about, Mr. Brenner." The unexpected firmness in her voice made it clear the subject was closed. She reached hastily for a checkered woolen scarf lying on one of the cabinets. "I'd best be getting along. He needs soothing down when he gets upset like this by strangers, and I've wasted enough of your time as it is."

''We enjoyed talking with you,'' Matt said, ''and we appreciate having the place ready for us.''

''Mom?'' Joshua leaned around the corner of the kitchen doorway. ''You okay?''

''We heard you yell,'' Katie said, standing back behind her brother, not sure if it was safe to get in yet.

''Everything's fine,'' Matt said. ''Your Mom dropped some frying pans.''

On her way out of the kitchen, Mrs. Wilkens stopped to give Joshua and Katie each a pat on the head. ''Such lovely children,'' she murmured.

''Mrs. Wilkens, I really am sorry.'' Robin stepped forward. ''About . . . Prather.''

Mrs. Wilkens turned around in the kitchen doorway, checkered scarf tied firmly under her chin. ''Mrs. Brenner, sorry changes nothing. So why be sorry? I learned that a long time ago.''

5

The Severed Tongue

"First you stand two waffles up together like a V." Joshua demonstrated on his breakfast plate.

Katie watched, her face tight with concentration.

"Then take a bite off another one," he continued, mouth full of waffle, "and lean it against the top of the V. Then put a sausage," he picked one up, "in the bit off place. See? A fort with a cannon."

"Neato!" Katie's eyes sparkled.

"Okay, guys." Robin looked up from the oranges she was feeding into the electric juicer. "Let's eat the breakfast, not play with it."

"I'm not hungry anymore." Joshua got up from the table, brushing waffle crumbs off his *Laser Warrior* T-shirt.

"You will be later. Finish those waffles."

Matt came into the kitchen dressed in a plaid

flannel shirt and faded blue jeans. "Fishing poles are ready. Let's go, scout."

"You better eat, too," Robin told him.

Matt took a glass of orange juice. "We'll grab something later on in town if we get hungry. Come on, fisherman." Matt and Joshua headed out of the kitchen doorway.

Robin shut off the juicer. "So that's how it works. The men go off fishing and leave the women home to clean up."

"Fishing's a pretty dangerous sport," Matt called out from the front door. "You never . . ." His voice dropped to a normal level. "Good morning, Mrs. Wilkens. Yes, they're both back there." He shouted again, "So long, Robin. Katie. Get the frying pan ready for fish!" The front door slammed shut.

Mrs. Wilkens appeared in the kitchen, a pair of rubber gloves and a dish towel draped over her left arm. "Hope I'm not here too early. Saw the men getting ready to go off fishing and I guessed I better start in on the breakfast dishes."

"The men were supposed to help," Robin said.

"Nonsense," Mrs. Wilkens objected pleasantly. "Cleaning up around here is part of my job. Besides, men have no business in a kitchen after they've finished eating."

The hell they don't, Robin thought, but she said, "Thanks, Mrs. Wilkens."

Robin and Katie walked into the living room, leaving Mrs. Wilkens humming cheerfully to herself over the breakfast dishes. "Don't worry, Mom," Katie told her. "Me 'n' you'll have a better time by ourselves anyway."

Robin smiled and put an arm around her daughter. "That's right, baby. We'll have the best time ever. We'll go look for flowers. Okay?"

Katie's eyes widened. "Really?" She had a pressed flower collection that was her special delight. The smile on her face wavered suddenly. "Will we meet any of those?" She pointed up at the stuffed grizzly looming over them.

"Not a chance. The last wild grizzly died in California a long time before you were even born." Robin looked up at the towering animal. "Good thing, huh?"

Matt Brenner pulled his Mercedes up to a weathered gray wooden building. Its neon sign read THE GRIZZLY BAR.

"Why're we stoppin' here?" Joshua asked as they walked in to the sounds of Hank Williams, Jr. reverberating from a jukebox near the bar.

Matt leaned down to make himself heard above the music. "I promised your Mom no business up here. But I have to make a quick call back to the office. So this is a secret, just between us men. Okay?"

Joshua nodded. "Sure, Dad."

"Here." Matt fished out some quarters. "See if you can win a few freebies while I'm on the phone."

"All right!" Joshua grabbed the quarters and headed for the row of video games on the far side of the large, barn-like room.

Matt kept his eye on Joshua as he gave the operator his credit card number, then listened to the ringing on the other end of the line. "Hello, Sarah? Matt . . . Not so bad, thanks. How about yourself? . . . Good. Listen, put Ed Jackson on the line, would you? . . . He is, huh? Well, go interrupt him, Sarah. This is important."

Even from across the room Joshua could see that they had a *Laser Warrior.* Its flashing crossed laser swords stood out like beacons against the bar's murky interior. Joshua put two quarters in and pressed Extended Play. He was pretty good at it, but *Laser Warrior* was tough. You almost never got the free game score on your first try.

He was at Third Level of Master Duel, his laser sword crossed with that of the Imperial Warlord, when he heard the voice behind him ask, "Do you play often?"

It was a lady's voice, not like his Mom's, but sort of deep and funny, with maybe an accent. Joshua's mother raised him to be polite, but no power on earth could make him stop at Third Level of Master Duel. He almost had a free game. He nodded in response to the lady's question without turning his head from the video display and parried the Imperial Warlord's thrust.

"You're quite skillful," the lady observed.

"Thanks," Joshua said, and landed two quick blows on the Imperial Warlord's Deflector Shield. When the Shield tilted up slightly to ward off the blows, Joshua rammed home a thrust to the Imperial Warlord's midsection. The Imperial Warlord exploded in a dazzling burst of multicolored microdots. The computer's sound effects beeped and honked. FREE GAME flashed on the video display.

"Congratulations!" The lady smiled down at him.

She had dark eyes and dark hair cut short. Behind her smile, her teeth were strong and white. She wore a black sweater and black leather jacket. Her diamond earrings glittered like shards of crystal in the sun.

Joshua smiled back. She looked like one of those tall ladies in his Mom's fashion magazines.

"So talented a young man. And handsome, too." She brought her face down close to his. "Is that your father over there at the telephone?"

Matt Brenner frowned as he saw the attractive young woman in black leather bending over Joshua. "No, he can't return the call here, Sarah. And we don't have a phone out at the House of Usher. Just make sure he gets the message, okay? And tell him I'll try again later today. Thanks, Sarah."

Matt hung up the phone, then walked past the long wooden tables over to the video games against the wall. The woman in black leather turned to him. She had a cool, self-possessed beauty and one of the most direct, penetrating stares he had ever seen. Her smile should have been hard enough to break bones, but when it came, it was warm and pleasant, even a little shy.

"Joshua has been explaining to me the finer points of *Laser Warrior,* Matt. He's quite good." She extended a white, long-fingered hand. "I'm Adriana Velotti, but Ana is easier for most people." The smile grew warmer. "I hope I didn't interrupt the telephone conversation with your architectural colleagues in Los Angeles."

"I didn't get through to the one I was trying to reach." Matt shook her hand, but did not return the smile. "You seem to know something about me, Miss . . ."

"Ana. Joshua and I have been talking. You must forgive me. I'm curious by profession." Her r's were slurred slightly by traces of an accent Matt could not place. "I work as a research assistant to Dr. Geza Todor, the Berkeley anthropologist.

Geza's here at Black Cavern to study the folklore and tribal myths of the Caiyallah Indians, the ones who settled this area centuries before the white man arrived." Adriana Velotti smiled again. "I'm so glad I met you, Matt, because . . . you don't mind if I call you Matt? My pet project here is helping with the restoration of Mission San Miguel, and, Matt, it would be so much fun to have a real architect—"

"Miss Velotti," he cut her off, "I don't like it when people try to pump information out of a child. It's the sort of trick cheap bill collectors use."

Her smile disappeared.

"If you want to know something about me, ask. But leave my son out of it."

"If that's what you wish. . ."

"That's exactly what I wish."

As they rounded the small tree-lined square in the center of town, Joshua turned to his father. "She wasn't that bad a person, Dad."

"I never said she was, scout." Matt parked the Mercedes in front of a redwood-paneled building. A large sign announced HANK'S HARDWARE AND BAIT SUPPLIES, and in somewhat smaller letters, WILDERNESS BACKPACK CAVER GEAR. "She just had no damn business trying to find out about me through you."

Inside the store, Sheriff Buck Cody leaned against the front counter, Stetson tilted back on his head, cigar clamped between his teeth. He was listening to a short, round-faced man in a black suit with a priest's collar. A lean, balding man who looked like the store manager rested his knobby elbows on the countertop and stared at the priest. All three men looked up when Matt and Joshua entered.

"Well, if it ain't the Good Samaritan hisself." Cody nodded at Matt for the benefit of the other two men. "Fella here was a real big help with that smash-up out west o' the Junction last night. Tried to save that poor sucker's life." When he saw Matt frown, Cody explained, "Boy you drug outta that wreck there went th' other way last night. Hauled him back here to the Jeter funeral home. Never even got him down to the vally before th' ambulance turned off their siren."

"I'm sorry to hear that," Matt said.

The priest adjusted the thick-lensed, black-framed glasses on his round face. "Sheriff Cody says you risked your own life to try and save that young man. Such compassion is uncommon, Mr. . . . ?"

"Brenner." He shook the priest's hand. "Matt Brenner. This is my son, Joshua."

"Father James McKerry. The only clergyman in town, I'm afraid." Father McKerry smiled at Joshua, then addressed Matt again. "Sheriff Cody tells us you're with an L.A. architectural firm, Mr. Brenner. Just the man I need for my restoration of Mission San Miguel."

"I've heard about it," Matt said.

"Oh? Our reputation grows. It's a lovely old place. The town was originally named after it. I wish it still were." Father McKerry sighed. "But you know how the tourist business goes. Entice the multitudes. Fill up the lodges . . . By the way, how do you like Kemmering House?"

"Mrs. Wilkens is taking good care of us."

"A dear woman, isn't she? One of the true pillars of our community, Mr. Brenner. The generous things she does for other people." Father McKerry stopped, shook his head slowly. "And yet her own burdens . . ."

"We met Prather," Matt said. "What kind of accident made him that way?"

A sudden silence fell over the room. The store manager looked down at the countertop, while Cody stared at his ornate belt buckle. Father McKerry took a deep breath, then let it out slowly.

"It was terrible," the priest said at last. "Prather was only about ten years old. He'd gone out alone one spring morning to explore the caverns. His mother warned him not to go there by himself, but you know how headstrong young boys can be, Mr. Brenner." Father McKerry hesitated. "When he didn't return home that evening, his mother came to me. She had no one else to turn to. Charity Wilkens' husband, Jacob, died when Prather was very young. I . . . there wasn't much I could do. I appealed to Ben Hawkins, Sheriff Cody's predecessor. He led a search party into the caverns, but they found nothing."

Father McKerry stared at his clenched right fist. "The next morning, some tourists were picnicking in Caiyallah National Forest, not far from the caverns. Prather staggered up to them, delirious with pain and shock. His appearance was much as it is now, except then the wounds were fresh and bleeding." The priest raised an unsteady hand to the side of his head and adjusted his glasses. "He tried to talk, but only blood came from his mouth. His tongue had been cut out of his head."

Joshua asked quietly, "Who did it?"

The priest looked startled, as if he had forgotten

Joshua was there. "No one knows. The poor boy couldn't tell what happened. Couldn't even write it down. Whatever learning he had before seemed to have been burned out of his mind. And he never learned much of anything afterwards." Father McKerry took another deep breath. "There were lots of irresponsible rumors about witches' covens and satanic cults. All nonsense, of course. Poor Prather was probably the victim of a sadistic psychopath. But the rumors persisted, perhaps because no solid evidence ever came to light." Father McKerry shook his head sadly. "I really don't know how Charity Wilkens stood up under it all."

The silence grew heavy again until Matt Brenner asked Buck Cody, "Anything like that happen recently around here?"

Cody frowned. "Just what do you mean by that, friend?"

"My son and I plan to go fishing at Mirror Lake."

"So go ahead. Ain't nothing to worry about over thataways." Cody scratched behind his right ear. "Only, I wouldn't stick around too long after dark, if I was you."

"Oh?" Matt raised his eyebrows. "Why not?"

"Slippery rocks near the water's edge. Easy to fall in. Get yourself drowned." Cody cleared his throat loudly. "Lost some tourists that way a few years back."

"They turn up looking like Prather?"

"Never turned up at all."

6

Axman

"The mountains look close enough to touch," Robin said, as they crossed the footbridge spanning the small stream near Kemmering House.

"And the air smells like Christmas trees," Katie exclaimed.

They headed out across the wide mountain meadow surrounding Kemmering House. Alpine flowers blossomed in dazzling abundance—yellow, orange, white, purple. A soft wind moved small cumulus clouds across a cobalt blue sky. The pines, firs, spruce and incense cedars of Caiyallah National Forest stretched out from the edge of the meadow into a hazy distance. Beyond that the sharp peaks of the Sierras rose like ancient sentinels above the small mountain valley that sheltered Kemmering House and Black

Cavern.

Katie already had her specimen bag half full of flowers. Robin carried the Hasselblad in a case over her shoulder. This light is so perfect, she thought, like something magical from an undiscovered world.

Katie was bending over to pick a dark purple blossom, her blond hair blowing in the wind and the forest dark green in the background, when Robin said, "Hold it right there, baby."

Katie looked up. "Huh?"

"Just stay like that." Robin had the Hasselblad out and was adjusting the focus.

"I'll fall over if I don't move."

"Just one more . . . there!" Robin squeezed the shutter of the Hasselblad. It clicked and whirred.

Katie pitched headfirst in a clownish somersault, landing on her back with both legs sticking up out of the flowers. She let out a loud peal of laughter.

Robin reached down and pulled her to her feet. "Come on, Buster Keaton." She smiled at her. "Let's go."

"Does Daddy know you brought the camera?" Katie asked, brushing meadow grass out of her hair.

"No," Robin admitted. "I made him promise not to bring any of his work along, so this," she patted the Hasselblad case, "is a secret, just between us girls. Promise not to tell?"

"I promise," Katie said solemnly. "Cross my heart and hope to die, stick a million needles in my eye."

"Just a promise is good enough."

The clouds began to pile up as they entered Caiyallah National Forest. The deeper they went, the more isolated Robin began to feel. Kemmering House was lonely enough to begin with, but at least Mrs. Wilkens was there. And her son Prather, Robin thought with a shudder. But out here in the forest, sunlight falling in long shafts through a canopy of pine boughs, it seemed that they were the only two people in a silent world of trees. Bird cries echoed through the forest, emphasizing the isolation and emptiness.

Katie wandered off the trail toward a patch of golden yellow wildflowers growing beside a moss-covered boulder.

Robin went over and grabbed her by the hand. "Let's stay on the trail, baby."

Katie tried to twist loose. "I want those." She pointed to the wildflowers.

"You've got enough for—"

The sound stopped her.

A slow, steady, *thock, thock, thock,* reverberating through the trees. Robin listened closely, tilting her head to one side. She could not tell if the sound was stationary or moving toward them.

"Mommy," Katie whispered, tightening her grip on Robin's hand. "What's that?"

"I don't know, baby," Robin hesitated, then made her decision. "Let's keep moving."

They continued along the trail, Robin walking rapidly with long, jerky steps, Katie struggling, at times running, to keep up.

The sound grew steadily louder and seemed to be coming toward them.

Robin's face was damp with sweat. She stopped, then turned to Katie. "Stay here, baby. I'm going to go see what that is."

"Don't leave me!" Katie grabbed onto her

mother's arm with both hands.

"There's nothing to be afraid of," Robin said, wishing she could believe that lie herself. "Just wait here."

"Mommy . . ." Katie stretched out a hand toward her.

Robin moved off the trail, through trees and underbrush, toward the sound. Thorns tore at her T-shirt and scratched at her bare legs. The *thock, thock, thock* grew louder and stronger. Robin swallowed hard and pushed on.

A bluejay exploded from the underbrush in front of her, screeching and flapping his wings.

Robin gave a stifled cry, both hands raised to her mouth. The other sound stopped momentarily, like music skipping a beat. Then it began again, resuming its slow, steady rhythm. *Thock, thock, thock . . .*

Robin moved cautiously through the clump of tangled undergrowth, around a tight stand of trees, and past an enormous boulder that blocked a narrow trail opening out onto a small clearing.

She saw him then.

And caught her breath.

He was young, about Robin's age, late 20's, early 30's. He was stripped to the waist, revealing a tanned, muscular body, gleaming with sweat. The muscles in his arms and shoulders rippled as he lifted the ax above his blond, bearded head, then brought it down on the log in front of him with a solid *thock* that echoed against the surrounding trees. Robin watched him raise the ax, bring it down, *thock,* raise it again, bring it down—the glistening sweat defining the musculature of his upper body and the tight faded blue jeans accentuating everything below the waist.

Robin felt a hot quivering between her thighs and realized with sudden embarrassment that she was becoming aroused.

She blushed fiercely and took the Hasselblad out of its case. It's just a nature study, she told herself. There's nothing wrong with photographing the male nude, and this guy isn't even nude. But as she thought it, in her mind's eye she saw him walking toward her, fully exposed, his gray eyes locked on hers. Her fingers trembled as she started to screw the telephoto lens onto the Hasselblad.

"Mommy!" Katie poked her in the ribs.

Robin cried out and dropped the telephoto lens.

"Who's that guy?" Katie whispered, pointing.

"Goddamn it, Katie." Robin bent over to pick up the telephoto lens. "Don't sneak up on me like that." She straightened up and saw him resting on his ax, staring directly at her.

Robin dropped the lens again. "Sorry," she called out. "Just going to take a picture."

He smiled easily. "No charge to tourists, but you'll do better up close with a wide-angle. And from over there." He pointed. "From where you are now I'll be all back lit. Causes exposure problems, unless you're going for a special effect."

"Thanks." Robin put the telephoto lens back in the camera case and took out the wide-angle. "You sound like someone who knows something about photography." She moved in closer.

"I'm a painter," the bearded man said, "but the two media are closely allied. They both create images with light." He smiled again. "My name is Gordon MacLeish."

"I'm Robin Brenner. We're leasing Kemmering House for the next two weeks. That's my daughter Katie over there."

"Hi, Gordon." Katie waved at him.

MacLeish waved back, then turned to Robin. "Have you ever exhibited your photographs?"

"A few gallery shows." Robin shrugged. "Nothing special."

"I'd like to see your work sometime."

"Thanks." Robin raised the Hasselblad. "I'd like to see yours."

"Why not now? My cabin's less than a mile's walk from here."

Robin lowered the camera, a nervous smile on her face. "I don't know . . . I . . ."

"How about it, Katie?" MacLeish called out to her. "Want to come see my paintings?"

"Sure, Gordon." Katie called back.

Robin laughed. "All right. Why not?"

Dr. Pepper bubbled into the glass. "Say when," MacLeish told Katie.

Katie waited until the foamy head was almost ready to spill over the top. "Stop! Thanks, Gordon."

"I have some very good Via Antinori Chianti Classico for us, Robin, unless you'd rather have Dr. Pepper, too."

"The wine sounds fine," Robin said.

They were sitting on MacLeish's redwood sundeck. It extended from the studio that occupied the entire second floor of his two-story cabin. The deck's elevation gave it a spectacular view of Caiyallah National Forest and the majestic Sierras ringing the horizon. MacLeish got up easily from the table and moved over to a wine rack. He had on a thin beige shirt that covered his well-developed torso, but Robin could imagine everything she had seen in the clearing. And some things she had not.

Get hold of yourself, girl, she thought. You're a happily married woman with two lovely children—pretty happily married, anyway.

MacLeish poured the Chianti into two Bacarat glasses. "You might want to inhale the bouquet before you taste." He handed the glass to Robin. "It's really quite exceptional."

An electric current coursed through Robin's body as MacLeish's hand grazed hers lightly. Her heart beat faster and her cheeks felt flushed. She sipped at the wine and didn't taste a thing but said, "It's wonderful."

"So's my Dr. Pepper," Katie announced.

Robin drew a hand across her flushed forehead and tried to smile. "I'll have to send you a check. This stuff must cost fifty bucks a bottle."

MacLeish stared at her with his light gray eyes. "You've already paid me the gift of your and Katie's company. That's worth more than a cellar full of the wine."

She saw MacLeish again holding the ax above his head, naked. Stop this shit, she told herself. "Do you live here alone?" she asked.

MacLeish smiled. "Is a man ever truly alone when he's doing work he loves? Yes and no. I don't see many people. You miss hearing other voices once in a while, but I'm always busy." He took a sip of wine. "When I get tired of holding a paint brush, I pick up my ax and go chop wood for the fireplace until I'm ready to get back to the easel."

"It must be lonely, though," Robin said,

wondering what would happen next if she and MacLeish were alone.

But even as she thought it, she saw MacLeish and herself, both nude, lying on the redwood planking, his strong brown hand moving slowly over her breasts, her stomach . . .

Robin set down her glass suddenly, some wine sloshing over the brim. She stood up unsteadily. The hot, quivering sensation was burning between her thighs again.

''Where are the pictures?'' she asked, her voice huskier than usual.

MacLeish's studio was filled with light. Three glass walls enclosed a large room with a beamed cathedral ceiling. Katie was outside on the sundeck going through her bag of flowers. Robin felt better now that she was moving around. She kept a set distance between MacLeish and herself as she gripped the wine glass like a dagger and forced herself to concentrate on the paintings.

They were unlike any she had ever seen. Maybe something like Edvard Munch's haunted landscapes crossed with the shocking savagery of the German Expressionists—only darker, more violent. One painting, *Dead Child,* showed a small girl being torn to pieces by huge, deformed vultures while her mother, on her knees, screamed in horror, her nails clawing bleeding tracks down her face. Robin turned away in revulsion. Her stomach lurched slightly and she tasted sour wine.

She moved on to the next painting, *The Waves.* A nude woman with long golden hair blowing loose in the sea wind, one arm raised above her head, mouth wrenched wide in agony, struggled hopelessly against rough waves while beneath the water's surface, clearly visible to the viewer, a school of voracious sharks dismembered her. Intestines drifted in the bloody water like the tendrils of an undersea plant. Her other arm, slashed off above the elbow, stretched out across the water, blood spurting forth against the slate gray of the stormy sky.

Robin saw again the young girl with the severed leg, blood pulsing out onto cold gravel while the wreck burned a horrible, brilliant orange. She put a hand to her mouth as bitter wine-flavored bile rose hot against the back of her throat.

She looked away from *The Waves.* And dropped the wine glass. The Bacarat crystal shattered on the wooden floor in slow motion.

The third painting, *Watcher in the Shadows,* showed two younger children, a boy and a girl, about Josh's and Katie's ages, gathering wild flowers in an open meadow. Behind them, in the shadows of the forest, half-seen, half-imagined was . . . Robin did not know what it was . . . some kind of animal in human form or what a human being might look like if he became an animal and turned the evolutionary clock backward. Pale white eyes burned in the forest's dim light, nostrils flared in a gray, dog-like muzzle, feral jaws bristled with long, sharp fangs that dripped slaver and filth.

The livid eyes stared intently at the children—and the viewer of the painting.

Robin shut her own eyes and turned away. "My God," she whispered hoarsely, "that's disgusting!"

It was out before she realized what she had said. She looked up at MacLeish, lounging against an easel, wine glass in one hand, watching her. "I'm sorry," she began. "I . . ."

"Don't apologize. The goal of art is not beauty but emotion—stimulus—and not all stimulus is pleasant." He picked up a rag and walked over to the puddle of wine spreading out from the shattered Bacarat glass.

"Gordon, I'm sorry." She reached down to help him.

"Forget it." He looked up and caught her extended hand in his. "You've paid me the supreme compliment. You were so overcome by my art you lost your senses." He grinned at her. "At least you acted like it. I've never seen anyone toss a glass of vintage Antinori before."

The physical contact of his hand touching hers blinded Robin. She forgot about the paintings, the studio, her daughter sitting not more than 50 feet away. All she wanted was Gordon MacLeish—in her arms, inside her, now!

She turned from him and saw the paintings again. A wave of nausea rushed over her. She was torn by a physical horror of the paintings and a burning desire for the man who had painted them, a desire so strong it seemed to shatter her consciousness. It's finally happening, she thought calmly to herself. I'm losing my mind.

She wrenched her hand free from MacLeish's grasp. "I've got to leave," she said, her voice harsh and unsteady.

"You've only just arrived." MacLeish started to rise.

"No!" Robin cried, and rushed out of the studio onto the sundeck, picked up Katie, and hurried down the wooden steps toward the trail that led back to Kemmering House.

They returned hot and exhausted, gasping for breath.

Katie threw herself into an armchair and tossed her head back, fanning herself with both hands. Robin leaned against the marble fireplace mantel, arms trembling, heavy breathing slowly subsiding.

"You didn't like Gordon, did you?" Katie asked. "That's why we left so fast, wasn't it?"

"We left because we had to get back." Robin went into the kitchen and came back with a glass and a half-empty bottle of Scotch. She poured herself an undiluted double. She swallowed most of it in the first gulp. "I'm a little sticky. I'm going to go take a shower and change." Robin headed for the stairs.

Katie jumped up from the armchair. "Mommy, it's still light. Can I play outside?"

"There's storm clouds out there, baby."

"Please . . ."

"All right. But only for half an hour. And stay close to the house. No going off by yourself. Okay?"

Hot water gushed into the bathtub. Robin unhooked her bra and threw it on top of her shorts and T-shirt. She wriggled out of her panties and tossed them onto the clothes pile. She smelled hot and musky. Sweat glistened between her breasts. She lifted her hair up from the back of her neck and studied her reflection in the old-fashioned gilt mirror above the bathroom sink.

Her cheeks were flushed, her dark blonde hair wild and disheveled, the curls across her forehead damp with sweat. Her lips were parted and she breathed heavily through an open mouth, her breasts rising and falling with each breath. The pale pink areolas surrounding her nipples swelled out with heat and dampness. The nipples themselves were dark red and inflamed, the way they always got when she was aroused.

She touched them lightly and felt them stiffen. The hot quivering began between her thighs again. She caressed her erect nipples and they grew longer and harder. Robin closed her eyes and moaned softly. Gordon MacLeish was with her—nude, fully erect, his hands on her breasts, stroking her sensitive nipples, pulling on them gently.

She reached down to touch the quivering heat between her thighs.

The two children from the painting flashed before her eye, vivid to the last detail. And the thing in the shadows, moving out toward them, slowly, quietly, pale white eyes on fire, jaws gaping, slaver drooling from sharp fangs.

Robin stared at her reflection in the misted glass, eyes wide with fear. The burning sensation was gone. Everything was gone except a black chill that crept over her body, making her tremble in the steamy heat of the bathroom.

Goddamn paintings! She leaned over to turn off the bathwater. He's a sick man. Beautiful, but sick.

She straightened up suddenly and saw the two children from the painting again. The little girl with the flowers was so like Katie . . .

Katie!

Robin opened the bathroom door and called down the stairs. "Katie?"

No answer.

She threw a towel around her and hurried downstairs, hardwood squeaking beneath her bare feet. She yanked open the double doors and rushed out onto the front porch.

But Katie was nowhere to be seen.

7

Water's Edge

Matt cast the lure out onto the lake, the reel whirring as it fed line. The lure hit the water with a soft *plop*. The floater bobbed on the highly reflective surface that gave Mirror Lake its name.

He handed the rod to Joshua. "Just hang onto it till something bites, scout."

Matt cast his own lure, then sat down on one of the boulders that lined the water's edge. It had started out as a great day for fishing—blue sky and hot sun—but dark clouds were piling up on the horizon, dimming the light. A cold wind started to blow across the lake.

Matt lit a cigarette, shielding the lighter's flame with his hand.

"Mom thinks you're quitting," Joshua said.

"She's partly right." He put the lighter back in his jeans pocket. "I'm trying to quit."

A hawk, wings extended, circled slowly high above the lake.

"Dad?" Joshua turned to his father. "Do you believe in . . . space monsters?"

"You mean like E.T.?"

"Dad!" Joshua looked put out. "That's a little kid's movie, like a fairy tale."

"I thought it was pretty good, and it's been a while since I was a kid."

"I mean . . . " Joshua shivered in the cold wind. ". . . like bad space monsters, who do awful things to people."

"What kind of things?" Matt made a mental note to check out the comic books Joshua was reading.

"Well," Joshua said, moving closer to his father and lowering his voice, "like those people's bones that the old guy at the gas station told you about."

"I told you those were cow bones, scout."

"You told Mom the old guy said they were people's bones."

Matt frowned. "You were supposed to be asleep."

"I wasn't really," Joshua admitted.

"I see." Matt made another mental note. Check out sleeping kids before discussing anything confidential in front of them.

"What if the space monsters landed in their spaceships and killed some people and . . ." Joshua swallowed hard. He saw the girl in the forest again with the dark shadows swarming over her. "What if they . . . ate 'em?"

Matt crushed out the cigarette underfoot and stared at his son. "Space monsters who eat people. Where'd you get that idea? From some movie?''

Joshua shook his head. What he saw in the forest last night was no movie. He knew that now. Whatever they were, they were real. They did that to the girl. They hurt Prather when he was little, when he was my age, Joshua thought to himself. A chill came over him that had nothing to do with the cold wind blowing across the lake.

''It's like those tore-up cows on that TV show. Remember?''

Matt remembered. It was a special on livestock mutilations that had been occurring in certain parts of the country. Robin had not realized at first how tasteless a program it was. By the time she shut it off, Katie was terrified, and had screaming nightmares about it for two weeks.

''What if the space monsters did the same thing to people instead of cows? What if they came down and killed 'em and cut 'em up and ate 'em and left parts of their bodies layin' around like with the cows?'' Joshua's face was feverish, his eyes bright with fear.

''I think,'' Matt said quietly, ''that if something like that was happening, we'd know about it.''

''But those two government guys saw it,'' Joshua insisted. ''They saw the bones all piled up inside the cave, and the space monsters knew they saw it, so . . .'' Joshua stopped. That was the awful part. They kill the ones who know. And he knew. ''So they killed those two guys,'' he went on, ''to keep 'em from talkin'. Then they took away all the bones so no one else'd know.''

Matt waited a while before answering. ''That's a pretty scary story there, Joshua,'' he said at last.

"Scary stories can be a lot of fun, long as you don't really believe them, and I don't think you do."

Joshua looked at his father. They were sitting on separate boulders about two feet apart, but Joshua felt like they were standing on opposite sides of the lake.

He doesn't understand, Joshua thought to himself. He's not even trying to understand. He just thinks I'm lying. But what would he say if I told him what I saw?

But Joshua knew he would never tell him. Not now. Not ever. "I guess you're right, Dad," he said. "I don't really believe it."

They finished without talking. Matt was thinking that Robin was right. It's a good thing we came on this damn vacation. You really never knew what your kids were thinking about until you spent some time with them and gave them the chance to open up. He'd have to see to it that Joshua started getting involved in more activities. He and Robin had made a point of not pushing him into too many organized sports, but there was a time when it was better to push a little than let him mess up his mind with too many video games and movies.

"Dad!" Joshua leaned forward on the boulder. His rod was slightly bowed with the weight of something dragging on his line. "I've got a fish, Dad!"

"Take it easy, scout." Matt put down his own rod. "Don't pull on him too hard. Just reel him in nice and slow."

"Like this?"

"That's the ticket."

Joshua's eyes shone with excitement. He had caught only one other fish in his life, and that was a small perch at a specially stocked children's pond. He reeled in his line at a slow, steady pace.

"I can see him, Dad."

A small, whitish object was visible just beneath the surface of the water. Joshua almost had it reeled in to shore.

"Keep it slow, scout. Lift him out. Don't jerk on him."

Joshua kept turning the reel as he lifted the rod to pull the fish out of the water. It broke surface with a soft splash and dangled there, twisting right, then left, water dripping from it in a steady cascade.

It was a naked human foot, small and delicate, amputated crudely at the ankle. Strips of withered flesh surrounded the shattered bone, as if the foot had been torn violently from the leg. A cheap ankle bracelet, still fastened to the foot, glittered against the dead, gray flesh.

Joshua saw again the gleam of metal under moonlight on the girl's foot as she lay face down on the forest floor, dark shadows closing in on her.

"Give me the pole, Joshua," Matt said evenly.

"No!" Joshua whipped the rod back over his head, making the foot swing around in circles like a grotesque tetherball.

Matt grabbed for the rod.

Joshua snapped it forward and let go. The rod sailed end-over-end out across the lake, the foot acting as a counterweight to increase the momentum.

"Nooooo!" Joshua stood bent forward, fists

clenched, breathing fast and hard, tears spilling from his eyes.

Matt turned on him, furious. Two hundred fucking bucks down the fucking drain! What the hell's got into him? Then he realized that Joshua had not simply panicked. He was terrified. He's trembling like an old man, Matt thought.

"It's okay, scout," he said, putting a hand on his shoulder. Joshua jerked away violently. "Things like that happen. They're not very nice, but they happen. We'll report it to the police. Try not to think about it. It doesn't mean anything."

But Joshua knew what it meant. They had torn her apart, ripping off her legs and arms the way he and Katie tore off chicken drumsticks and thighs. The images spinning in his head made him sick, and he felt his stomach heave. He could hear the sounds of her bones breaking when they tore off her legs—and her still alive, screaming. Then one of them didn't want the foot because there wasn't enough meat on it, so he threw it away.

Joshua leaned over and vomited.

Matt held him. When the spasms passed, he washed off his son's face with lake water.

"Rinse your mouth, scout, but don't swallow it."

Joshua spit out the water, then looked up, his eyes swollen, face pale. "Let's go home, Dad."

"Sure." Matt helped Joshua to his feet, then picked up the other rod. "Let's get out of here."

The dark clouds had almost blotted out the sky, and daylight was fading to a dull gray. A cold wind blew white caps across the lake's surface, making the trees near the shore creak and moan.

They're here! Joshua realized with woozy

alarm, glancing at the swaying pines and firs crowded tight against the shore. This is where they brought her, because this is where they live. Joshua looked back into the dark depths of the shifting forest. Something was out there, waiting for him.

"Dad." His voice was strained and high-pitched. "There's something back there."

Matt looked at the forest. "It's only the wind, scout."

"Something's there!" Joshua screamed.

Matt frowned. They would have to make an appointment for Joshua to see a child psychologist when they got back home. It was one thing to get shaken up by the severed foot, but it was another thing—

The smell hit him then—raw, bloody, rotten—the same smell that had gagged him the night before inside the trees looking for Joshua's imaginary injured girl. It was the smell of unearthed corpses, dug up from beneath the ground by an unholy predator.

Matt looked uncertainly into the forest. Something moved, something not a tree, something that might be part of the smell and part of its evil. His nerve broke. It's the stench, he told himself. The fucking graveyard stench! He wanted to pick up his son and run and keep running until he got far away from this lake with the severed foot floating somewhere in its depths, fish nibbling at the ragged gray flesh, but there was no place to run. In order to leave the lake they had to cross through the forest to the main road.

And the graveyard smell was coming from the forest.

Joshua screamed in terror.

A figure shambled out from among the trees.

He was tall, almost seven feet, clad in black, completely bald, with a heavy, muscular body and powerful hands. The face was sharply chiseled and defiant, eyes dark and piercing. One eye seemed to glitter with an unnatural intensity.

"Who the hell are you?" Matt demanded hoarsely.

"You should not be here, my friend." The voice was deep, resonant with the rich accents of another language. "You are in great danger." The glittering eye fell on Joshua. "The boy especially."

"What are you talking about?" Matt clenched his right hand into a fist. "Who are you?"

The dark eyes narrowed, like those of a predator stalking its prey. "I am speaking of your physical safety, perhaps your very survival. This is far more important than my identity. Leave. Now!"

He turned to reenter the forest.

"Son of a bitch," Matt growled, and moved forward. "Hold it right there!"

The tall man spun around with cat-like agility, his huge hands spread wide like claws, raised in defensive position. The dark eyes stopped Matt where he stood. The right eye glittered with hallucinatory brilliance.

Matt felt his mouth go dry. His throat tightened, and breathing became difficult. He was no coward, but he could not move against the sense of deadly power that confronted him now.

The tall man held Matt's eye with his own for several long seconds.

Then he turned toward the forest and disappeared within its depths.

8

The Animal God

Katie was in the meadow picking wild flowers when she saw it.

Lean, black, part of his fur and left ear missing, the cat stalked the butterfly with single-minded determination. He stopped and crouched low, tail twitching. The butterfly hovered over a white blossom. The cat pounced. The butterfly slipped easily through the outstretched claws and skittered away across the open meadow.

Katie moved up to the cat, carefully, trying not to startle him. "Hello, kitty," she said quietly.

The cat looked at her with yellow cat-eyes, tail still twitching.

"You hungry, kitty?" Katie took some M & M's out of her jeans pocket. She had carried M & M's daily since seeing E.T., in hopes of finding a lost extraterrestrial to take home. A stray cat was almost as good.

"There you go." She placed the M & M's on the ground in front of her, then drew back to give the cat some room.

The cat came forward, cautiously, and sniffed at the candy. He ate it, so Katie tossed him some more. He ate that. A few more tosses and she was able to get close enough to pet him as he ate, snapping at the M & M's like insects on the ground. Katie put what was left of the bag in front of him. While he tore at it, she took a long red ribbon from her jeans pocket and tied it around his neck.

She stood up. "Now I have a leash for you and you're mine," she announced.

The cat did not seem to mind that. When he finished the candy he began on the M & M's bag.

Katie took it away from him. "I'm going to call you Darth Vader." She tugged at the ribbon. "Come on, Darth Vader. Let's go."

The girl and cat wandered out into the meadow, away from Kemmering House. Katie crossed the mountain stream that cut through the meadow by jumping from rock to rock. The cat did not like this, but he jumped with her because he had no choice. Katie picked more wildflowers. The cat stalked bees and dragonflies, and chewed on meadow grass and leaves and the occasional handful of M & M's that Katie tossed to him from a newly opened bag.

"When we get back home I'll give you a great big bowl of milk," she promised.

They were at the edge of the meadow, and the dark forest loomed ahead. Clouds had blotted out the sun. A cold wind began to blow, making the meadow flowers dance and the forest trees creak and groan. Two ravens landed on the bough of a high pine and began to caw noisily. The cat watched them, head raised, tail twitching.

"Mommy said I'm not s'posed to go into the trees," Katie explained to the cat. "I guess we better go home, huh?"

The cat kept watching the two ravens. Katie looked into the forest. It was filled with shadows and strange sounds and it went on forever. It was not a nice place, she decided, almost as bad as Almond Creek. Almond Creek was a small but steep canyon not far from where they lived. Once Joshua dared her to go down in there with him, and they both got lost and her father had to come get them out. Katie shivered as the cold wind blew over her. She had enough flowers for today. She would not enter the forest.

She tugged at the cat's ribbon. "Let's go home, Darth Vader."

One of the ravens left the pine bough and swooped down to the forest floor. The cat leaped at him, the ribbon jerking out of Katie's hand. She bent down and grabbed at it, but the cat was off in hot pursuit of the raven.

"Darth Vader, come back," she called, following him into the forest.

If it hadn't been for the red ribbon, she would have lost him, but it trailed out a good three feet behind the cat as he raced over pine needles and pine cones. The raven rose effortlessly to a low-hanging bough and perched there. The cat scrambled up the tree trunk, his claws digging into the bark. He edged his way out gingerly onto the branch, which began to sway with his weight. The raven cawed loudly and flapped his wings, while the cat moved closer. The raven waited until the cat was almost within striking distance before he fluttered off the branch.

The cat swiped at him, and fell, tumbling head over heels down to the forest floor. He did not land on his feet, but seemed to be all right.

Katie grabbed the red ribbon. ''Bad Darth Vader! We're goin' home.''

Something shifted out in the underbrush, not too far from where Katie stood tugging on the cat's ribbon.

Katie froze. She turned her head slowly to where she thought she had heard something move. It moved again. Alarm bells went off in Katie's head. Bears! She saw the huge stuffed grizzly, towering above the Kemmering House lilving room, jaws gaping. She remembered vividly Joshua's horrible stories of bears attacking picnickers and dragging the half-eaten bodies back to their caves. She never should have left the meadow. Tears gathered in her eyes, and she started shivering, but not from the cold wind that whistled through the pines. Please don't let him be hungry, she prayed.

The underbrush moved again. Branches crackled.

''Let's go,'' she whispered to the cat, tugging at his ribbon as she backed away, her eyes on the underbrush.

But the cat would not move. He stared fixedly at the underbrush, his long tail twitching.

''Come on, Darth Vader,'' Katie pleaded, ''let's—''

She stopped, and wrinkled her nose. Something smelled awful, like garbage cans behind the school cafeteria. It made her sick to her stomach. She pulled hard on the cat's ribbon, but he kept staring at the underbrush, leaning forward like a pointer. A cold drop of water fell on Katie's right hand, then another drop. The rain began to splatter on leaves and tree branches and pine needles on the forest floor.

It was dark inside the forest now. The cold rain was falling hard. She could not see well, but she saw something lying on the ground, not far away. It might have been an animal, except it was lying there like something human.

Katie backed away from it, past tree trunks and under pine boughs, her vision blurred by tears and rain.

The arms grabbed her from behind.

She shrieked at the top of her lungs, struggling desperately to get loose.

Suddenly she heard someone say her name and looked up to see her mother's face, fearful, wet with rain, bending over her own.

9

Aftershock

"A severed human foot?" Robin stared at her husband.

"Not so loud. They'll hear you."

They were talking in the kitchen with the door closed. Katie and Joshua were out in the living room roasting marshmallows at the fireplace.

"Did you report it?"

"I will tomorrow. Josh was pretty upset. I wanted to get him home."

"Jesus Christ . . ." Robin put a hand to her forehead, closed her eyes, then opened them abruptly. "Matt, there is something very wrong here. I don't know what it is, and I don't want to find out. I just want to get us away from here. Now!"

Matt remembered the ominous warning of the tall, bald stranger with the glittering eye. "I think you're jumping to conclusions, Robin."

"Jumping to con—"

'I don't like what happened any better than you do, but I can think of at least a few logical explanations for it that don't have anything to do with maniacs running around cutting up bodies."

"What do you think attacked Prather Wilkens?"

"That was a long time ago," Matt said. "Besides, we paid for this place in advance."

The kitchen door opened. "Mom? Dad?" Joshua poked his head in. "Wanta come see our marshmallows?"

"Sure, honey." Robin forced a smile and headed for the living room. She stopped at the kitchen door, then turned to her husband. "We can get the money back. And if we can't, screw it. I care more about our kids than two weeks of goddamn rent!"

"Our kids are fine," Matt said.

She looked hard at him. "I want to make sure they stay that way."

They put the roasted marshmallows on graham crackers and topped them with squares of chocolate. Katie had learned to do this at summer camp. Matt's marshmallows fell off the graham cracker onto his jeans, and part of Joshua's landed on the rug in front of the fireplace.

Katie took a bite of her marshmallow and sniffled. She had caught a cold in the rain.

"I'll bet it was a bear," she announced suddenly. "Big as him!" She pointed at the huge stuffed grizzly by the double front doors.

"Bull!" Joshua sneered at her, his mouth full of marshmallow. "If it was half that big you'd be in his gut right now gettin' digested."

"Joshua!" Robin glared at him.

"He would of eaten me, if Darth Vader hadn't of saved my life." Katie offered the cat her marshmallow. He accepted.

"You'll make him fat as ol' Superman back home," Joshua warned.

"Don't let him eat your food, Katie," Robin said.

"Besides." Katie turned to Joshua. "He smelled awful. Just like a bear."

"Probably a skunk." Joshua belched.

"Only . . ." A troubled frown crossed Katie's face. "He didn't look like a bear. He seemed more like a person."

Matt looked up, and Robin stopped chewing. Joshua put his marshmallow and graham cracker down on the plate. Suddenly he wasn't hungry anymore.

"What do you mean?" Matt asked slowly. "He *seemed* like a person. *Was* it a person?"

Katie shook her head vigorously. "No! It's just . . ." She thought about it. "He looked like a bear, I guess. I couldn't see too good 'cause it was rainin' real hard. He smelled like a bear for sure. But he was layin' down like a person." She thought about it again. "Layin' down the way a animal would if he was a person instead of an animal."

Joshua's stomach twisted into a hard knot, the pain causing him to lean forward. He looked at his sister, damp blonde curls plastered to her skull, cheeks bulging as she chewed a large mouthful of marshmallow and graham cracker. They almost got her, he thought to himself. They'll get all of us before they're through.

They ate in silence for a while, except Joshua,

who stared into the fireplace and felt cold despite the heat of the flames.

"I think," Robin said, wiping her mouth with a paper napkin, "that tomorrow we should do something together. All of us."

Matt cleared his throat. "Josh and I were planning on a little stream fishing tomorrow."

"You two have done enough fishing for a while," Robin said evenly. "There must be something interesting for all four of us to do together."

"Let's play croquet," Katie suggested.

"The croquet set's at home, airhead." Joshua turned away from the fireplace. "We could play double teams on *Laser Warrior,* Mom. Me 'n' Dad against you 'n' Katie."

"That wasn't exactly what I had in mind," Robin said.

"Yeah." Katie sneered at him. "Airhead!"

"I guess we could all visit the caverns together," Matt said. "They have group tours."

"All right!" Joshua's spirits rose. They live in the trees, he reasoned, so they can't be underground, too. "Dad, can we go way down to the bottom . . ." He remembered then the pile of human bones inside the cavern and the two explorers who never returned. " . . . and see things?" he finished lamely.

"I don't want to go down into no dark scary old hole," Katie objected.

"Any dark scary . . ." Robin began.

"Any dark scary old hole." Katie grimaced. "Gross!"

"You'll like it better than you think, Katie," Matt told her.

That night Matt approached Robin again and, too tired to resist, she let him make love to her.

But as he moved his hands and mouth over her body, she imagined that it was Gordon MacLeish and not her husband who was fondling her, sucking her, bringing her slowly, steadily to climax.

Stop it! she told herself. This is wrong. It's sick.

But as he entered her, and as they moved together in rapidly increasing rhythm and the physical world began to dissolve around her, it was Gordon MacLeish who rode her, his powerful muscles flexing as he thrust deep inside her, again and again.

And as she came in a series of sustained, shimmering orgasms, she looked up into a blond-haired, blond-bearded face whose cool gray eyes stared back intently into her own.

10

The Sealed Tomb

"Welcome to Black Cavern, folks." The tour guide was a buxom, suntanned girl with a big smile and bright blond hair worn long underneath her forest ranger's flat-brimmed hat. "Largest cavern system in the Sierras. Only a small part of it's been opened recently to the public, but you won't think it's so small by the time we're finished here." She laughed at her own joke.

The tourists stood clustered at the mouth of the main entrance, shifting uncomfortably, clutching cameras, carrying children too young to walk.

" . . . have all brought jackets or sweaters, because as you can feel already," the guide said, waving a hand in the air, "it gets pretty cold here underground. Mean cavern temperature is a year-round fifty-six degrees Fahrenheit. That's because factors determining surface temperature . . ."

Robin pulled her own thin sweater up close and shivered. Katie tugged at her left hand. "Mommy, I'm freezin'."

" . . . and if you haven't worn a good pair of walking shoes . . ."

The stocky, bearded man standing next to Matt Brenner nudged him. "No such thing as good walkin' shoes, right?"

" . . . covering a total distance of only three miles today, but you'll soon discover it's all uphill. . ."

The bearded man shook his head sadly. "I knew I shouldn't've let Shari talk me into this one. What's your excuse?"

Matt laughed. "Same as yours."

"Hey, Roy Danforth." He extended a hand.

Matt took it. "Matt Brenner."

"Matt, you and me, we should've been smarter. We could've at least smuggled in a six-pack, right?"

" . . . an eye on the little ones at all times. No running or pushing . . ."

The frail, little boy with thick-lensed glasses whispered to Joshua, "Ever see anything this dorky before?"

Joshua shook his head. "Mom and Dad took me to Carlsbad Caverns once, when I was a little kid, but I don't remember it."

" . . . not touch any of the cavern rock formations. And please—absolutely no taking any pieces as souvenirs. Leave Black Cavern the way you found it, undisturbed . . ."

"My name's Kyle Danforth," the boy said. "What's yours?"

"Joshua Brenner."

"I got a cousin named Joshua," Kyle said. "Where d'you live?"

"Pacific Palisades."

"Hey, all right! We live in Woodland Hills."

"We're starting now," the guide announced. "Keep in orderly formation, don't get separated from the group, and remember, please hang on to your little ones."

The tourists began filing down into the cavern.

Katie tried to twist free from Robin's grasp. "I'm not a little one!"

"Hey, Matt, we should've used our heads," Roy Danforth said. "We could've at least rented a golf cart, right?"

The tourists formed a circle around their guide. They stood in a small cavern beneath dozens of long, slender stalactites descending from the darkness above, water dripping from some of them. Children squealed and laughed when cold cave water fell on them. Adults grimaced, drawing up their sweaters and jackets.

"We call this one the Rainfall Room," the guide said, "and I guess I don't have to tell you why. What you're seeing and feeling right now is cave building in action. Every single stalagmite and stalactite in this room—and every one you'll see on the rest of the tour—was formed by billions of water droplets, just like the ones falling in here right now. The droplets contain a mineral deposit called calcite. When the water evaporates, it leaves the calcite behind, and all those calcite deposits become the beautiful stalagmites and stalactites you—"

"How do you tell the stalwhosits and stalwhatsits apart?" Roy Danforth called out in a loud, echoing voice.

"Good question." The guide beamed at him. "And the answer's super easy. All you have to remember is that the stalactite"—she pointed her flashlight at a spear of hanging stalactite—"hangs on tight to the ceiling. While the stalagmite"—she aimed the light at a bulky column on the cavern floor—"just might make it all the way up to the ceiling if it . . ."

"My husband asks the dumbest questions," the plump, short-haired woman next to Robin whispered. "I always tell him, listen and you'll find out, but he never does." She sighed. "And now he's bothering that nice man next to him."

"The nice man's my husband," Robin said, "and he doesn't look the least bit bothered. I'm Robin Brenner, by the way. This is my daughter Katie. And my son, Joshua, over there."

"Hi, Katie." Shari Danforth smiled brightly. "Looks like our men are already getting acquainted. That's my Kyle over there talking to your Joshua. And my husband, Roy, of course, he's the one asking the dumb questions."

" . . . formed millions of years ago when the limestone in these caverns . . ."

"This is worse'n the locker room in gym class," Joshua complained to Kyle Danforth. "Drippin' all over you."

"Yeah," Kyle agreed. "Hope it gets better fast."

"We're going down to the next level now," the guide announced. "It's not far. But it's a pretty steep descent, so watch your step. And all you kids, remember—no running or . . ."

"Let's wait till the back of the line," Joshua

whispered, "and I'll race ya."
Kyle beamed. "All right!"

The group of tourists huddled together on a limestone ledge. Below, a small stream splashed and echoed against cold stone. Beyond the glow of artificial lights, the cavern receded into impenetrable blackness.

Robin shivered, wishing she had brought a parka instead of her thin sweater. "God, I'm freezing."

"I'm already froze," Katie said through chattering teeth.

"It is cold, isn't it?" Shari Danforth rubbed her heavy arms. "You'd think if they could put in lights, they could put in heat."

". . . water in the stream, like the water in the Rainfall Room, comes from glacial melt in the mountains above us. Farther down in the caverns are true underground stream systems that originate from unknown sources beneath the earth." The guide flashed her light at the ceiling. "If you look up here—"

"Any body ever live in this hole?" Roy Danforth asked, his loud voice echoing off the far cavern wall.

The guide hesitated before answering. "The Caiyallah Indians lived here in this mountain valley for hundreds of years before the white men came. The Caiyallahs knew about the caves, of course. From artifacts found near the main entrance—arrowheads, pottery shards—we think they may have tried to live down here. In the beginning . . ." She hesitated again. "But not for long."

"Too damn cold, right?" Roy Danforth's loud

laughter sounded ominous as it echoed back across the dark emptiness of the cavern.

"No." The guide was not smiling now. "According to Caiyallah legend, Black Cavern was . . . *mhr'shna.* Taboo. Forbidden. The Indians believed it was haunted by hideous demons who ate the flesh of human beings. *Kt'sa hulai nagrom.* The People of the Dark."

Something seemed to rattle on the far cavern wall.

Heads turned in that direction, and peered into blackness. It sounded like gravel sliding down an incline, but it had an irregular rhythm to it, a hesitancy that gravel does not have.

"You all right?" Kyle asked Joshua in a low voice.

Joshua's face was damp with sweat. His mouth was open, his breathing uneven. "Sure," he whispered, "I'm fine."

"Where are all the Caiyallah Indians today?" asked a pretty red-headed young woman with a little girl about Katie's age in tow.

"I don't know if there's any left alive," the guide answered. "When the Spanish fathers first settled this area back in the 1700's they found very few Caiyallahs still living here."

"What happened?" The young woman drew her daughter closer. "Disease?"

"According to what the Caiyallahs told the fathers," the guide looked over her group, "it was the *kt'sa hulai nagrom.*"

Matt broke the uncomfortable silence. "I thought the Indians steered clear of the caverns."

"They did," the guide agreed, "but, according to Caiyallah legend, the flesh-eating demons would leave the caverns to . . . go hunting."

The gravel rattled again on the far cavern wall. Then it stopped.

It's all true, Joshua thought to himself, heart beating wildly. They've been here forever.

"Did the Spanish missionaries ever see any of these . . . things?" asked a thin, balding black man with a gray moustache.

"No." The guide shook her long blonde hair emphatically. "The fathers recorded all those Indian legends, but they didn't believe them. No more than we do today. The early Spanish fathers were really practical. They built things, like the beautiful Mission San Miguel. You can go visit it on the other side of the Paso Perdido Ridge, not far from Caiyallah Lodge. Admission free. The Black Cavern Historical Society is helping restore the mission to its original condition. It's been completely abandoned for over—"

"Why was it abandoned?" asked a voice from the crowd.

The guide forced a smile. "No one really knows. When the first party of U.S. Cavalry scouts entered this area hunting renegade Indians in the 1870's, they found the mission deserted. No sign of life for miles around."

The guide stopped speaking. The profound cavern silence was broken only by the splashing of the underground stream.

"The original mission community might have been attacked by hostile Indians," the guide continued. "Or by—"

"Or maybe the whadayacallits ate 'em!" Roy Danforth laughed loudly, some other tourists joining in nervously.

Joshua again saw the girl in the dark forest, surrounded by shadows, shadows with claws. He saw the mutilated foot, dripping water, turning slowly from side to side as it dangled from his fishing line.

He put a hand over his mouth to keep from screaming.

"Did those Cavalry dudes, you know, ever, like, go jammin' on inside this place?" asked a young girl with a punker haircut and a WHAM! T-shirt.

"We think so," the guide answered carefully. "Some members of the scouting party rode back to the fort to report on what they found. The rest . . . stayed." The guide looked up with her clear, guileless blue eyes. "We don't know what happened to them. They were never heard from again."

Something shifted in the darkness, beside the underground stream.

Tourists cast nervous glances in that direction.

"Time to move on," the guide announced brightly, her cheerful smile back in place. "We've got lots more to see and not much . . ."

When they stopped again, they found themselves in a long, dark corridor that curved upwards on either end, dropping slightly in the middle. A massive slide of rocks and boulders blocked off what looked like an entrance to another cavern. Dim lights illuminated small pockets of the long corridor.

"This is the Sealed Tomb," the guide explained solemnly, her voice echoing down the corridor. "Here Black Cavern's brief mining history began with high hopes and ended in horrible tragedy. After the Cavalry scouts rediscovered this area, independent prospectors began to arrive on the scene, lured by rumors of fabulous gold deposits deep in the caverns. Few became permanent residents. Some simply disappeared. Most of the others returned home with tales of a terrible curse guarding the vast wealth of Black Cavern.

"The rumors of gold deposits reached Marius Kemmering, a millionaire miner who made his fortune from the silver lodes of Leadville, Colorado. Kemmering brought money and prosperity to Black Cavern. A real community flourished here for the first time since the founding of Mission San Miguel more than a century earlier. Marius Kemmering entertained lavishly in Kemmering House, the elegant home he built for himself, his beautiful young wife and two children. You can still see it today if you take Black Cavern Road—"

"That's where we live!" Katie shouted. Robin shushed her.

"But fate turned against Marius Kemmering." The guide's bright voice grew somber. "Miners began quitting the Kemmering Mine, despite good pay. Kemmering doubled their wages, but still they quit. Unconfirmed reports of attacks on the miners inside the mine—"

"Attacks?" Matt interrupted her. "By what?"

The guide looked at him. "The records don't say." A tourist scraped his foot against the cold stone floor, the sound echoing in the darkness. "Kemmering continued to lose miners," the guide went on. "He began hiring outsiders—drifters, thieves, murderers. Still he lost miners. Marius Kemmering became melancholy and withdrawn. He changed the interior of Kemmering House, had it redesigned to look dark and threatening."

The guide's voice dropped to a theatrical

whisper. "One night, his two children died at Kemmering House under mysterious circumstances. His beautiful wife left him . . . and so did his miners."

"Finally," she continued in a normal voice, "Marius Kemmering led a group of fifty-seven miners down into the main shaft to disprove the rumors that were destroying his mine. Things went well for the first two days. Then, on the third day, Marius Kemmering and fifty-seven other men perished. Their bodies were never recovered."

She moved her flashlight beam dramatically over the rock slide blocking the entrance to the Sealed Tomb. "The bodies of all those men are locked forever behind this slide."

Small cries of dismay came from some of the tourists. Mothers drew their children closer.

"So the cave-in killed them,' Matt said.

The guide turned on him. "The slide took place after the Kemmering Mine Disaster."

"How do you know?"

"Because . . ." The guide's voice flared sharply, then resumed control. "Because there was actually one survivor, a crazy old miner. He didn't live long after he got topside, but the thing is, he couldn't have reached the surface if a slide got them."

"What did get them?" Matt asked.

"No one knows."

"What did that crazy old miner say?"

"No one paid attention." The guide smiled tightly. "He was crazy."

They killed 'em, Joshua thought, the pit of his stomach contracting.

"Mommy . . ." A child's voice cut through the darkness.

"Who's that?" Katie whispered to her mother. Robin shushed her.

" . . . few sticks of dynamite," Roy Danforth was saying to the guide, "and then, *Kabloom!* Blast them suckers right outta there. Then you could go in and count the—"

"Excuse me, please . . . ." A woman's voice, sharp with distress, rose from the back of the group.

"A major fault line runs through these caverns," the guide explained to Roy Danforth. "That's one of the things that limited Marius Kemmering's original operations. And it's kept us from using explosives to open up the Sealed Tomb. Setting off anything down here could bring—"

"Excuse me!"

Heads swiveled in that direction, and murmurs rose from the group. People stepped back out of the way to reveal the pretty redhead holding on to her obviously frightened daughter.

Kyle Danforth's thick plastic lenses reflected the dim lights of the corridor as he glanced over at the woman and her daughter. "What's up?" he asked Joshua.

"I . . ." The young woman was not used to attracting public attention. "My little girl ran into something over here on the floor. I don't . . ." Her voice caught again. "It doesn't feel . . . right."

"Just a stalagmite, ma'am," the guide said cheerfully. "Your little girl wasn't hurt, was she?"

"Look." The woman's anxiety was escalating. "I don't know what this is, but I think someone better come over here and take a look at it. Now!"

The guide gave the weary sigh of one much put upon. She started edging her way through the group toward the woman and her young daughter.

Joshua moved closer to see what was going on. The woman had her arms wrapped tight around the little girl, who was sniffling to herself, one hand at her mouth. Her mother glanced occasionally at something on the ground, only to turn away immediately with a look of mixed fear and disgust.

The guide approached them. "Now where is this?" she asked, much of her cheerfulness gone.

The woman pointed toward the ground at a dark form without shape or definition.

The guide turned her flashlight on it.

The woman's scream exploded inside the narrow corridor, setting off a chain of vibrating echoes. She covered her daughter's eyes, then turned her own head in revulsion from what was on the stone floor, clearly outlined by the steady flashlight beam.

A severed human head was lying sideways, the top of its skull missing, as if someone had torn it off and scraped out the insides, after first ripping almost all the flesh from head and neck. Fresh blood glistened where skin had been. Eyeless sockets seemed to stare straight at the horrified observers.

"Holy shit!" Kyle Danforth exclaimed, eyes wide behind his thick plastic lenses.

"What the fuck's goin' on over there?" Roy Danforth yelled, bellying his way through the crowd.

"Joshua!" Robin called out above the excited babble.

Joshua backed away from the horror of the flayed head, his own jaw slack. This is what they do to the ones who know!

The guide turned off her light, and the horror dissolved into darkness.

11

Intruder

Robin looked carefully at Joshua across the speckled formica table top. "Sure you're okay?"

"I'm okay," he said.

"I'm okay too, Mommy," Katie chimed in.

"Good." Robin nodded firmly, as if to convince herself. "Both of you stay here and eat your ice cream. When your Dad gets back . . ."

Tires crunched on gravel, a motor died, and a car door slammed.

"I'm not hungry for ice cream." Joshua started to get up from the kitchen table.

"Eat it anyway."

Joshua, recognizing the edge in his mother's voice, sat down and began to eat his ice cream.

Matt climbed the steps slowly to Kemmering House, a cigarette burning in his right hand.

Robin stepped out onto the porch, closing the

double front doors behind her. ''Did you report it?''

''Yes.''

''Well, what did Cody say?''

''Said he'd look into it.''

''Look into . . .'' Robin broke off in exasperation. ''Jesus Christ!''

''He's a small town cop, Robin.'' Matt took a deep drag on his cigarette. ''This is a great big can of worms. All he gives a shit about is getting the lid back on tight.''

''What about us?'' Robin's eyes burned with anger. ''What about protecting us?''

''Don't let the kids play in the caverns by themselves. Or in the woods at night. Usual bullshit advice.''

''I cannot believe this . . .'' Robin shook her head in disgust. ''The hell with it. We're going back.'' She turned for the double doors. ''Get the car ready, and I'll start packing.''

''Robin . . .'' Matt ground out his cigarette underfoot.

She whirled on him fiercely. ''You still think this is all Josh's imagination?''

He started to say something.

''You think that . . .'' Revulsion crossed her face. '' . . . that *thing* in the cavern is something he just made up, too?''

''That was very real.''

''Then what the hell are we waiting for?''

''Something's going on all right,'' he agreed. ''I'd like to know what.''

''Who gives a holy goddamn anyway?'' Robin shouted.

''Look, there's got to be a reason—''

''Screw reason!'' Robin's face flushed an angry

red. "There's a reason for every sick, filthy thing that's ever happened, but that's not our problem. Our problem's keeping our kids safe from—"

"Nothing's happened to our kids," Matt said calmly.

"Nothing's happened?" She stared at him. "What do you want to happen?"

"I'm not running from shadows, Robin, or spooks in the night."

She flashed him a steel-belted smile. "Fine. Stay here! Show 'em what kinda stuff you're made out of, tiger! Meanwhile, us cowards—"

"Pardon me . . . Mr. and Mrs. Brenner?"

Startled, they both turned toward the intruding voice.

It belonged to a small, thin man with stooped shoulders. His rimless glasses glinted in the afternoon sun. He stood next to a late model maroon Oldsmobile Cutlass parked neatly in the Kemmering House driveway. His whole posture, hands thrust nervously into his pockets and head cocked shyly to one side, suggested someone stepping forth with great embarrassment to ask the world a question he knew it didn't want to hear. But the eyes behind his rimless glasses were drawn tight with pain.

Robin, still angry, gave him a look that should have melted the glasses off his face.

"Help you with something?" Matt asked coolly.

The shy little man adjusted the rimless glasses on the bridge of his nose. "Mr. and Mrs. Brenner, I'm Walter Selwyn. Awfully sorry to bother you like this. I . . . Edna and I, we read about it—the accident—in the *San Diego Union.* And the *L.A. Times,* but they didn't say anything about Ginny. That's why I came up here. All the way from San

Diego. Sheriff Cody . . . he said both of you . . . saw it." Walter Selwyn pushed at his glasses again, his hand trembling. "Ginny's our only child. She's all we . . ." His voice caught awkwardly.

The hard anger in Robin's eyes softened. "I'm sorry." She came down the front steps toward the small, lonely man in the driveway. "She was so beautiful. Such lovely blond hair . . ."

"No." Walter Selwyn looked up at her. "Ginny had dark hair, short dark hair. The girl with the blond hair was her best friend, Cheryl Holmes. We read about Cheryl in the paper." He moved toward Robin, desperation in his eyes. "But we didn't read anything about Ginny."

"There were only three people in that car," Matt said, descending the stone steps. "Two boys and one girl. The boy behind the wheel was dead by the time we got there, and the girl died right after I pulled her out of the wreck. The other boy died on the way to the hospital." Matt came up to Walter Selwyn and looked down at him. "There weren't any others. I looked."

"Ginny was with them." Walter Selwyn's face contorted in agony. His right hand clenched into a fist so hard that nails dug into his palm. He was not used to arguing with strangers.

Matt stared at him. "How do you know?"

"I saw them. I . . ." Walter Selwyn's voice caught again. "I was there when Ginny got into that car—some secondhand Toyota, bright yellow, sitting there idling in our driveway. She kissed her mother good-bye." His eyes began to water behind the rimless glasses. "She kissed me good-bye, and I made her promise to be careful. She said, don't worry, she was always careful."

Walter Selwyn bit his lip and looked down at the gravel driveway.

Robin put a hand on his shoulder. "I'm sorry," she said quietly.

Selwyn flinched at the touch and Robin withdrew her hand in embarrassment. He looked up at her, then at Matt. "What happened to her? She was with them. What happened to her?"

Walter Selwyn's desperation had an almost physical presence to it, huge and threatening, out of all proportion to his small size.

"Maybe they let her off somewhere," Robin offered. "Before the accident."

He turned to her, his upper lip quivering. "Why? Why would they do that? Why would they let a young girl out by herself on a mountain road in the middle of the night?" He was shouting now. "Why in hell would they do a damn stupid thing like that?"

"Just back off." Matt's voice carried a warning note. "We didn't do anything to your daughter."

Walter Selwyn put a hand over his mouth. The eyes behind the rimless glasses were wet with tears. "I'm sorry." His voice was muffled by the hand and he took it away. "I'm so sorry, Mrs. Brenner. I don't talk to people that . . . I . . ." He swallowed hard. "I've had this with me all day long, like a time bomb ticking in my gut the whole way up here. Is she alive? Is she hurt? Is she . . ." He choked back a sob. "I finally get here and no one knows anything. The police don't know. You don't know." He drew a harsh breath. "I could live with an answer, any answer . . ." Tears coursed down his pinched face. "But I can't live with nothing! I've got to know what happened to my little girl!"

Walter Selwyn winced painfully, grabbing at his stomach with both hands. Matt reached out to him. Robin stood there, tears in her own eyes.

"She's the girl I saw."

Walter Selwyn looked up at the boy standing in the doorway of Kemmering House.

"She's the one I saw in the woods," Joshua said, eyeing his father cautiously. "The night of the wreck."

12

The Official Version

Matt Brenner parked his Mercedes between Buck Cody's dusty black-and-white patrol car and a red four-wheel-drive pickup with mud-caked fenders.

The Black Cavern sheriff's office sat by itself at the west end of the town square, a mottled beige stucco building with a fake redwood front. A small sign on the front door announced in formal block letters SUMMIT COUNTY SHERIFF. Without the sign it could have passed for a taco stand.

The interior was cramped and plain—bare walls and unvarnished hardwood floors, gray metal filing cabinets with several sprung drawers, a smell of pine trees drifing in with the breeze through open windows. Beneath one of the windows a tall, lean woman with short gray hair was hunched over a typewriter dabbing at the paper in the carriage with correction fluid. The nameplace on her desk read VIOLET GREENWAY. No title. No flourishes. Straight, simple, to the point, like the woman behind it.

She looked up, correction fluid brush poised in midair. "What can I . . ." She squinted at Matt Brenner, then Walter Selwyn. "You been here already today. Both of you."

Walter Selwyn started to apologize, but Matt said, "There's a few things we both forgot."

Violet Greenway leaned back in her secretary's swivel chair and frowned. "Buck won't be any too wild about seein' you boys again."

"To be honest with you," Matt said casually, "we're not crazy about it either."

Violet Greenway gave them a long, level stare as she reinserted the brush into the correction fluid bottle, twisting the cap hard to the right. "He gets paid to keep the peace in Summit County, not babysit tourists." She looked over at an electric wall clock with an old-fashioned 7-Up logo. "Now's about the time he heads on down to the G-Bar for his afternoon break."

"This won't take long," Matt promised.

"Tell *him* that." She nodded at Cody emerging from an inside door with another man.

The other man wore a short-sleeved khaki deputy sheriff's uniform with a small breast pocket tag that read KESSLER. He was in his early 20's, lanky, dark-skinned, a shock of greasy black hair falling over the right side of his sharp-featured face. His eyes were dark, small and close-set. He grinned at something Cody said, revealing a mouth full of strong, white teeth.

Cody was starting to say something else when he looked up and saw Matt and Walter Selwyn. He nodded at them. "Afternoon, gentlemen.

Anything you forget the last time you was here?"

"Something I just learned about," Matt said.

Cody frowned at the 7—Up clock on the wall.

Matt added, "It won't take all afternoon."

Cody turned back from the clock. "I'll hold you to that." He clapped a hand on Kessler's shoulder. "Kess, boy, I reckon you get to start settin' 'em up without me. Save me a place, hear?"

"Will do, Chief." Kessler put on a pearl gray Stetson and started for the front door. When he passed by Matt, he stopped. "You make sure this is real important now."

Matt stared at him. "And if it's not?"

Kessler's face convulsed into a threatening sneer. He took a step forward.

"Kess!" Cody interrupted in a loud voice. "Get your ass on down to the G-Bar, would you?"

"Talk to you later," Kessler muttered to Matt, then turned on his heel and walked out the front door, slamming it hard behind him. Seconds later a pickup engine roared into life.

Buck Cody unwrapped the foil from a piece of chewing gum. "Well, let's hear it."

"Mind if we use your office?" Matt nodded at the inside door.

"Ain't no secrets from Vi here," Cody said, popping the gum into his mouth.

"Let's just say we're shy about talking in front of strangers, okay?"

Cody shrugged. "Anything to keep a tourist happy."

As Matt and Walter Selwyn followed Cody into his office, Violet Greenway gave them a look that could have drawn blood.

Inside, Cody eased himself into a padded swivel

chair behind a scuffed wooden desk. Matt and Walter took hardwood chairs facing it. The room was similar to the larger outer office, except for the animal heads—bear, deer, mountain lion, coyote—all mounted with their mouths gaping wide, glass eyes glaring down at the occupants of the room. Like the ones at Kemmering House, Matt thought.

"Good hunting around here," he remarked.

"Yeah." Cody snapped his gum. "Now, if you boys don't mind my rushin' things just a little, what is it?"

Walter cleared his throat, but Matt spoke first.

"I think we're all aware of the separate facts," he began quietly. "It's just a matter of bringing them together. Wally's daughter was in that car with those three other kids before the accident. She wasn't there by the time we showed up. I searched the interior. If there'd been another body, dead or alive, I would have found it."

Cody unwrapped another piece of gum. "Most likely."

"So what happened to her? Wally doesn't think they let her out sometime before the accident, and neither do I. Wally said they were all headed for the same destination, a campground higher up in the mountains. Besides, you don't just dump someone out on a dark road in the middle of nowhere." Matt remembered the argument he and Robin were having when the flaming wreck burst upon them. "Even if you're mad at them," he added.

Cody chuckled, but there was no warmth to it. "You'd be real surprised to learn what people do to each other once they get mad enough."

Matt ignored that. "I don't know exactly what

happened." He kept his voice quiet, matter-of-fact. "I think maybe she was thrown from the car when it crashed, or maybe she crawled out of it afterwards. But whatever happened . . ." He hesitated. "I think she's the same girl my son saw in the woods that night."

Cody frowned like a man hit by a sudden migraine. "Goddamn it, Brenner, we have already gone through this whole damn nine yards once before. You said yourself the boy's scammin' us!"

Matt nodded. "That's what I thought at first—that there were no other victims. But don't you see? It's just what Josh described. A fourth victim. An injured girl, lying on the ground . . ."

"Where she'd disappear to?" Cody leaned back in the chair, hands behind his head. "Got a answer for that one?"

"I can't explain it," Matt admitted. "But I think . . ." He saw again the mutilated head on the cavern floor, eyeless sockets staring up at him. He looked at Cody. "It's not the only thing in Black Cavern I can't explain."

Cody snapped his gum irritably. "I ain't got time for no mystical experiences, Brenner! I don't give a damn what you *think* happened. Or what your kid *said* he saw. Alls I want to know is what *did* happen! And one thing I know for damn sure *didn't* happen—"

Matt interrupted. "It's not what I think—"

"—is no hurt girl scrambled outta that mess and crawled over into the woods. Because if she had done it, we sure as hell would of found her body. And we have went over that area time and —"

"Sheriff Cody." Walter Selwyn's thin, nevous voice echoed harshly in the small room. "My daughter was in that car. I know she was. I've talked to a few people up here. You. Father McKerry. Mr. Jeter at the funeral home. Mr. Gormley, manager of the Caiyallah Lodge." He pushed at his rimless glasses. "All of you, with the exception of Mr. Brenner here, have tried to convince me that I don't know what I'm talking about. That I don't know whether or not my own daughter was inside a car I saw her get into with my own eyes!"

"Wally . . ." Cody's brow contracted. His eyes became somber and somewhat sorrowful. "This ain't the first time she's ran away from home, is it?"

Walter leaped to his feet. "I resent that!" Flecks of saliva flew from his mouth. "I resent that very much, Sheriff Cody. She was not running away from home. She had our permission to go with—"

"Has she ever ran away from home before?" Cody interrupted in a loud, accusatory voice.

Walter stepped back, his upper lip quivering. He swallowed hard. "She's . . . Once before. She was only a child. She . . . she didn't know what she was doing."

"Runaways usually try again," Cody said. "Sometimes, second or third time around, they ain't so lucky." Cody shrugged. "Or maybe what really happened is her pals let her out somewhere along the way for a little rendezvous."

"Liar!" Walter shrieked. He covered his face with both hands and fell back heavily into his chair.

Matt stared hard at Cody. "That's bullshit, and you know it."

"Prove it." Cody shifted the gum to one side of his mouth. "Makes more sense than that bullshit you 'n' him been feedin' me about bodies that float outta wrecked cars.''

''It didn't float anywhere!'' Matt protested.

''Then where in hell did it go to?''

''Maybe . . .'' Matt gestured vaguely. ''Maybe someone moved it.''

''Moved it? Shit!'' Cody leaned across his desk. ''Who? How? When? Where to? Why? Goddamnit, Brenner, this ain't no Alfred Hitchcock mystery hour. I'm a busy man. You give me somethin' to check out, I'll go check it for you. But you give me bullshit and I'll let you eat it up all by your lonesome.''

Walter took his hands from his face. His eyes were red, glistening with tears behind the rimless glasses. ''You think she's dead, don't you?'' he asked Cody.

''I never said nothin' about—''

''Why don't you say it?'' Walter Selwyn's eyes burned behind the rimless glasses with an unnatural brightness. ''Why don't you say she's dead?''

''No!'' The cry came from behind the closed door.

All heads turned in that direction. Matt got to his feet and Cody started to rise from his chair.

The door flew open. Mrs. Wilkens staggered into the room, gray hair disheveled, eyes wide with terror. Behind her Violet Greenway held fast to the shoulders of Mrs. Wilkens' purple cardigan.

''Mr. Brenner!'' Mrs. Wilkens reached out to him.

''Charity! For God's sake—'' Violet Greenway glanced at Cody. ''I tried to keep hold of her, Buck.'' She turned back to Mrs. Wilkens. ''Move it, Charity, and get your wrinkled butt back in there." She jerked hard on the sweater.

Mrs. Wilkens turned suddenly and slipped out of her purple cardigan. Violet Greenway staggered back, still gripping the sweater. Mrs. Wilkens, though smaller and older, shoved her hand fiercely, palm outward, into Violet Greenway's face. The taller woman stumbled back out of the room and fell down hard on her bottom.

"You goddamn bitch!" she screamed from the next room.

Mrs. Wilkens slammed the office door, cutting Violet Greenway off in midscream. Then she turned to Matt, her shoulders rising and falling rapidly as she struggled for breath. "Mr. Brenner, you've got to come back home!"

Her voice dropped to a terrified whisper. "The evil has returned to Kemmering House."

13

Forbidden Image

At Kemmering House, Robin was in the pantry off the kitchen. It was not an ideal darkroom, but it would do. She stepped back and brushed a dark blond lock out of one eye with a damp wrist. A smile crept over her face. It looked all right—stop bath, timer, drying line, portable color enlarger on a table by itself. Before long she would be contentedly immersed in the lock-step process of developing and enlarging photographic prints.

It had always been that way for her. Whenever she reached the point where the tensions were beginning to take over and she wanted to start smashing things, and people, there was the darkroom—a separate place, away from the outside pressures, where images came to life magically like visions in a crystal ball. A friend of hers who had majored in clinical psychology told her once that it was all symptomatic of a desire to return to the womb. That was bullshit and Robin told her so. And there went that friendship. It had nothing to do with wombs. The darkroom was special because it was hers.

There was a knock at the pantry door.

"Mom," Joshua called through the closed door, "can I come in?"

"No. I've got exposed film out on the table."

That wasn't true, but she didn't want the kids barging into her darkroom. Not now. She wanted to be alone, without other people nagging and picking at her. The guilt hit her then, like a lead weight from above.

"Mom," Joshua called through the closed door.

"What?"

"Can I go and see Kyle?"

"No, you . . ." Robin frowned. "Who's Kyle?"

"That kid I met at the cave."

"Oh, yeah." Robin remembered plump Shari Danforth and her little boy and that airhead husband of hers. "Where are they staying?"

"Caiyallah Lodge. Can I go?"

"No. It's too far."

"I'll be careful."

"The answer is no, Joshua."

"Aw, Mom . . ." The darkroom door rattled as Joshua gave it a sullen kick. "You never let me do nothin'."

"Anything. And if you don't shape up in five seconds flat, you'll get to do something. You'll get to go straight to your room and stay here."

There was a long silence then, "Can I at least go outside and play?"

"No. I want you and your sister to stay inside."

"Mom!" Joshua wailed in protest. "What am I

supposed to do all day with her?"

"It's not open to negotiation, Josh. Understand?"

No response.

"Joshua?"

"I understand." His voice was small and defeated.

Robin heard a curious sound that might have been muffled sobbing, then the slap of running shoes on linoleum as Joshua left the kitchen.

The guilt hit her again, but she couldn't let them outside today—not after what had happened in the caverns. She shuddered as the horrible image threatened to flare up in her mind again. And with the disquieting sense of a prophecy coming true, the words of the old man at the gas station came drifting back to her.

Some of them bones still had pieces o' fresh meat stickin' to 'em.

Robin trembled, then flicked on the infrared bulb. The pantry was suffused with a dark red glow. She removed the film from its container and placed it in the first tray, then set the timer. While waiting for the negatives, she took out the right number of contact print papers and arranged them. The roll of film was the one shot yesterday when she and Katie went walking in the woods. Not much to get excited about. Ought to let Fotomat have it, she thought. But she was doing it herself because she was mad at Matt and he wasn't there to yell at and she didn't want to yell at the kids.

And because the photographs reminded her of Gordon MacLeish. Admit it, she told herself.

The images came unbidden, flooding into her mind. MacLeish nude, ax raised above his head, penis monstrously engorged, a pagan statue of a priapic god. Him on top of her, pushing inside the quivering heat between her thighs, opening her wide, filling her up with the heat and hardness of his own thrusting passion.

The timer went off with a jarring electronic buzz.

Robin jumped, muscles contracting violently. She was breathing heavily, cheeks flushed. Her hands trembled slightly as she removed the negatives from the tray and began the process of transferring them to contact prints. Lifting prints out of the stop bath, she drained excess fluid back into the pan and hung them on the drying line, like sheets on a Saturday afternoon, fingers clumsy from the chill of the stop bath. She stepped back and studied the hanging prints carefully. They looked better than she had expected. There was Katie outside Kemmering House, holding up her flower bag, her hair golden, the sky deep blue. The house loomed huge and dark behind her, its black windows staring like the empty sockets of the flayed head on the cavern floor.

Robin hugged herself to keep from shuddering. Stop it!

There was Katie crossing the bridge over the meadow stream, waving at the camera, the waters beneath the bridge rushing white and black, the flowers of the meadow dazzling as a flock of brightly colored birds in flight. More shots of Kemmering House. The stream. The meadow. The mountains hazy in the distance, rising above the dark forest. The forest itself, dim and gloomy like the interior of a great cathedral. The weak dappled light among the branches devoured by hungry, overpowering darkness.

Should have opened it a full stop, Robin

thought, making a mental note to reprint the forest shots and leave them in a bit longer.

Then she saw the one she wanted to enlarge.

Katie was in the meadow, right on the edge of the forest, bending over to pick the purple wild-flower, her blonde hair blown back from her eyes, glowing golden against the bright light that faded into the green and black of the trees.

Robin smiled. It was perfect. A blond forest elf picks the first flower of spring. Who knows? she thought. It might even sell. She frowned. The background was far too dark. In an enlargement, the darkness would completely overshadow Katie's blonde hair and her purple wildflower. The shot would look underlit, like vintage Orson Welles.

Robin prepared another print. This time she left it in long enough to lighten the image one full stop. When she pulled it out and hung it up to dry, she could see some improvement. There was more detail in the forest background now—different shades of green and brown, outlines of branches that had been invisible in the first print.

But it was still too dark, especially right behind Katie. There was a solid dark mass, like a boulder. Robin frowned. She remembered taking that shot. Nothing that large had been there in the background. She would have seen it through the Hasselblad's reflex viewfinder.

She prepared another print, opening it one more stop.

The color balance was off now. Katie looked washed out, the details gone from her face and clothes. She seemed to float in front of dark three-dimensional trees like a pale, transparent ghost. But the dark shape behind her was clearer now, more sharply defined.

It was no boulder.

Tangled undergrowth and lingering shadows obscured it. But it seemed to be some kind of forest animal, waiting patiently in the darkness, watching the pale little girl bend over to pick a faded purple flower.

It was a large animal.

But that's impossible! Robin protested, her heart beginning to pound rapidly. I would've seen it!

Her hands shook as she placed the print in the enlarger, made the necessary calculations and turned it on. She waited impatiently, thinking that there was no way she could have missed something standing right behind Katie!

The trembling in her hands was worse now. She lifted the print from the enlarger and hung the enlargement on the drying line. It took several tries. Her hands were shaking so badly she had trouble opening the clasps. When the print was secured, she stepped back to look at it.

A horrified cry escaped her.

Katie was a pale blur now, an albino shadow falling across the dark trees. The flower she was bending over had become a shapeless blot, like a Monet water lily, its purple color distorted by the stop increases and the enlargement until it appeared as a splash of blood bursting in front of—

The Watcher in the Shadows.

Gordon MacLeish's hideous painting materialized before her eyes again. The Watcher, fanged mouth gaping, stared at the children picking flowers, white eyes on the fire with a hatred that yearned to destroy them.

"Dear Jesus . . ." Robin put a hand to her mouth.

With a hunger that sought to devour them.

That was the real horror in MacLeish's painting. The obscenity. The thing in the shadows wanted more than death, more than mere destruction.

But this is no painting, Robin's mind screamed. This is a photograph, and I know it's real because I took it.

The Watcher, still dim within the tangled undergrowth, stared out at the ghostly blond vision that was Katie. Staring at her hungrily, its burning eyes reached out for her from the darkness.

"It's a trick of light," Robin muttered softly to herself. "A sunflare . . . A reflection on the lens."

But the white eyes continued to burn in the forest, staring deep into Robin's own eyes.

She screamed in helpless terror, and groped for the darkroom door, knocking over a stop bath tray and slamming her right thigh hard into the enlarger table. Screaming again as a wet, cold thing wrapped itself damply around her face, she battled frantically with the hanging print and ripped it from the line. Fumbling for the doorknob, she grasped at it feverishly, the old metal slippery as oiled steel.

Then she was out in the kitchen, late afternoon sunlight streaming down through high, narrow windows. She fell across the kitchen table, gasping for breath, her own screams still ringing in her ears.

Except they were not her screams.

She straightened up suddenly, her face frozen in horror.

They're outside, she thought, tears flooding her eyes, a sharp pain searing her chest.

But the screams were not coming from outside. They were coming from the basement.

14

Basement

Luke Skywalker and Princess Leia sat astride the Imperial Walker like Indian royalty on a palace elephant. Down below, Han Solo and the robots C3PO and R2D2 stood surrounded by furry Ewoks. One of the Ewoks fell over and Katie repositioned him.

Joshua sat listlessly in an overstuffed armchair. He looked up at the huge grizzly rising on its hind legs beside the double front doors and the eagle descending from above and the moose head with branching antlers and flat, black eyes. The wild boar's head had fierce, curving tusks. Just like a saber-tooth tiger, Joshua thought, recalling the dramatic picture of the giant cat trapped in a tar pit in his *Child's First Book of Prehistoric Animals.*

As he watched the mounted animal heads, a chill crept slowly up his spine. They're all dead, he thought uneasily, but you can feel 'em still alive. He turned from the dead, staring animal eyes.

And saw the basement door.

Late afternoon sunlight drifted in through a high living room window, slanting in long shafts across the hardwood floor. Dust motes danced in the light, making the barred basement door look like the entrance to an old vault—or subterranean tomb.

Joshua rose from the armchair.

Katie formed a circle of Ewoks around the Imperial Walker. "Wanta play, Joshua?" she asked.

He reached out to touch the heavy bar, its dark iron nicked and rusted. The bar was bowed slightly in the middle as if some great pressure had been applied to it. The metal was cold and rough to the touch. He traced the flat rectangular shape of the bar and the strong iron brackets supporting it.

"I said you wanta play, Joshua?"

Something tried to break out of here, he realized, sweat forming suddenly on his upper lip.

"Joshua!"

Seems to go on for acres, Mrs. Wilkens had said. Joshua visualized a vast, dark world stretching out beneath him. He moved his hand slowly to a large iron knob protruding from one end of the bar; he grasped it and pushed hard to the left. The rusted metal gave out a long, high-pitched *screeee.* The sound made his back stiffen. But the bar moved easily, with a lightness out of all proportion to its dark, dead weight.

"Joshua!" Katie cried out from behind. "Don't!"

He continued to slide the iron bar across the door.

"I'm gonna tell." There was real fear in Katie's voice.

The bar came to a stop with a heavy, metallic thud that echoed inside the large living room and was answered by a similar sound, only heavier, coming from the basement.

"Don't open it!" Katie scrambled to her feet.

Joshua turned to her, his palms resting flat on the wooden door. "It's okay, Katie." Sweat glistened on his upper lip. "This'll be like a real adventure—"

"No!" Katie stamped her foot on the hardwood floor. "Downstairses are gross."

"We might even find some old dolls—"

"I don't care. Lock it back up."

"Don't you even wanta see what's down there?" he asked innocently.

"I'm tellin' Mommy," Katie threatened.

Joshua grabbed the iron bracket handle of the basement door—*Why are you doing this?*—and pulled. *Because I have to.* The door opened slowly, with a stuttering groan of aged wood and rusted metal.

"Close it, Joshua!" Katie screamed.

He continued to pull until the door stood fully open. A low, slanting stairway ceiling dropped down into darkness. It was only late afternoon, but no light reached the basement.

"Joshua," Katie whispered, digging her fingers into his arm, "turn on the lights."

They stood at the head of the stairs, peering down into darkness. Joshua turned on the switch. Dim light from below revealed the sloping stairway ceiling, mottled gray stone flecked with cobwebs. A solitary spider moved slowly across its web.

"Spiders!" Katie whispered in horror. "Gross!"

Joshua looked down at the basement steps. They were unfinished pine boards. A flimsy length of wood served as a guardrail. The steps were covered with the dust and grime of years, but the dust had been disturbed recently by someone going down into the basement—or coming up out of it.

Bullshit! Joshua thought. Nothin' down there except old junk. But as he looked down the darkened stairs, a vision flickered before his eyes —a circle of naked adults, standing in the living room, beneath the animal heads, facing the basement stairs and waiting . . . waiting for what? The vision passed with an abruptness that made Joshua shudder. He placed a tentative foot on the first wooden step. The step groaned and shifted slightly.

"Be careful," Katie gasped.

Joshua put his other foot on the grimy pine plank. It shifted again. His heart skipped a beat, but the board held. He put a foot gingerly on the next step, reaching out for the guardrail with his right hand. The railing creaked.

"Joshua!" Katie pleaded. "Come out of there!"

The sweat stood in beads on his forehead as he moved down the stairs, testing every step, gripping the unsteady railing in his right hand and balancing with his left. When he reached the bottom, he turned and looked up at his sister silhouetted against the fading living room light.

"Come on down, Katie," he called up. "It's okay. A little wobbly, but it's okay."

Katie did not see anything okay about it, but she dreaded the thought of waiting upstairs alone. She descended the stairs fearfully, hands clasped in front of her, shoulders hunched, wincing every time a step creaked.

As she reached the last step, she wrinkled her nose. "It stinks down here."

"That's the way basements smell," Joshua said, but he knew what she meant. There was something else underneath the usual moldy basement smell, something that made your throat close up and your stomach sick.

He looked out over the dim interior. The ceiling was low, under seven feet. Thick rectangular pillars of crudely mortared stones rose from the dirt floor to the low ceiling at regular intervals. The stones were streaked with dark stains. Leaning against one of the pillars was an old-fashioned spoked carriage wheel with several spokes missing and a cracked rim.

"Hey, neat!" Joshua cried. "A stagecoach wheel."

"I don't like this place," Katie whispered nervously.

Joshua looked back at the rest of the basement. The dirt floor was rough and uneven, littered with old wooden crates, metal pipes, broken boards, torn gunny sacks, piles of frayed rope, glittering shards of broken glass. A pitchfork leaned against one of the stone pillars, its thick strong tines bent and twisted, covered with rust, as though someone had carelessly dropped it into a giant garbage disposal. Beyond the forest of stone pillars, on the far wall of the basement, barely visible under the dim light, stood a low, narrow doorway gaping at them like an empty socket in a dead man's skull.

"A secret passageway!" Joshua exclaimed. "Let's go see what's inside!"

As they neared the far wall, they found themselves in a part of the basement that was more open, less cluttered by debris. The rough stone pillars thinned out, and the crates and broken glass disappeared. But the smell, the familiar sick-to-your-stomach smell of something dead and rotting, grew worse, heavier, ranker, filling your nose and mouth until you had trouble breathing.

They stood before the cramped doorway. A world of unknown darkness waited on the other side, silent as death.

"Joshua . . . " Katie began to whine.

Gripping her firmly by the hand, Joshua stepped through the low doorway, stooping slightly.

They found themselves in a small stone-walled chamber. The weak basement light picked out a flat stone slab, about seven feet long, raised above the dirt floor on piled stones. Crude clay pots lay scattered around the slab. Joshua stared at them and at the strange, childlike drawings of animals that covered all four walls of the chamber, their bright primary colors leaping out of the darkness. They were so poorly executed that Joshua could not tell what kind of animals they were supposed to be. It was as if some lonely, demented child, a prisoner in the darkness, had scribbled out his deepest fears in brightly colored chalk on the empty walls.

"Weird," Joshua whispered to his sister.

"Joshua . . ." Katie's fingers dug into his arm. "I wanta go back."

"Sure," he nodded, "after . . ."

He stopped, and Katie yelped in alarm.

In the opposite wall, partially obscured by chalk drawings, stood another, darker doorway. At one time someone had completely sealed it off with heavy bricks and thick layers of mortar. Now most of the bricks were gone, as if blasted loose by an explosion or knocked out by a wrecking ball. Only a jagged outline remained, framing the blackness beyond.

Joshua's throat went dry. "It's the tunnel," he whispered to Katie. "The one the old lady told us about. The one that goes all the way back into those caves."

Back to where they live, he thought. They're part of this house.

He moved forward, breaking loose from Katie's grasp.

"Joshua," she gasped. "Are you crazy?"

He was close enough now to see the heavy, rough-hewn timbers bracing up the tunnel. The torn-out entrance led in sideways. Joshua leaned inside, hoping to peer around, without going all the way in.

He heard it.

Something was breathing—slow, heavy, wet, with a kind of liquid gurgling at the end of every long-held exhalation.

Joshua heard the sound as clearly as he heard his own frightened breathing, but he also felt it, felt it moving through his body, shuddering in perfect synchronization with his own breathing. He tried to turn a little more to the right, to see it once and for all.

He stared into the blackness. He saw, or thought he saw, a darker form faintly outlined against the tunnel darkness. He saw it move, slowly, lift its shaggy, misshapen head and look upon him with pale, dead eyes glowing like phosphorous in the dark.

Eyes that stared at him from the forest.

It was the same one—the one who had risen from the feast of the dead girl, sniffing him out in the night air, seeking his blood, even behind the glass and metal barrier of the Mercedes, even as it was doing now. Joshua heard the sniffing this time, saw the burning eyes widen, and then saw —or imagined he saw, though it was so dark he could see nothing else—a mouth full of sharp, savage fangs. Twisting into an evil smile.

You are mine.

Joshua did not hear this, but felt it, hammering into his brain like shock waves from an explosion.

I have claimed you.

You are mine.

Joshua's scream was beyond terror—the hoarse, despairing wail of someone at the edge of madness.

But his survival instinct was still in working order. It threw him into automatic pilot, made him turn from the tunnel, grab his sister, and run. Katie protested shrilly as Joshua pulled her across the broken dirt floor of the chamber. He slowed down long enough only to duck through the narrow doorway into the main basement, pushing her ahead of him. Then he was running again, so fast that he pulled her behind him like a water skier, her feet skimming the ground on every other step. Behind them, he could hear something breaking from the tunnel into the chamber, clattering over loose dirt and clay pots, breathing rapidly as it gave chase. Joshua ran, driven on by sheer terror. Ignoring the pain in his lungs and Katie's screams, he zigzagged through the forest of pillars, dodging old crates and metal pipes.

He did not look back, but he could hear it gaining on them.

When they reached the foot of the stairs, Joshua pushed Katie up ahead of him. She stumbled. The rickety staircase groaned, swaying from side to side like a tree branch in a storm.

"Climb!" Joshua ordered her.

"I—" Katie gasped for breath. "Joshua, I'm so tired!" She started to cry.

"Climb!" He gave her a violent shove that sent her half-flying, half-falling almost to the top.

She glanced back, to make sure he was following her. Then she turned around.

And saw the figure at the head of the stairs.

A long butcher knife was raised in its right hand.

15

Confrontation

Katie cried out and fell to her knees.

The figure with the knife bent over her.

Katie saw who it was. "Mom . . ."

Joshua clambered up the stairs. "Shut the door! Quick!"

Robin stared at Katie. "What happened down there?"

"It came outta the t-tunnel. It ch-chased us!"

"What tunnel?" Robin demanded. "Who chased you?"

"Mom," Joshua pleaded, "could we shut the door first?"

Robin stared down the dark stairs. She tightened her grip on the butcher knife and motioned Joshua and Katie away.

"Go find Mrs. Wilkens and tell her to get Daddy." Robin's voice caught. She swallowed.

"Then get away from here. And stay away from here."

"What are you gonna do, Mommy?" Katie asked fearfully.

"None of your damn business. Just do like I say."

"Mom," Joshua began, "shouldn't we—"

"Get outside and stay there!"

Joshua and Katie backed up quickly to the double doors, opened them and stepped outside, all the while watching their mother as she turned toward the basement stairs.

Robin gripped the knife. She did not know what had attacked her children—or watched Katie from the forest—but if it could be photographed, it was real.

If it was real, it could be killed.

The first step gave under her weight. She jumped back, regaining her balance. Christ, they could've gotten killed! A few more cautious steps brought her to the middle of the stairs. She crouched down to survey the basement's expanse.

"Jesus . . . " She looked out over the uneven dirt floor, stone pillars, wooden crates, broken glass.

She wrinkled her nose as the smell assailed her. Rising from beneath the basement smells of mold and damp and dirt was the graveyard stench of death and liquid decay.

She winced in disgust. "Shit!"

Her voice echoed faintly in the dim light.

Then seemed to echo again.

Her whole body tensed. She gripped the butcher knife hard. The wooden handle felt wet and slippery. She moved up one step. The sound came again. Not an echo. A separate sound. Moving closer now. Coming through the half-light and shadow toward her. Robin strained her eyes. It was impossible to define shapes clearly. Everything looked abstract and diffused—shadows and substance, light and dark.

The sound came again, closer than before. There came a quick movement over dirt, somewhere out in the darkness, slithering toward her. A drop of sweat fell from the tip of her chin onto the hand that held the knife.

"Who's there?" she called out.

The slithering sound stopped.

She moistened her lips. "I said who's there?"

The light bulb flickered, then went out.

Robin screamed as the basement fell into darkness.

Nothing answered her scream.

Nothing moved.

Then came a sound, unlike any she had ever heard before, except in nightmares—the deep guttural murmuring of something that wanted to speak but was incapable of producing fully human sounds.

"Dear God . . ." Robin's right hand began to tremble, and she almost dropped the knife.

The murmuring sound moved closer. The graveyard stench grew stronger and warmer.

Robin backed up two steps on shaky legs. "I've got a knife," she warned, her voice quivering. "Come any closer and I'll kill you!"

The murmuring grew louder, like someone trying to speak through a mouthful of blood. Robin stared into the darkness at the foot of the stairs. She could hear the horrible sound and smell the stench clotting in her nose and mouth, but she could see nothing.

Then two points of white light in the darkness stared up at her from the foot of the stairs.

Robin tried to raise the knife to strike but her arm would not move.

"Mom!" Joshua's voice carried down the stairs. "Get outta there quick!"

Her son's voice saved her. She threw herself up the stairs. Down below, the liquid murmuring rose in harsh crescendo to an angry, full-throated snarl. A heavy foot fell on the bottom step, sending a tremor through the entire stairway. Claws clicked over wooden boards as something made its way quickly up the stairs after her.

Robin burst into the living room, feet skidding across the polished hardwood floor. She grabbed wildly for the door. A small cry of despair escaped her as it seemed to swing shut so slowly, so very slowly, falling lightly like a gentle curtain over the horror that rushed up from the darkness below.

The door slammed shut with a solid thud. Robin drove the bar home, scraping its rusted length across the brackets with a strength she did not know she possessed. The bar fell into place just as the thing on the other side hurled its full weight against the basement door.

The door shuddered under the impact, the iron bar vibrating like a tuning fork. Robin jumped back.

It struck again. This time with a force that should have ripped the door loose from its hinges and thrown it across the living room. Robin and Joshua hugged each other in helpless terror as they felt the impact course through the floor beneath them like an earthquake.

"Mom," Joshua whispered, "is it gonna break it down?"

Robin, too stunned to reply, only shook her head as she watched the basement door strain against its hinges, wood splintering, the iron bar actually starting to bend, the whole door beginning to give under the pressure of the savage, snarling thing that attacked it from the darkness on the other side.

16

Passenger

Walter Selwyn turned the key in the ignition of his maroon Oldsmobile Cutlass. The engine caught, and he pulled out of the Kemmering House driveway and onto the narrow dirt road that led to Black Cavern Road and, eventually, back to his empty room at the Caiyallah Lodge.

Matt Brenner had pressed him to spend the night with them at Kemmering House. He was grateful for Matt's help and for his support, but he did not want to be with the Brenners for the rest of the evening—not tonight, not with what he had to think about, his little girl gone forever.

He turned onto Black Cavern Road. The Cutlass swayed on its springs as it pounded over the broken surface. He noticed that the passenger door was unlocked. He leaned over and locked it, but the truth was that he didn't care anymore.

Thieves could strip the car and demolish it. He had already lost more than any thief could ever take from him.

It hit him then. The sense of terrible, final loss crushed him like an iron weight. His chest ached, and his throat closed up. The tears ran down his face, dripping onto his hands as he clutched the steering wheel. The road ahead swam in front of his eyes, blurry and distorted.

"Oh Ginny . . ." he whispered brokenly. "Oh, my poor baby . . ."

It was then, when the pain was at its worst, that Walter Selwyn became aware of his passenger in the back seat.

At first he had not noticed the sounds behind him—or the smell.

A nauseating stench seemed to infect the car's interior, foul and unspeakably evil, as though something unclean had crawled in to die and was now lying there, dead, dissolving into thick putrescence on the dark red velveteen upholstery.

Cold sweat broke out like a rash along his upper lip. He took his foot off the accelerator and the Cutlass began to slow down. He was aware of his heart thumping wildly as he glanced up at the rearview mirror, dreading what he might see.

He saw nothing.

Only the blackness of the road behind him was reflected in the dark mirror along with the cold mountain sky touched with dim stars and a pale low-hanging moon.

He had not paid much attention to the commotion at Kemmering House. He did not understand what Matt Brenner's wife and children thought they had seen in the basement. He did not really care. But now he recalled Matt's vivid description of the flayed head in the cavern and his account of the hideous fate that had befallen Prather, the widowed caretaker's son.

Walter looked down at his hands gripping the steering wheel. They were trembling.

Something moved suddenly in the back seat, then snorted, like an animal clearing its nostrils.

Cold fear crawled up Walter's spine. His hands began to shake so badly that he could barely hold onto the wheel. His breathing grew uneven, labored.

The Cutlass slowed down to almost nothing and began to weave along the narrow two-lane road.

Walter glanced at the driver's door, calculating how quickly he could open it, throw himself out of the car, and then . . . And then what?

That was when he felt the breath on the back of his neck—hot, humid, stinking like fumes from an open grave.

He struggled to speak, but his mouth was dry.

Then he found his voice. "Look," he croaked, "I don't know who you are. I don't . . . You can have all my money . . ."

The Cutlass rolled to a stop in the middle of the road.

"You can take the car. You can . . ."

The sounds came again, something shifting in the back seat. Then a different sound, low and wet, like a liquid growling, only softer. Almost like a dark, evil purring.

Walter began sobbing like a frightened child, hard, dry sobs without tears this time.

Turn around, he ordered himself. Be a man and turn around and look at it!

The dark purring stopped abruptly.

Walter Selwyn turned around.

He beheld a terror he knew did not exist, even as he stared at its grinning horror, face to face.

He opened his mouth to scream.

But he never got the chance.

17

Night Music

The sounds came to Joshua in his dreams—harsh, discordant, the wails of something dying on a distant world.

His eyes opened. He was in his parents' bedroom on the second floor of Kemmering House, staring up at the ceiling, at the elaborate ornamental moldings, rinsed in pale moonlight filtering through drawn lace curtains.

The sounds from his dream continued, loud, jarring and unreal.

Joshua sat bolt upright, his body damp with sweat. He listened to the unearthly sounds echoing up from the main floor as he tried hard to figure out what they could be and who was—

A hand grabbed his shoulder. He started to scream, but another hand clamped his mouth shut.

"Keep it down, scout," his father whispered. "We don't want your Mom and Katie to hear it, too."

A sense of relief washed over Joshua like a great weakness. His Dad heard the sounds!

Katie stirred in her sleep. "Mommy . . ."

Matt pulled the covers up over her. "Go to sleep, baby."

Robin stretched and turned over on her side, but the slow, even breathing of her deep sleep continued without interruption.

Joshua watched his father as he got out of bed, pulled on his jeans, picked up the emergency light and took a .38 snub-nosed revolver out of the side table drawer.

Slipping quietly out of bed, Joshua ran over to him and whispered, "Can I come too?"

"No. Get back in bed."

"Dad!" Joshua's face fell. "I heard them, too."

He saw Ginny Selwyn in the forest, Matt remembered, and didn't get any credit for that. "Okay, but put some clothes on so you don't freeze your ass off. And keep it down, okay?"

Outside in the second-floor hallway, Matt locked the bedroom door with a heavy, old-fashioned key. Then he turned on the emergency light, right hand shading it so only a small circle of light fell on the floor directly in front of them. In the same hand he held the .38.

"Dad," Joshua whispered, one hand clutching his father's belt, "what's makin' the noise?"

"The piano," Matt said, his voice quiet but grim.

"The piano?" Joshua shivered at the thought of some uninvited . . . something seated at the grand piano. "Who's playin' it?"

"That's what we get to find out."

They moved slowly down the dark hallway. Just before they reached the staircase to the main floor, Matt stopped. The moment they rounded the corner they would become easy targets. Paranoid overreaction, he objected automatically, but in fact, it was fairly plausible. Whoever was seated at the grand piano intended no good for the Brenner family.

Matt turned to his son. "Okay, scout, I'm going down there by myself."

"But, Dad—"

"No buts about it." Matt uncovered the emergency light and raised the .38 for firing.

He ducked around the corner, sweeping the light down the stairs and over the living room. It outlined only the legs of the grand piano. He charged down the stairs, keeping the light in front of him. When he was halfway down, he swung the light directly onto the piano as it continued to send forth jumbled, grating chords.

No one was seated at the instrument.

The back of Matt's scalp began to crawl. He advanced on the playerless piano, offkey notes ringing shrilly from its sounding board. He swallowed hard. He did not believe in haunted houses or haunted pianos, but right now, in this dark house at the dead of night, he was in no mood to see a keyboard playing itself.

As he rounded the side of the grand piano cautiously, he shined his emergency light down onto the keyboard.

The thing sprang at him with a blood-freezing yell.

"Darth Vader," Joshua cried out from the stairs.

The startled cat leaped past Matt and landed clumsily on the hardwood floor. Heart racing out of control, Matt raised the .38 in a shaking hand.

"Dad, wait!" Joshua came thundering down the stairs. "It's only Darth Vader. Don't shoot him!"

Matt kicked savagely at the black cat, who easily avoided him. "I ought to have him skinned and stuffed," he muttered, sitting down heavily on the piano bench. "Where the hell did that come from?"

"Katie found him in the woods," Joshua explained, bending over to pet the cat. "When she—"

The sound from behind the basement door stopped him.

Something pushed against it, hard from the other side. Door timbers creaked, and the iron bar rattled faintly.

Matt turned the emergency light on the door.

Something slammed into it this time, buckling the door against its strained hinges, then again, even harder than before. Accompanied now by loud, savage snarling, whatever was trying to break out was frustrated and furious.

"Oh shit," Joshua whispered weakly. "Not again."

Matt moved up to the door.

"Dad, don't," Joshua shouted.

Matt raised the .38 and fired.

Joshua covered his ears against the roar of the gun. Matt fired again, and bullets tore through the thick wood. He fired three more times. Joshua started to choke on cordite fumes.

A long, shattering wail rose from behind the door.

Joshua heard it clearly through ears temporarily deafened by gunshots—the howls of a dark, inhuman thing gripped by pain and rage. Joshua went numb with fear.

Cries came from the upstairs bedroom along with the distant rattling of a doorknob.

"Dad," Joshua asked, his ears still ringing, "don't we wanta let Mom and Katie out?"

Matt put his hand on the iron bar. He drew it back. The rusted metal screeched in protest.

"Dad!" Joshua cried in horror. "Don't!"

Matt opened the door.

Nothing stood at the top of the basement stairs, but the emergency light, shining down onto the unfinished pine steps, revealed large, scattered splotches of blood and bloody prints of naked, deformed feet—human feet with claws!

Matt slammed the door shut and threw the bolt into place.

He turned to his son. "Joshua," he said quietly, "I think it's time you told me everything you saw that night."

II: The Offering

18

Vanished

"Look, Katie." Joshua pointed through the Mercedes windshield at the grounds of Caiyallah Lodge. "They got a pool!" He reached for the door handle.

Robin grabbed him by his T-shirt collar. "No running or shoving near the pool. And no jumping in with your clothes on. Okay?"

"Sure, Mom." Joshua pushed open the car door and started running toward the pool nestled at the foot of the five-story redwood building that overlooked Caiyallah National Forest from the top of the Paso Perdido Ridge.

Katie scrambled out after him. "Joshua, wait for me."

Matt smiled as he watched them through the windshield. "You'd think they didn't have their own pool at home. Wonder what makes this one so special?''

''Maybe it reminds them of home.'' Robin shot him a pointed glance. ''Maybe that's where they'd rather be.''

Matt frowned. ''Look, Robin—''

''No, you look.'' She twisted in the car seat to face him. ''When are you going to admit the danger—''

''I admit it!'' he snapped back at her. ''I'm the one who suggested moving into the damn hotel.''

''Big fucking deal!'' She pulled off her sunglasses and glared at him. ''That's like putting a Band-Aid on a broken arm. You had enough sense to move us out of a place where we almost got killed.''

''I—''

''But do you have enough sense to take us home? No!''

He looked at her. ''About finished?''

She tossed her head angrily. ''There's plenty more to say, but you wouldn't listen anyway. So what's the point?''

He took a deep breath. ''The last thing in the world I want to do is put you or the kids in any kind of risk. For any reason. Period. That's why we're moving into the hotel.'' Matt looked out the windshield at the peaks of the Sierras rising above Caiyallah National Forest. ''But I'm just not leaving without trying to find out what's going on here in Black Cavern.''

Robin toyed with her sunglasses. She looked up at him. ''You going to put some kind of time limit on this investigation of yours?''

''If I don't find out anything today,'' Matt promised, ''after talking with Father McKerry again, then we go home first thing tomorrow morning. Deal?"

She leaned over and kissed him on the mouth. "Deal."

As they approached the swimming pool and the main entrance to the lobby, two BMX bicycles cut in front of them. Joshua was on one, Kyle Danforth on the other.

Joshua wheeled to a stop. "Neat, huh?" He grinned at his parents. "Kyle's Mom rented 'em for us."

He pointed to a lounge chair beside the pool. Shari Danforth waved, then got up and headed toward them, a tall drink in one hand.

Robin cocked her head at the two boys. "And just where do you two gentlemen plan on going with these things?"

"Not far." Joshua looked down at the ground.

"Real close by," Kyle added. "My Mom said she'd kill us if we got lost."

"And I meant every word of it," Shari Danforth wheezed, winded by her walk from the pool. She turned to Kyle and Joshua. "You two dudes gonna haul ass or what?"

"Bye, Mom. Dad." Joshua waved as he and Kyle moved out from the parking lot.

"And don't run them bikes off no cliff," Shari Danforth called after them. "I got fifty bucks down on deposit."

Robin looked at the swimming pool. "I don't see Katie."

"Your little girl?" Shari Danforth pointed to a metal table with an umbrealla. "She's sitting down over there. Said she was hungry so I bought her a triple fudge sundae."

Robin tried to smile. "Thanks."

Shari Danforth shrugged. "The way I see it, you take 'em to the dentist twice a year anyway. So why shouldn't they enjoy a little, right?"

The lobby of Caiyallah Lodge was a high-ceilinged, wood-beamed affair with animal heads mounted in an unbroken line around all four walls. Like the heads at Kemmering House, they seemed to stare down at the occupants of the room with a fierce, predatory intensity.

"I'm sorry, Mr. and Mrs. Brenner." The short, plump desk clerk looked up from his registration book. "There are no rooms available at present. Perhaps if you'd like to check back with us tomorrow afternoon . . ."

"We won't be here tomorrow afternoon," Matt said.

The desk clerk shrugged indifferently. "Then I'm afraid we can't help you."

"You got that right." Matt turned irritably from the registration desk.

Robin put a hand on his shoulder. "Matt," she whispered, "we are not going back to that house."

"I know, I know." He let out a deep breath. "We'll just have to change our plans."

"How?" she asked suspiciously.

"By leaving here tonight instead of tomorrow."

"Really?" Robin's eyes lit up.

"Unless . . ."

"Unless what?" Her eyes grew hard.

He turned back to the desk. "What room is Walter Selwyn in?"

The desk clerk looked up coldly. "The name again?"

"Selwyn. S-E-L-W-Y-N. Walter Selwyn."

The desk clerk studied his list, then looked up again. "We have no one here by that name."

Matt frowned. "I know he's staying here. He told me so himself just yesterday. Look again."

The desk clerk's eyes narrowed. "I looked carefully the first time. We have no one here by that name."

"That's impossible." Matt leaned over the desk.

"A problem, Leonard?" The question came from a tall, gaunt man with close-cropped white hair and cold gray eyes who had appeared suddenly from a door behind the desk.

"Not really, Mr. Gormley." The desk clerk turned to his manager. "This gentleman seems to think we have a guest who isn't on the register."

"The name?" Gormley asked, his gray eyes on Matt.

The desk clerk started to answer. Matt cut him off. "Walter Selwyn. That's S-E—"

"Of course." Gormley gave the S a sibilant hiss. "Mr. Selwyn *was* a guest of ours. He checked in yesterday morning." Gormley flashed a cold smile. "Unfortunately he chose to leave the same day. He checked out last night."

"He didn't mention it to me," Matt objected.

"Perhaps," Gormley suggested, eyebrows raised, "he doesn't tell you everything."

Matt ignored that. "Did he say why?"

"He said he was leaving because he had found what he was looking for."

19

Dare

"Wait up," Kyle yelled from down below.

Joshua wheeled to a stop, one foot on the ground, balancing his bicycle. He was breathing hard, mouth open, heart thumping like a fast engine on idle. From this part of the Paso Perdido Ridge, southwest of Caiyallah Lodge, you could see for miles—across Caiyallah National Forest to the north and across the town of Black Cavern to the south. In the distance Joshua could see the meadow surrounding Kemmering House and the house itself, small and indistinct, like a block of wood dropped in a clearing. Joshua shivered as a cold wind whipped at his hair and clothes.

Kyle finally made it up on top of the ridge beside him, leaning hard on his pedals, mouth hanging open, chest heaving from the effort. It was several long minutes before he caught his breath.

''See that road way over there?'' Kyle pointed to a squiggly line that looped around Caiyallah National Forest, past the caverns and then back by Mirror Lake up to the lodge. ''Well, this other road here,'' he pointed to a sharp turnoff ahead of them that plunged straight down to Mission San Miguel, ''leads to that one.'' He pointed again to the loop around the forest. ''So if we take this sucker down past the old church, we can go all the way round and wind up back at the hotel.''

Joshua stared at the proposed route, frowning. ''Will your Mom let us go that far?''

''Shit no,'' Kyle admitted, ''but if we listened to her, we'd just be draggin' our butts in circles around the ol' parkin' lot all day.''

''Yeah,'' Joshua agreed, ''guess so.''

They sailed down the steep road past Mission San Miguel and out through Caiyallah National Forest, moving under tall pines and cedars, the blue sky bright and cloudless, Mirror Lake glittering in the distance like a medallion in the sun, the mountains rising sharp and bold above them.

The road they were on was the old San Miguel Trail that the mission fathers had developed from a Caiyallah Indian footpath. It cut across Mirror Lake Road and Black Cavern Road, winding up through Caiyallah National Forest to the cavern entrance. The formal entrance, with its parking lot, historical marker and restrooms, stood at the end of Black Cavern Road. But before you reached it on the old San Miguel Trail, you came upon an entrance sealed off with barbed wire and a dark redwood warning sign, its yellow lettering faded and peeling:

DANGER—ABANDONED MINE

Original entrance to main shaft of the Old Kemmering Mine, 1884-86. Extreme danger from poisonous gases, open pits, cave-ins.

NO TRESPASSING—VIOLATORS WILL BE PROSECUTED

BY ORDER OF SUMMIT COUNTY SHERIFF

They stopped, resting on their bikes. A hot sun beat down on them and the dark entrance to the abandoned mine. Wind whistled through the pines behind them.

"This is the way in," Kyle said excitedly. "Right into the good stuff. None of that Rainfall Room horseshit."

"Yeah." Joshua nodded, thinking that this is where they live. This is the darkness that is their home.

"Right where all the good stuff is, you bet." Kyle turned to Joshua. "Wanta go inside?"

You are mine, echoed the voice in Joshua's head, drumming up out of the dark tunnel in the Kemmering House basement and out of the darkness before him. *I have claimed you.*

"No," Joshua shouted, jumping off his bike and letting it crash to the ground.

Kyle frowned. "Somethin' wrong?"

"No!" Joshua shook his head violently.

It did no good. They had climbed inside his head. Somehow they were in there now—the white, burning eyes that came whenever he shut his own eyes. They were everywhere—in the trees, beside the lake, at the door to the basement, scratching and clawing to get in, sniffing him out, hunting him down. Every road he took, no matter where he wanted to go, led back to them—because they were part of him.

"No," he whispered, tears coming to his eyes.

Kyle cocked his head and stared. "Don't wanta go, huh? Little bit of the ol' chicken blood there? The ol' bright yellow stripe down the back?" Kyle grinned at him. "Scared?"

Scared shitless, Joshua thought. He looked at the dark entrance to the abandoned mine, gaping like an open mouth, hungry to swallow him and keep him forever.

"Scared?" Kyle taunted. "Startin' to grow a few feathers?"

No one could help him. He was alone. Joshua looked at the dark entrance to the mine again. He raised his chin defiantly. He would take them on, then, alone, like Laser Warrior, the colorful image of the video game hero forming in his mind's eye. He would hunt them down and go up against them on their own ground.

"Well?" Kyle demanded, slightly irritated. "You wanta go in or what?"

Joshua turned to him, face shining with sweat. "We don't have a light," he said thickly. "We can't go in without a light."

Kyle dug deep into his jean pockets, pulled out a small penlight and snapped it on. "We got one."

20

Impulse

Katie lay fast asleep on a lounge chair beside the Caiyallah Lodge swimming pool. In the next chair Shari Danforth read a paperback novel. Robin sat at the umbrella table, trying to read a day-old *Los Angeles Times* as she batted occasionally at flies buzzing around the remains of Katie's hot fudge sundae.

Finally Robin rolled up the *Times* and took careful aim at three flies perched on the edge of the plastic dish. She brought down the paper hard. The flies escaped unharmed, but the plastic dish and spoon flipped off the table and went skidding across the poolside concrete.

Robin got up from her chair. "I'm going inside for a drink."

"You can order one out here." Shari Danforth

pointed to her tall glass, watery with half-melted ice.

"Thanks, but I don't want to share it with the flies." Robin glanced at Katie. "Keep an eye on her for me, would you?"

"Sure." Shari Danforth nodded, turning a page of her novel.

Robin knew she did not really need a drink. Her nerves were on edge, trembling like taut wires. Drinking would only make things worse, but she was damned if she was going to spend the rest of the day lying around the pool while Matt cruised all over town playing Macho Cop. Inside the large, high-ceilinged lobby of Caiyallah Lodge she glanced around, hating the place, especially the mounted animal heads lining the four walls. She turned in disgust from their flat, glassy, staring eyes, and saw the neon sign to the Wigwam Room.

It was a bar like any other—dark and dirty, music too loud, people clustered in small groups at tables, solitary drinkers on barstools, mingled odors of cheap beer and bourbon and cigarette smoke.

Robin was still looking around, letting her eyes adjust to the smoky half-light, when a woman's voice called out, "Hi! By yourself?"

Robin turned toward the sound. At first she could make out nothing among the dark shadows at the tables, then she recognized the attractive red-haired young woman who had been part of the cavern tour, the one whose little daughter found the severed head.

Robin smiled self-consciously. "Hi." She hadn't counted on running into anyone she knew.

"So have a seat." The redhead pushed out a

chair on the other side of the table with her foot. "Unless you've got to run."

"Thanks," Robin took the offered chair, wishing she had stayed by the pool where at least she didn't have to talk to anyone.

"By the way," the redhead said, smiling at her, "I'm Ellen Riordan."

"Robin Brenner." Robin returned the smile.

"So where's your daughter? That was your kid with you yesterday? Cute little blond?"

Robin nodded. "Out by the pool. Fast asleep."

Ellen laughed. "Mine, too, in our room upstairs." Her smile faded. "I'm glad she can finally get to sleep without sedatives."

Robin saw again the flayed head lying sideways on the stone floor and suppressed a shudder. "It must have been awful for her," she said sympathetically, remembering how she had covered Katie's eyes the instant she realized what had been found.

"Yeah, it was bad." Ellen Riordan took a long, reflective swallow of her drink, ice cubes clinking against the side of her glass. "But you know what was even worse?" she asked, looking up over the glass. "Trying to get those assholes at the sheriff's office to do something about it. The way they acted, you'd think it was some kind of teenage prank, like dumping over a trash can."

"I've heard Buck Cody's not too helpful," Robin said.

"Cody's at least polite," Ellen went on, her eyes glowing faintly with alcohol. "Dumb as a horse's ass, but polite. But that greaseball sidekick of his. What's his name?" Ellen frowned, trying to remember. "Kessler. That's it. Floyd Kessler." She shook her head and jabbed viciously at the ice in her drink with a plastic straw. "A real prick, believe me."

"That bad, huh?"

Ellen nodded. "A world-class prick."

"Got a mouth on you for talkin' shit behind people's backs, ain't ya?" Deputy Floyd Kessler stood over them, dirty hair slicked back across his skull, one hand holding a can of beer, the other hooked through his belt.

Ellen looked up, startled. "I . . .'

Kessler slammed his beer can down onto the table. Ellen Riordan cried out as flecks of foam spattered the table top.

Kessler was breathing heavily now, his anger at breaking point. "I could run you in on a drunk and disorderly so fast it'd make your fuckin' cunt shrivel up."

"I didn't—"

"Maybe we'll just pretend you didn't. Long's you get your butt the fuck outta here. Now!"

Ellen rose unsteadily. "My purse . . ." She reached for it.

Kessler grabbed it first and held it away from her, leering, then he let it drop onto the table top. There was the tinkle of shattering glass. Ellen's eyes flared with anger, but she picked up the purse without saying a word and left.

Floyd Kessler eased himself into the vacated chair.

Robin started to get up.

Kessler gripped her arm, hard.

"Take your hands off me," Robin said evenly, "or I'm calling the police."

Kessler laughed, revealing strong white teeth. "Lady, I am the police."

Robin sat down again, fighting to control her

panic. "I don't know who you are . . ."

Kessler leered at her. "But I know who you are. You're the wife of that smartass city fucker's always stickin' his dick into where it don't belong." He kept his tight grip on her arm.

A wave of nausea burned Robin's stomach. Who is this creep? she wondered anxiously. And where's Matt? "Look," she said carefully, "if you don't let go of me . . ."

"What?" Kessler leaned across the table, bringing his leering face so close to hers she could smell the revolting sourness of his breath behind the beer. "If I don't let go of you, what?"

"I'll break your arm backwards for starters," said a deep, quiet male voice.

They both looked up to see Gordon MacLeish standing over them. His blue cotton work shirt was unbuttoned midway to reveal a heavily muscled chest, sleeves rolled back over thick, corded forearms. He stood at ease, but his gray eyes were narrowed on Kessler.

"Hey, pretty boy." Kessler turned on him, without letting go of Robin's arm. "Whyn't you take one of them long-handled paint brushes of yours and ram it sideways up your asshole?"

MacLeish moved while Kessler was still speaking. He slammed the cutting edge of his right hand hard against the Deputy Sheriff's chest, square on the sternum. The air rushed from Kessler's lungs with a strangled *huuuuuunh!* His nerveless hand dropped Robin's arm. He flipped over backwards out of the chair and onto the sticky floor of the Wigwam Room with a tremendous crash.

MacLeish bent down and yanked Kessler up to an awkward sitting position on the floor, pinning both arms behind him.

"You fucker!" Kessler gasped.

"Do I have to start breaking bones, Kess?" MacLeish asked quietly, pulling back on the pinned arms until Kessler cried out in pain. "Because if I do, I'll break both arms. Then you'll have to hire someone to wipe your ass for you."

MacLeish jerked back the pinned arms and Kessler screamed.

The bartender, a fat man with sandy hair, reached under the bar for something, calling out to MacLeish. "We don't want no trouble here, friend."

"Then stay out of it," MacLeish warned.

"Don't!" Kessler panted, coughing. "Don't . . . do that . . . no more."

MacLeish let go of Kessler's arms and stepped back, poised to attack again.

Kessler got to his feet with difficulty, stumbled, then regained his balance. His right hand brushed the butt of the .38 Smith and Wesson holstered on his leg. He wanted to draw the gun and kill MacLeish, but he knew that before he could unsnap the holster, MacLeish would be on top of him. He glared at MacLeish for several long seconds, the hatred burning in his dark eyes, then he turned around awkwardly and stomped out of the Wigwam Room. The look on his face dared any of the spectators to do so much as smile.

No one did.

MacLeish turned to Robin. "You're okay, I hope?"

She smiled with a mixture of relief and embarrassment. "I'm fine, thanks. Thanks very much."

"Sorry about our rustic police force." MacLeish

took Kessler's vacated seat unselfconsciously, as though he had been asked. "That's one of the drawbacks of living in a small town, I guess."

"Really." Robin smiled again, then looked down at the table top. She looked up again. "Look, about that time we left your place in such a hurry. I'm sorry—"

"Don't be." MacLeish shrugged casually. "A lady has the right to leave whenever she wants to. Without apologies."

"I still owe you for that broken wine glass."

"You don't owe me anything." MacLeish leaned forward over the table, folding his heavy brown forearms in front of him. "But you never did finish your wine. Can I buy you a drink?"

Robin looked uncomfortably around the Wigwam Room where the other customers were murmuring, heads together, glancing at her and MacLeish. "I'm not sure I want to stay . . ."

"Then why not come back to my place?" MacLeish asked casually. "And take up where we left off?"

Robin sucked in her breath. It was happening—the object of her daydreams, sitting across from her, looking more attractive and desirable than ever. And now he was inviting her to turn those daydreams into reality.

Robin ran a hand distractedly through her hair. This is all Matt's fault, she thought. He's the one forcing us to stay here, and if anything happens, he'll have no one but himself to blame. She knew this, but she also knew what she had to tell Gordon MacLeish. Even though she was angry with Matt, and frightened and lonely and horny as hell in a way she could not begin to understand for this strange, quiet, considerate handsome man who painted hideous pictures—she knew what she had to tell him.

The sounds of the bar came rushing in on her.

And she said, "All right."

21

Mission

Matt parked his Mercedes between a white Ford Escort and a weathered blue Dodge van in the dirt lot of Mission San Miguel. The crude adobe tower of the mission rose starkly against a background of blue sky and gray mountains. The chapel, a large rectangular structure, ran about 60 by 120 feet. A colonnaded cloister extended from chapel to tower. Electric sanders, paint buckets and a few old sawhorses gave mute testimony to the restoration that was supposed to be going on inside, but Matt could hear no work in progress.

He stopped at the double wooden doors of the chapel. They were carved with crude bas-relief figures. On the right top panel Christ raised Lazarus from the dead. On the left, Christ was being nailed to the Cross. Both lower panels depicted the torments of Hell, the demons looking especially gross and disgusting. They seemed to be feeding on the bodies of the newly damned, but the wood carving was primitive and awkward. It was hard to tell exactly what the sculptor had meant to convey.

Matt pushed open one of the doors. The interior of the chapel was cold and dark, untouched by the brilliant sunshine outside. The only light came from three emergency lamps hooked over sconces along one wall of the narthex. No one was in sight. An inside set of double doors led into the sanctuary and were closed. Electric wires trailed across the floor, issuing from a generator at the side of the room. Three wires led to the emergency lamps; the others snaked under the closed double doors and into the sanctuary. At the far end of the narthex a door opened onto a small room.

Matt stepped inside the room. Originally it must have been a cubicle for the mission head, but now it was someone's office. A metal desk covered with papers stood against one wall. Light from a small tensor lamp fell in a tight white circle on the desk top. Along the other walls of the room stood metal shelves filled with books, and Matt looked at some of the titles.

The Golden Bough
Witchcraft in the Middle Ages
Demonology: History and Theory
The Blood Cults of Western Europe
The Masks of God
Primitive Man: Myths and Symbols
Early Hunting Societies:
Animal Gods and Masters of the Hunt
Pastoral Care of the Sick and Elderly
Forbidden Food:

THE FEEDING

A Psychoanalytical Study of Cannibalism
Human Sacrifice in Primitive Cultures

Matt turned from the bookshelf. On the desk top, harshly illuminated by the tensor lamp, lay various pieces of paper, some covered with typing, others with handwriting. One stood out among the rest. On it were written:

Mother	CONSORT
Child	HEIR

THE OFFERING

THE FEEDING

The Offering was circled in black ink, *The Feeding* in red. Below that were several lines written in a language Matt could not even identify, let alone read. He reached out for the paper.

A hand snatched it away from him.

Startled, Matt looked up to see Father McKerry standing beside him, eyes emotionless behind thick, black-framed lenses as he crumpled the piece of paper in his right hand.

"If you want a guided tour, please ask." The priest's voice was soft, but edged with tension. "These are private papers."

"Sorry," Matt apologized, wondering what the priest was hiding. "Unusual books." He nodded at the shelves.

The priest smiled faintly. "A specialized collection, reflecting my interest in anthropology and primitive cultures." He stepped toward the office door, making it clear that he wanted Matt to follow him.

"A man of many interests," Matt said as they moved out into the narthex. "Architectural restoration. Anthropology . . ."

The priest maintained his faint smile. "This is a small town. The needs of the parish are few. My outside interests help me understand a little better the place where I am called to serve. Restoring the mission teaches me about the early fathers who settled this area. My anthropological studies reveal to me the life and culture of the Caiyallah Indians."

The priest stopped in the middle of the narthex. "But I'm surprised to see you here, Mr. Brenner. I had understood that you had little interest in our . . . project."

"I came here to ask about someone you talked with just the other day. A man from San Diego named Walter Selwyn."

The priest frowned. "Selwyn? Walter Selwyn?" He pursed his lips, trying to remember, then shook his head. "I talked to no one by that name."

"Maybe he didn't give you his name," Matt persisted, "but he talked with you. I'm sure of it. He mentioned you specifically."

Father McKerry frowned sympathetically. "I'm sorry. I didn't talk to many people yesterday. If I'd spoken with someone from San Diego named Walter Selwyn, I'd remember him."

Why would he lie about it? Matt wondered. Or why would Selwyn lie? "I'm sure you talked with him. Little guy." Matt indicated Walter Selwyn's height. "Wire-rim glasses. Jittery, worried-looking. Drove up here from San Diego looking for his daughter, Ginny. Talked with Cody about her. Claims she was the fourth passenger of that yellow Toyota—"

"No fourth body was found in the car," the priest interrupted with quiet conviction. "You know that better than anyone, Mr. Brenner."

Matt stopped. "No fourth body" was beginning to sound like a sales tract. How the hell do they know? Why are they all so goddamn sure?

"I didn't see a fourth body," he admitted, "but that doesn't mean there wasn't one."

Father McKerry shrugged. "My heart goes out to the poor man, this Selwyn. He didn't speak with me, but I wish he had. He sounds like someone in desperate need of counseling."

Matt's eyes narrowed. "What he needs is a straight answer."

The priest started to respond when a woman's voice called out, "Matt, you changed your mind. You decided to come help us after all."

He looked up to see Adriana Velotti emerging from the wooden doors of the sanctuary. He knew then who had told Father McKerry about his lack of interest in the restoration of Mission San Miguel. She was coldly beautiful as ever, dressed in black pants and a black cowled sweater. An amulet hung from a gold chain around her neck, and diamond earrings glittered against her short black hair.

As the doors swung open behind her, Matt could see inside the sanctuary, dark except for a bright light falling on the altar. The altar itself had no lectern or communion rail. A large, circular stone platform rose several feet above the altar floor, but no crucifix hung behind it. Painted instead on the wall was a fresco of Christ with the crown of thorns, blood flowing down his face and onto his white robes as he raised his hands in what looked like a gesture of benediction for the animals gathered around him.

They were not peaceful lambs and doves, but wild predators of the dark mountain forest—wolves, bears, mountain lions, eagles. Savage and dangerous, powerful bodies tensed, they seemed subdued by the dramatic figure with the blood-stained robes and the crown of thorns, but it was not love that commanded them. The blood-streaked face of the Christ on the sanctuary wall was cruel and fierce, distorted by a wolfish grin and strong white teeth. His arms were raised not in benediction but in a defiant show of power. The predators did not bow their heads in love and humility. They cowered.

A chill came over Matt Brenner that had nothing to do with the clammy darkness of the sanctuary.

"Christ triumphant, commanding the natural world," Father McKerry murmured behind him, voice hushed with awe. "You can actually feel the life force, can't you?"

Matt said nothing, repulsed by the fierce painted Christ and his predatory worshippers.

Adriana Velotti moved in close behind him, her perfume rich and musky. "This fresco is the work of a local artist," she said in a softly seductive voice. "His name is Gordon MacLeish. He has a powerful, original vision, don't you think?"

"It catches your eye," Matt agreed. "But what does it have to do with the Christian chapel?"

She smiled at him, her strong white teeth dazzling against the blackness of her hair and sweater. "It represents a symbolic union of Christian and

Indian beliefs. Christ as Master of the Animals. The Lord of Creation as the god of nature. It's probably the way the early Caiyallah converts saw Christ—as the great tribal magician controlling the natural world." She raised her shoulders in a pretty shrug. "That's what the experts say."

Matt frowned. "And what do they know?"

"Not much, my friend," boomed a deep male voice from the darkened sanctuary, startling Matt.

Out of the darkness stepped a tall, powerfully built man clothed in black. His skull was entirely bald, and his right eye glittered with an unnatural intensity. The shock of recognition was visible on Matt's face as he saw once again the figure in black emerging from the forest beside Mirror Lake, but this time Matt noticed that the right eye glittering so brilliantly was made of glass. It stood immobile in the lean, cadaverous face, staring at Matt with a cold luminosity.

"My science," continued the tall man, "anthropology, is comprised of much guesswork, like most sciences." The deep voice had the same accent as Adriana Velotti's, the same strange R's and odd lilt. "But, of course, there are good guesses and bad guesses. The Caiyallah Indians seem to have had an almost purely Neolithic religion, one that worshipped animals, especially beasts of prey, as gods. The shaman who could control them through magic, the Master of Animals, was a god of gods. If you will, the Lord of Hosts." The heavy eyebrows rose slightly. "When the first Caiyallahs accepted Christianity, they could hardly have envisaged Christ in any form other than the Master of the Animals."

Adriana Velotti grabbed Matt's arm. "Matt, Dr. Geza Todor, renowned authority on primitive cultures and visiting Professor of Anthropology at Berkeley. Geza, Mr. Matt Brenner, distinguished Los Angeles architect in charge of a major project for CalForm."

Geza Todor grasped Matt's hand in a powerful grip. "An honor, sir." He bowed formally.

"Same here." Matt studied Todor's impassive face, thinking that the bastard was pretending not to recognize him.

"We've been trying to get Matt to help us with the restoration," Adriana Velotti explained.

"There is little here to interest a professional architect," Todor said, watching Matt's face for a reaction. "The structure is, for the most part, crudely designed. Is it not, Mr. Brenner?"

"A type of folk architecture," Matt agreed, then asked, "What interests you about it, Dr. Todor?"

"The curious intermingling of Indian and Spanish beliefs. Usually the Spanish Christian missionary culture dominates, but here in Black Cavern, this seems not to have happened. For example," Todor said, pointing to the raised stone altar inside the sanctuary, "that altar reflects Neolithic rather than Christian beliefs." The glass eye turned back to Matt. "From what we can determine, blood sacrifices were performed on such altars. The nature of the victims, whether animal or human, cannot be determined as easily."

A heavy silence fell over the room. Matt could hear his heart thumping inside his chest, and he was sure the others could hear it too. He's taunting me, he thought, staring at the tall figure in black. He knows why I've come here. Matt glanced at Father McKerry for support, but the round-faced priest seemed curiously detached, waiting patiently, hands folded, as though Geza Todor had been discussing weekly church attendance instead of blood sacrifices.

"Well . . ." Todor extended his hand again. "It has been a pleasure, Mr. Brenner, but I'm afraid I have work that won't wait any longer. I will leave you in the company of the good Father and the delightful Miss Velotti." A cold smile flickered across the cadaverous face. "Be careful, sir, or you may find yourself enlisted in their . . . project."

Todor turned to leave.

Adriana Velotti grabbed Matt's arm and started to pull him toward the sanctuary. "Matt, come and see—"

"Dr. Todor!" Matt called out sharply.

Todor stopped and turned around, the cold glass eye coming to rest on Matt.

"I want to talk with you," Matt said.

Todor frowned.

Matt's face tightened with anger. "What did you mean," he demanded, "that day at Mirror Lake?"

"I meant exactly what I said."

"You told us to get out of here," Matt shouted at him. "You threatened us!"

"I . . . advised you to leave. At once. It was good advice." Todor fixed Matt with a steady stare, electric light flashing off the glass eye. "It is still good advice."

Matt moved in on the taller man. "Start talking sense, Doctor. What the hell do you mean?"

Todor held his ground. "I am in no position to explain myself, Mr. Brenner. And even if I were, I fear you would . . . disbelieve me." He stared at Matt thoughtfully. "It is good advice, however. Take it or leave it, as you will. If you can." Todor bowed slightly. ''And now I truly must be going. Good day, sir.'' He turned to leave.

Matt reached out to stop him.

Father McKerry stepped forward. ''We don't want trouble here, Mr. Brenner.'' The priest's round face hardened. ''And if you're looking for trouble, we don't want you.''

22

Interlude

It was not until they were standing at the front door of Gordon MacLeish's two-story redwood cabin that Robin remembered his hideous paintings. The mutilated bodies, the blood—the mere thought of them made her stomach contract.

"Are there . . . any . . . new paintings?"

"I'm working on a large canvas right now," MacLeish said, leading the way through a spacious living room with fireplace and outside onto the redwood deck. "But we're not going to look at my stuff today." He turned around on the sundeck and smiled at her, his blond hair ruffled by a sharp mountain breeze. "This time I want to hear about your work."

As Robin smiled back at him the tightness in her stomach was replaced by a flushed excitement that made her breath come faster and her face feel hot. He's so beautiful, she thought. The familiar quivering started between her thighs again. You're married, she warned herself, with two wonderful children.

"Well?" MacLeish raised his eyebrows. "What about it?"

Robin's breath seemed to stop. She licked dry lips. "About . . . what?"

MacLeish laughed. "Your work. Do we get to hear about it? Or are you one of those modest artists? Unlike me."

"Oh, yeah . . . " She smiled as waves of relief and disappointment washed over her in turn.

MacLeish poured the wine, and they talked. For the most part, Robin talked, but it was hard for her at first. She was serious about her photography and loved doing it, but she did not talk about it much. Matt was too preoccupied with his own work, and her married friends only wanted to talk about the standard topics of money, kids, fantasy lovers. Once she had driven up to San Francisco to visit an old college friend who was also a professional photographer. They had spent the whole weekend talking about money and kids and fantasy lovers. But Gordon MacLeish was a good listener. He made her feel that he cared about her work, that he wanted to hear about it.

So she talked, excited by the idea of communicating, one artist to another.

And even more exciting was the physical presence of Gordon MacLeish himself, sitting casually there in one of the deck chairs, blond hair blowing in the mountain wind, open shirt revealing his muscular chest, his long, powerful legs stretched out comfortably in front of him, his clear gray eyes directly on hers, making the quivering sensation throb within her even as she talked.

The afternoon shadows lengthened, and the wind grew colder.

They moved inside.

They sat on a long, dark blue couch. MacLeish started a fire, then poured more wine. Robin was wearing shorts and a thin, sleeveless cotton blouse. The cool mountain wind had chilled her, and the heat from the crackling fire felt good. She slipped out of her sandals and tucked her legs up underneath her on the couch. The wine intensified the heat within her and the heat from the fireplace flames. She began to feel deliciously high, slightly dizzy. The couch on which she and MacLeish sat seemed to be a boat rocking gently on a golden sea of late afternoon sunlight. Her curls clung to her forehead, and brushing them back, she realized that her hand was trembling, along with the rest of her.

She took a slow, careful sip of wine to steady herself. As they continued talking, she noticed the way MacLeish would occasionally drop his eyes from hers to glance directly at her breasts or at her left hand resting lightly on a tanned thigh. Her heart began beating wildly. She found herself wishing she hadn't worn a bra. Her large nipples stiffened at the thought, and she wanted MacLeish to see them through her thin cotton blouse. She wanted to display herself to him, naked, here beside the warm glow of the fireplace on the couch that rocked gently out into the golden afternoon. She desperately wanted him.

MacLeish's painting *The Watcher in the Shadows* flashed before her eyes. In place of MacLeish's own handsome face there appeared the distorted canine visage of the Watcher, fangs dripping slaver, as it moved out from the forest undergrowth toward the two children—*Joshua! Katie!*—playing in the meadow. Like my photograph, she thought, with a calm, unreal panic.

Robin set the wine glass down on MacLeish's coffee table with an audible clink and rose from the couch.

She turned to him. "Thanks for everything, but I've got to go. My little girl's back at the hotel by herself." Robin's voice caught. "My husband will be worried about me."

MacLeish looked up at her. "Husbands and children are rather like parents, aren't they? We tend to worry about them more than they worry about us."

Robin flushed, and reached awkwardly for her purse, aware of MacLeish's eyes on her as she bent over to retrieve it from the sofa. "I shouldn't be here," she said, straightening up, brushing distractedly at a stray curl. "I never should have come here. I've really got to go."

MacLeish shrugged slightly and leaned back against the dark blue couch, his eyes fixed on hers. "If you have to leave, I'll drive you back. But I don't think you really want to go." He got easily to his feet. "I think you want to stay. I think that's why you came over here in the first place." He took a step toward her. "I want you to stay."

Robin moved back. She turned toward the fireplace, stared into the flames, shivering. This is wrong, she told herself firmly. But he was right. She did want to stay. It was why she had accepted his invitation back at the bar. It was what she had wanted from the first moment she saw him there, chopping wood in the clearing.

MacLeish put a hand, lightly on her shoulder. A

shudder coursed through her.

She moved away. "Really, no . . . don't."

The hand moved up to her neck and turned her head, gently, toward his.

Her mouth fell open. "I . . ."

Their lips met. The purse fell from her hand, bouncing on the hardwood floor.

She jerked her mouth away from MacLeish's and looked down. "Oh, shit . . ."

"Don't even think about it," he whispered, and kissed her again, putting his arms around her, drawing her in close against him.

Robin shuddered violently and threw her arms around his neck, their tongues thrusting deep into each other's mouths as he guided her slowly, imperceptibly across the floor and back toward the couch. This is wrong, Robin tried to tell herself again. She started to break away, but MacLeish's grip on her tightened. She embraced him passionately in response. He reached up and began unbuttoning her blouse. His hands grazed her breasts lightly as he worked at the buttons. She raised a hand to stop him, then rested it gently on his hand as he undid the last button.

The blouse fell open, and the heat from the fireplace felt good on her bare stomach. He unfastened her bra. It parted in front, the two cups dropping away to reveal her small white breasts, the dark red nipples jutting out hard and aroused from the soft pink, almost colorless areolas encircling them. He began to stroke her swollen nipples slowly, pulling on them gently. Under his light touch they stretched out incredibly long and hard, like the huge, thrusting nipples of a nude model she had seen once, so big they hardly seemed real.

Robin leaned back her head, mouth open, moaning softly. He bent down and took one of the swollen, straining nipples into his mouth, his beard scratching the soft skin of her breast. He teased her erect nipple, bit down on it lovingly, then sucked on it until Robin felt the room start to whirl around her. He eased her down onto the couch, removing her open blouse and shorts. Robin helped him, her hands trembling, eyes feverish with desire.

Her whole body was trembling. She could see her flesh quiver as MacLeish took his mouth from one of her hugely erect nipples, glistening now in the firelight, and moved slowly down her torso and over her belly. When his lips touched her labia she gasped. Then his tongue probed at her clitoris and she cried out. Her breathing became harsh and erratic. He continued to push against it with his tongue, sucking harder on it, adding to her own wetness until she felt she must be staining the couch and tried to move, but then her body stiffened and a tremor jolted through her as she cried out again and the whole world, sunlight and firelight, seemed to fall away in one sweet rush.

Then he was kneeling in front of her on the couch, his own clothes removed, one hand on his penis as he guided it into her. It was much larger than she had expected. It's too big, she thought groggily. It'll tear me open. He'll hurt me! She gasped as the head pressed against her wet labia, then entered her with a sudden thrust. The whole huge length of the shaft was inside her now, filling her up with its warmth and its hardness. MacLeish began rocking inside her with a steadily accelerating rhythm, the great hard length of him thrusting in and out of her. She moved with him and against him, increasing the power of his thrusts with her own frenzied urgency, time and space dissolving in one blinding orgasm after another, the passion growing with each climax, damp flesh pressing damp flesh, bodies locked together, hearts and blood pounding furiously in unison.

It came out of nowhere like a rush of cold air.

Ice cold, the chill gripped her heart and spread through her body like a malign, living presence. She saw Joshua. She felt him, heard him, alone, frightened, surrounded by darkness, in mortal danger.

Robin, her face damp with sweat, looked up at MacLeish and saw by firelight his steel gray eyes, his handsome face expressionless, sweat beading his smooth forehead as he thrust mechanically into her with grim determination. Taking his pleasure, she thought suddenly, recalling that faded expression from another, distant age. But there was no pleasure to it. He was like a machine, a household sex aid programed for maximum enjoyment. The deep thrusting was no longer a shared, sensuous frenzy. It hurt, like being battered by a blunt instrument, hammering away without passion or sensitivity.

Robin grimaced at the pain and the spreading coldness in her body. She tried to twist out from under him, but MacLeish kept on with his labors.

She sensed again the horror of Joshua's desperation, the mortal danger.

He's not in danger, she tried to tell herself rationally. He's out riding bikes with that Kyle kid.

But he *was* in danger. She knew that.

And there was nothing she could do to help him.

23

The Pit

The darkness had them.

Joshua knew it the minute he and Kyle stepped inside the abandoned Kemmering Mine.

The darkness and the damp and the strange, dank smell engulfed them. The soft, barely heard sounds of chill water trickled over cold stone, dropping slowly, drip by drip, onto more stone. The mine was its own world, and once inside, you were part of it. Joshua turned and looked back at their bikes outside propped against a pine, the sun shining through the pine needles, deep blue sky in the background streaked with thin wisps of scudding clouds. It was so close. A few steps and you were back out in the sunlight and safety.

But the darkness had them now, and the bright world outside was like a brilliant, flat photograph —unreal and unreachable. Even the outside sounds seemed to disappear. The rustle of wind through tree boughs and the chirping of birds were all swallowed up by the soft, sinister muttering noises of the darkness.

Joshua turned away from the distant brightness and hurried to catch up with Kyle, who was rushing forward into the darkness, the thin beam of his pocket flashlight bouncing in front of him. Damn his stupid ass, Joshua thought resentfully. This was all Kyle's fault. If he had brains instead of bullshit we wouldn't even be here now.

Kyle stumbled over something in the darkness. ''Shit!'' His voice rang off the cold stone walls.

''What's wrong?'' Joshua asked, moving up behind him.

The flashlight beam dipped to reveal a roughly pyramidal shape. ''One of those goddamn stalagmites,'' Kyle said.

Joshua squatted down to study it. After a few seconds he said, ''Looks more like a pile of horseshit or somethin'.''

''Horseshit?'' Kyle's laughter echoed in the darkness. ''When's the last time some horse dragged his butt in here?''

''It's not rock,'' Joshua insisted. ''That's for sure.''

''Horseshit!'' Kyle laughed again.

The sound came then, a sharp, squeaking sound, followed by a dry rustling of leathery wings, as if some dead, petrified bird had come to life suddenly, awakened from years of stony sleep by Kyle's laughter. The squeaking came again. The wings rustled.

''What the fuck's that?'' Kyle whispered, turning his narrow flashlight beam toward the sounds.

When the light fell on the bat hanging upside down from a supporting beam, the creature opened its mouth and screamed. The weak light outlined a mouth full of small, sharp fangs. Unfurling its wings, the bat dropped from its perch and began to swoop around the dark mine. In the middle of one swoop it veered suddenly and headed straight for the flashlight, missing it by inches. Dusty wings scraped Kyle's face as the creature shot past.

"Goddamn it!" Kyle roared, hands raised to protect his face. "Get it the fuck away from me!"

The bat swooped at him again. Kyle screamed in pure terror, drowning out the bat's own piercing squeals. He struck out awkwardly at it with his flashlight, but that only made things worse. In the darkness beyond Kyle's screams, Joshua could hear more squeals and flapping wings. Something hit the back of his neck and bounced off. Dry, leathery wings brushed his arm as one of the creatures flew past. He shuddered in disgust.

"They're everywhere!" Kyle shrieked, swiping at the darting bats like a crazy man, flashlight beam zigzagging through the darkness.

"Let's get outta here," Joshua shouted at him.

Kyle turned and ran, but not toward the entrance. That way out was now a gauntlet of swooping, squealing bats. Kyle plunged deeper into the darkness, the flashlight beam pointing up as he covered his head with both hands. Joshua protected his own head from the dive-bombing bats and ran after Kyle. Suddenly he stumbled, tripping over a pile of hardened bat guano. He threw out his arms as he pitched forward, regaining his balance at the last possible moment.

He heard Kyle yell and saw the flashlight beam

leap up into the air, turn over and fall to the ground, bouncing as it hit.

"Kyle!" Joshua ran toward him, trying to avoid more guano piles, even though he could see nothing in the darkness except the flashlight beam and the narrow stretch of uneven floor it illuminated.

Kyle was screaming for help as Joshua came upon the dropped flashlight, picked it up and shined it at the screams.

He gasped in shock.

Kyle was hanging onto a low, rusted metal bar that formed a crude barrier at the edge of a sudden drop into blackness. His legs and lower torso hung down into the dark cavity. His glasses were wildly askew, his face pale with terror as he screamed for help.

Joshua edged slowly over toward him, reaching out with his left hand, the right one clutching the flashlight. "Just grab hold and I'll pull you out."

"Can't reach it," Kyle whispered, his voice choked with fear.

Joshua was at the edge of the drop-off now. He leaned over carefully, left hand extended, feet planted firmly on the rocky ledge. And as he leaned over, the weak light shined down into the darkness below Kyle, revealing the dim outlines of a wide, deep shaft that seemed to drop away forever into blackness. Joshua closed his eyes and shuddered, the flashlight trembling in his right hand.

"What's wrong?" Kyle asked, turning his head to look.

"Don't!" Joshua warned. "Just grab my hand, now, and don't look down." Joshua's voice was shaking. "Don't even think about it."

Kyle grabbed at the outstretched hand with such desperate force that he almost pulled both of them back into the abyss. Small stones rattled beneath Joshua's feet as Kyle's weight dragged him perilously closer to the yawning blackness.

"Quit pullin' on it, dickhead!" Joshua screamed at him. "Just hang on, okay?"

Joshua braced his feet and began to pull Kyle slowly up out of the pit. It was hard work. Sweat broke out on his arms and forehead despite the chill inside the abandoned mine. The muscles in his forearms trembled.

"Lift your feet up and climb," Joshua gasped, his chest heaving. "I'm startin' to slip!"

Kyle scrambled up on top of the rusted metal barrier, his feet kicking out wildly over the black space of the pit. Then he was on the solid rock of the ledge. He stayed there on his hands and knees without moving, head down, gasping for breath like a winded horse.

After a few minutes Joshua asked, "You okay?"

"Sure." Kyle nodded. "Fuckin' piece a shit almost broke my leg." Kyle rubbed his right shin and winced. "Amost fell in that fuckin' hole."

"Maybe we better go back," Joshua suggested hopefully.

"Hey, man." Kyle turned to him, glasses still hanging lopsided on his face. "I'm the one almost got my ass broke. Where do you get off actin' so chicken shit scared?"

"Fuck you if I'm scared, asshole," Joshua shot back, his cheeks burning with shame.

"So if you ain't scared," Kyle got to his feet, wincing as he put weight on the bruised shin, "why go back?"

Because they're here, you poor dumb shithead,

Joshua wanted to say as his heart raced with terror and he looked out into the darkness. They're here and they'll find us and tear the meat off our bones.

"Long's we watch out for them fuckin' holes, ain't nothin' to it, man." Kyle pitched a rock into the darkness for emphasis.

Does it even matter, Joshua wondered, whether they come after you in your own bedroom or you go in to meet them? "Okay," Joshua agreed finally. All that really matters is, in the end they get you. "But I'm keepin' the flashlight."

"Bullshit! That's my light, sucker."

"Who almost lost it?" Joshua asked.

"Fuck you!" Kyle glared over the top of his crooked glasses. "That was a accident. Give it here!" Kyle grabbed for the flashlight.

Joshua backed nimbly out of his reach. "Accidents can happen more than once. 'Specially if you're a total and complete asshole."

"Fuck you!" Kyle grabbed for the flashlight again.

Joshua sidestepped him. "Either I'm keepin' it . . . or we go back. Now."

Kyle stopped, stared at Joshua, then shrugged. "So keep it. The batteries are almost run down by now anyways."

They continued their journey into the darkness. The sounds moved with them, only slight background noises at first—flutters, shifting movements, dim echoes. More bats, Joshua thought, and ignored them. But the deeper they went into the Kemmering Mine, the more noticeable the sounds became. At one point Joshua stopped abruptly, flashlight raised in front of him. The sounds stopped. When he and Kyle started moving again, so did the sounds. It was not good, and Joshua knew it.

They came to a triple fork, and after several minutes of argument and hesitation, they took the right fork. They had not gone far when they noticed loose objects underfoot that began to make walking difficult—hard, but slippery, like half-eaten ears of buttered roasted corn. Joshua pointed the flashlight down at the cavern floor.

The object in the circle of light looked like a white tree branch covered with mud. Joshua prodded it with his toe. Don't touch it, his mind warned automatically, but he ignored the warning and bent over to pick it up.

He smelled it then.

And knew exactly what he had picked up.

He gagged violently, throwing it down onto the floor where it clattered among the other bones. Joshua rubbed his hand furiously against his jeans, trying to get rid of the slimy feel of rotted flesh on a human bone. *Still had pieces of fresh meat stickin' to 'em.* Joshua remembered the old man at the gas station and his gorge rose again.

"Well?" Kyle demanded behind him. "What is it?"

"Shit." Joshua's voice was trembling. "Fuckin' shit!" He turned to Kyle. "Let's get outta here!"

"Hey, stay cool man, okay? What is it?"

"Look!" Joshua jabbed the flashlight at the bones on the floor. The blood on one of the bones still glinted a dull, coppery red.

"Holy shit," Kyle whispered. He knelt down and picked up one of the bones and sniffed at it. Then pulled his head back suddenly, teeth bared in disgust. "Jesus! Smells worse'n fuckin' dog barf!"

"Only a pervert'd stick his nose in it. I'm goin' back." Joshua turned abruptly, swinging the flashlight beam around with him.

It fell on the half-eaten corpse, leaning against the dark stone wall.

The corpse still had some pieces of clothing on, but not much flesh. It leaned back against the stone wall in a half-sitting, half-crouching position. Rats scurried over it like ants on a piece of rotted meat. The intestines had been gouged out. Several rats were crawling around inside the cavity that remained. Other rats chewed at stray scraps of flesh on arms and legs, although these were mostly bone by now. The top of the head had been torn off, like the one on the cavern floor outside the Sealed Tomb. The rats crawling over the face had pretty well stripped it, but a pair of rimless glasses, one lens shattered, still balanced grotesquely on a bare nasal ridge, framing a pair of empty, staring sockets.

Joshua remembered the rimless glasses Walter Selwyn had worn. A weight seemed to hit him in the chest. This time the gorge did not stay down, the vomit filling his mouth suddenly and spilling out over his lips.

Behind him Kyle let out an ear-splitting scream and started to charge madly forward into the darkness.

"Wait!" Joshua spit the vomit from his mouth and pointed the flashlight at the fleeing boy. "Not that–"

The shadow leaped from the darkness and grabbed Kyle. The boy cried out again, but it was not a scream this time. It was the deep, despairing moan of someone who knows that the end has come at last.

Joshua's mind was on fire. Save him! Help him! Don't leave him! But there was no saving him. Not now. He could try, and get killed along with him.

Joshua's mind was still in turmoil when his body made the decision for him. It turned around the other way and ran.

Into the face of the demon.

Open, dog-like, grinning mouth. Blood dripping from sharp fangs. Bits of flesh lodged between them. And the eyes—the horrible white, burning eyes that had claimed him the night of—

You are mine!

The cavern exploded then with the screams of a thousand demons, echoing off stone walls, shrieking into darkness, burning into his brain.

It was only when he felt the raw pain in his throat that he knew the screams were his own.

24

Unholy Visions

Robin woke in darkness.

In the first moment of complete disorientation that comes with awakening suddenly from deep sleep, she knew nothing—except that she was lying nude in a strange bed beside a strange male body, also nude, and that the window was open, letting in cold mountain air and pale moonlight, and that her body was encrusted with dried sweat, her mouth parched and foul-tasting.

Then the memories returned, fixing time and place and what had happened before she drifted off into a restless, nightmare-haunted sleep in which demons pursued Joshua and Katie through a vast underground parking garage while she watched helplessly over a video monitor. She sat up abruptly, shaking off the last traces of the dream. She winced at the bad taste in her mouth and ran a hand absently through her hair. It was tangled and matted. She turned to look at Gordon MacLeish's hard, muscular body outlined by moonlight, the suntanned flesh almost black against the white sheets. His back rose and fell softly with the even rhythm of deep sleep. Here was her dream lover, the man she had made passionate love to only hours before, surrendering herself to him as she never had to any man, not even Matt.

Matt, she thought, and her stomach felt queasy.

Now, looking at Gordon MacLeish sleeping nude beside her, his magnificent body on full display, she felt absolutely nothing. All the heat, the crazy lust and mad desire that had driven her into another man's bed for the first time in her married life was all gone, like burning whiskey poured from a bottle. And she was that bottle, empty and clear and cold in the white moonlight, watching a sleeping man who interested her now about as much as a sleeping dog. It's the guilt, she thought listlessly, but she did not feel guilty, just empty and cold and transparent as the glass in the bedroom window.

She swung her legs down onto the floor. Gordon MacLeish stirred slightly and muttered something, but did not break the rhythm of his sleep. She looked down at her body, washed pale as fresh milk by the moonlight. Her nipples still were fiercely erect, swollen to twice their normal size, jutting out dramatically from her breasts. Christ, she thought, after Matt divorces me, I can always get a job as a *Penthouse* centerfold. But the idea was not funny and she did not smile.

She rose from the bed, hands pressing down on the mattress so it would not spring back with the release of her weight. Her joints felt stiff, her body bruised. There was no more burning between her legs, only a raw soreness that reminded her of the days when she had gone horseback riding too long as a young girl. She groped for her clothes in the moonlit darkness without success, then she remembered that he had undressed her on the blue couch. They had made love there first, before he carried her into the bedroom.

She felt her way into the living room, the carpet cool beneath her bare feet. Large blocks of moonlight spilled across the living room floor. She picked up her scattered clothes. She was shivering now from the cold night air, her thin shirt and shorts hardly offering much warmth. She picked up her purse from a side table, then took out a comb and started pulling at her tangled locks.

What do I do now? she wondered. Go in there and wake him up and say, Hey, I've had my forbidden fuck and now I'm sick of you, so take me back to the hotel, would you?

It was a problem she had not considered, but she couldn't just stay there, not with him in the next room sleeping it off. Besides, it was late. She didn't even know how late. Robin disliked wearing watches and she hadn't noticed any clocks in MacLeish's house, but it was late enough to make Matt worried. Her stomach went queasy again at the thought of her husband and what she could possibly tell him. She pulled hard at a stubborn tangle and the pain made her yelp. It's his damn fault anyway, she thought resentfully. If he'd taken us back home when I asked him to . . .

But the blame felt hollow, the anger feigned. The truth was she missed Matt and wanted more than anything just to be with him again, wanted to lean against his calm reasonableness and stubborn practicality, wanted to be loved by him with his gentleness and patience, so different from the sleeping superstud in the next room. Please God, she prayed with sudden fervor, don't let him find out. Just let everything be like it was before.

But even as she prayed for it, she felt with a dreadful certainty that everything already had changed and nothing would ever be the same again. The feeling swept over her like a clammy mist. She shuddered. I've got to get out of here, she told herself, dropping the comb back into her purse, turning toward the front door.

Then she saw the thin shaft of white moonlight shining through the partially closed door to MacLeish's studio.

She knew what was in there. She had no desire to see those hideous paintings again, but she was angry with Gordon MacLeish now, disgusted by him. She wanted to force herself to look at those paintings one last time and fix his memory in her mind once and for all.

She moved up to the half-closed door and pushed it open. It was like stepping into a crystal palace of white light. The three glass walls revealed a breathtaking panorama of dark forests, moonlit mountains, and black sky speckled with bright stars. The studio itself was bathed in soft white moonlight, the paintings along the fourth wall.

She forced herself to look and turned away suddenly, revulsion twisting her stomach. The painting was called *The Offering.* It depicted a large room in a deep cavern. A young girl, her hair long, body soft and beautifully sculpted, lay nude on her back atop a raised stone platform, her hands and feet held down against the cold stone by . . . Watchers in the Shadows. Not just one obscene apparition, but a grisly throng, they crowded close around the helpless girl, her mouth wrenched open with pain and terror as she watched one of the disgusting creatures mount her, thrusting into her with all the finesse of a rutting bull, its claws digging into her soft flesh, its animal mouth gaping wide with sexual heat, fangs clotted with unspeakable filth, white eyes burning.

"God, no!" Robin backed away from the painting, hanging there ghastly in the moonlight, the monstrous creatures crawling over the wretched girl, coarse black animal hair covering misshapen gray-skinned bodies. Robin's forehead burned. Her throat ached. He's psychotic, she thought, real terror taking hold of her as she turned away from the obscene painting—toward the next one.

She was able to keep from screaming only by clapping both hands to her mouth, but the muffled wail that escaped was worse than any scream. The next painting, *The Wayfarer,* was Joshua's nightmare vision in the forest come to life. The pine trees gave way to a clearing in which another young girl, this one with short dark hair, lay on the forest floor while . . . Robin shut her eyes and trembled violently. She could not look at the abomination before her, the hideous creatures dismembering the young girl and tearing the limbs from her body. One monster crouched at the side of the clearing, fierce white eyes glaring out at the viewer as it gnawed on a severed arm, blood running from its canine mouth, teeth gnashing furiously to rend the still warm flesh from the bones. Two other monsters quarreled over a piece of bloody meat torn from the girl's body, snarling at each other like dogs fighting for a bone. A third creature stuffed intestines and other viscera into its mouth, the long intestinal ropes drooping down onto its chest.

Dear God, Robin thought hysterically, gorge rising at the back of her throat. Did Josh really see something like this?

She had no words for what she saw.

She backed away, heart pounding inside her chest, and moved toward the studio door. She had seen enough. Monsters! she thought savagely, and Gordon MacLeish the most horrifying of them all because he was a monster in human form. Dread seized Robin's heart. Did one of those things really come after Josh and Katie in the basement?

The rattling came from the far end of the fourth wall.

Something clattered down onto the floor.

Robin jumped at the sound, turning.

What she saw almost stopped her heart. A numbness crept over her, making her seem to drift in slow motion, like a dreamer fleeing the unseen horror of a nightmare. She saw the paintbrush that had rolled off its stand bounce on the floor several times, the long handle vibrating.

And she saw the painting behind the stand.

It was large, much larger than the others. It filled up over half of the fourth wall like an epic mural. The painting gave a very real illusion of depth. It seemed to draw you into it, entirely against your will—past the large oak trees at the edge of the small cemetery, past the black wrought-iron fence surrounding it, past weathered tombstones standing sharp and clear in the painting's own white moonlight. You felt as if you were really there, inside the painting, a viewer no longer but an actual observer of the event, a silent, unwilling participant.

A ring of monsters crouched like dogs in a circle, fangs sharp and bloody, burning white eyes fixed on the center of the circle, where a monster larger than the others, spectacular in its repulsiveness, conducted an unspeakable ritual.

A small boy, about Joshua's age, knelt beside the huge monster. One of its claw-like hands gripped the back of the boy's neck; the other held out a piece of bloody meat to the child. Before them on the ground sprawled a mutilated corpse, internal organs exposed, large chunks of flesh torn from the bones. A nearby grave lay unearthed, its coffin broken open, fresh dirt scattered across the cemetery grass. The child reached out toward the unholy food with obscene glee, his mouth already full, gobbets of flesh dribbling down his chin. The great demon seemed almost to be smiling, like an approving parent watching an infant's first meal of solid food. And in the child's eyes there burned a feverish, inhuman light.

The painting was called *The Feeding.*

"No," Robin whispered.

Then the terror overcame her. "Noooo!"

Her scream bounced off the glass walls, hammering at her eardrums. She did not feel the pain. She screamed again, then her voice broke, the scream rattling in her throat.

In another part of the house a door banged open and someone called out, uncertainly, "Robin?"

MacLeish!

She moved fast, out the studio at a dead run, her purse flapping against her side. Gordon MacLeish stood in the doorway to the bedroom, still nude, one hand on the living room light switch, the other rubbing at his eyes with the awkward movement of someone half-asleep.

"Robin!" He turned and reached for her.

She kept moving, out the front door and across the driveway and into the front seat of MacLeish's Cherokee. The keys were still in the ignition. She turned it on, and the engine caught. Please God, she prayed, let it be automatic. She threw it into drive and floored the gas. The tires spun with an earsplitting whine, kicking out gravel behind them.

MacLeish burst from the front door, still nude, a very wide-awake look in his eyes now.

Robin finally released the brake. The Cherokee leaped forward, veering crazily toward the edge of the driveway. She turned hard on the steering wheel and brought the vehicle screeching back into line. Jumping on the gas, she headed straight for the road back to Caiyallah Lodge.

MacLeish reached her just as she was negotiating a wild right turn onto the road. He grabbed hold of the door handle on the driver's side with both hands, running furiously to keep up with the vehicle's accelerating momentum.

"Robin," he shouted at her through the open window. "Shut it off! Now!"

She glanced fearfully at MacLeish's narrow gray eyes and open mouth, veins bulging in his neck. She kept the pedal floored. The Cherokee swung out into the road, fishtailing dangerously. MacLeish was still shouting at her. She kept her eyes straight ahead, fighting with the steering wheel to keep the vehicle on the road. MacLeish's voice rose in crescendo with the whining motor as the transmission jerked through the gears.

And then the screaming was gone.

She looked up at the rearview mirror and saw MacLeish rolling nude out into the middle of the road. Then there was a sharp curve and he was gone. Robin shuddered, tasting sour vomit at the back of her throat. She took her foot off the gas and hit the brakes as the Cherokee swung into another sharp turn, tires squealing.

She steered through it, then leaned back and gave a deep sigh of relief as the road opened out onto a long, tree-lined straightaway. Her foot rode the accelerator, and the Cherokee's speed increased.

The next curve came at her without any warning.

One moment she was barreling down the straightaway; the next she was heading for a wall of pines. She jumped on the brakes, cutting hard left at the same time. Tires shrieked, and the Cherokee tilted left, wobbling on two wheels. For one heart-stopping instant Robin knew it would tip all the way over, hit the embankment, and never stop rolling. But the Cherokee somehow righted itself, falling back onto all four wheels, fishtailing madly like a drop of water skittering across a hot greased skillet. Headlights flipped back and forth from road to pine trees.

She almost had it under control again when the Cherokee shot off the narrow shoulder and dipped down nose first into a shallow gully, bouncing so hard the headlights flipped straight up and the whole frame shuddered. Robin was thrown up out of her seat, knocking her head hard against the roof. The Cherokee jolted over rocks and holes. Dust whirled past the headlights and pine boughs snapped across the windshield.

The right wheel dropped into a deep hole. The vehicle flipped over onto its side, crashing down with a violence that almost threw Robin headfirst through the windshield.

Bruised, sobbing, terrified, she crawled up out of the driver's door. The left wheels were still spinning. Dust drifted in front of the headlights like fog in a horror movie. She climbed down to the ground on unsteady legs.

She stumbled toward the highway. Her breath came in short, ragged gasps. Her ears rang with the squeal of skidding rubber and the grinding of gears.

She did not hear the speeding car.

The driver leaned on his horn, then hit the brakes. The car began weaving out of control, and Robin threw her arms up in front of her.

The car skidded dangerously around her and came to a jolting stop. The driver's door flew open.

"Robin!" a voice called out to her.

MacLeish! she thought hopelessly, bending over double under the glare of the car's headlights.

But then the voice called her name again.

"Matt . . . " Tears came to her eyes.

"What are you doing here?" He grabbed her roughly. "Where the hell have you been?"

He knows, she thought wearily, too tired to run or lie.

"I've been looking everywhere for—" He took a quick, angry breath.

"Matt, I . . . ." She shook her head. The tears were coming too fast.

"Look at me."

"Matt . . ."

"Look at me!" He lifted her face until their eyes met. "Joshua's missing."

25

Victim

The ambulance was waiting for them.

Its red turret light revolved silently, bouncing off pine trees, parked cars, and the gray face of the mountainside looming above the entrance to the abandoned Kemmering Mine.

Panic-stricken, Robin turned to her husband. "You didn't tell me he was hurt."

"I didn't know." Matt cut sharply into the crowded turnout before the mine entrance. "All Roy said when he stopped me outside the bar was that Cody found the bikes. No sign of the boys. Anywhere."

Robin threw open her door before the Mercedes came to a full stop. She stumbled as her feet skidded over gravel, then she started running.

"Robin!" Matt turned off the ignition and jumped out of the car.

Beyond the parked cars a group of onlookers stood pressed around the loading end of the ambulance. Under the sharp bursts of bright red lights Robin could see Roy Danforth, face buried in his hands, shoulders shaking. Buck Cody stood beside him, Stetson tilted back, a flat, dull look in his eyes. When he saw Robin running toward him, Cody's eyes widened, and he started to say something.

Matt caught up with her, grabbing her left arm. "Hold on, okay?" She tried to jerk free. "Running won't—"

Roy Danforth pulled his hands away from his face, looking up at the sound of Matt's voice. Danforth's fat, bearded face went pale under the flashing red light. His lower lip started to quiver, and a thin trickle of blood burst from his right nostril.

"You did it to him," he shrieked suddenly. "Your goddamn fucking kid did it to him!" He pointed a trembling arm at the ambulance.

Matt and Robin stopped in their tracks. Matt stared at where Danforth was pointing, but he could see nothing beyond the crowd gathered around the ambulance, except the movement of two paramedics as they carried something toward a stretcher on the ground.

"It was his idea to go inside," Danforth kept screaming. "He fucking knew this would happen!"

Matt turned and stared at Danforth's haggard face, the thin line of blood glistening from his nose down into his beard. "Roy, what are you—"

"I'll kill you!" Danforth lunged at him.

Robin screamed. As Buck Cody grabbed at Roy Danforth's left arm, Danforth turned and swung at

Cody with a hard right. Cody dodged, taking it on the side of the jaw, but the force of impact staggered him. He stumbled backwards, the Stetson flying off his head. Danforth pulled back to let him have it again.

Floyd Kessler sprang out of nowhere and seized Danforth's right arm, whipping him around. Then he hit him, hard, full in the paunch of his soft stomach. Danforth bent over, the air leaving his lungs in a rush. Kessler hit him again. A smile glimmered on the deputy's lean face as he drove his fist deep into Danforth's gut. You could hear the soft smack of flesh against flesh and the gagging sound as Danforth dropped to his knees. Kessler drew back to strike again.

''Knock it off, Kess,'' Cody barked, rubbing at his jaw. ''Don't want to bust nothin' loose inside there.''

Matt stepped forward. He still had hold of Robin's arm, but he was pulling her now instead of holding back. At the sound of footsteps Kessler turned, his arm still cocked for another punch. His small eyes narrowed as he saw the two of them, but there was something in Matt Brenner's face that made Kessler step to one side. Matt brushed on past, through the crowd gathered around the ambulance.

Robin turned away with a cry of horror and disgust.

Matt felt the pit of his stomach burn hot, then cold, as he stared at the object beneath him. Underneath the steady bursts of red light Kyle Danforth lay. His blond hair was spattered with blood from his gouged-out eyes. His mouth moved spasmodically, blood welling up from where his tongue had been cut out. Someone had bound him crudely with barbed wire to a square made of weathered two-by-fours. The same person had cut off the boy's hands and feet before lashing the bleeding stumps to the wooden frame. Most of the clothes had been torn from his body, along with strips of flesh.

The red light flashed again. Matt saw blood on the steps behind the basement door, the severed foot twisting slowly on Joshua's line, the flayed head lying sideways on the cavern floor, Prather Wilkens' mutilated face staring in out of the darkness.

He raised a hand to his own eyes, his face damp with sweat. He heard labored wheezing and he turned to see Robin with both hands at her throat, eyes glazed with tears as she stared at the atrocity. He put a hand to her shoulder.

She turned to him. "Where is he?" she cried.

The two paramedics finished cutting loose the barbed wire bonds. A high, soulless wailing rose from the bleeding mouth. The paramedics lifted Kyle gently from the wooden frame and strapped him onto the stretcher. He struggled briefly, then lay still, but the wailing continued, an eerie a capella chant. One paramedic attached an IV to a mutilated forearm; another started to dress the wounded eyes. The high wailing shifted suddenly to a hoarse, agonized shrieking. The two paramedics performed their labors mechanically since they knew it was all an empty gesture, trying to save what little was left to save.

"Where is Josh?" Robin demanded, her voice breaking.

Matt moved over to where Buck Cody still held Roy Danforth, head drooping forward onto his chest, beard and jacket flecked with vomit. A short man with a red face was injecting the contents of a syringe into Danforth's left forearm. Deputy Floyd Kessler stood to one side, hands on his hips, chewing gum with an aggressive, even rhythm.

Matt faced Cody. "Where's my son?"

Cody looked up. "Only found the one boy. Little ways inside the main shaft. Didn't see no sign of th' other."

"Kyle . . ." Roy Danforth tried to raise his head, then dropped it again on his chest.

"They were together," Matt said.

Cody turned to the red-faced man who was replacing the syringe in a medical bag. "You take him back by yourself, Doc? Or you need th'ambulance?"

"We can manage." The doctor led Roy Danforth slowly to his car, guiding him by the arm like a sleepwalking child. "Short steps, Mr. Danforth." The doctor's voice carried across the darkness. "Nice and easy . . ."

Matt stepped in front of Cody. "If my son's still in there, I'm going after him."

Cody shouted over his head to the crowd around the ambulance, "All right, you folks step back outta the way. Give them boys some room. Go on home. All of you. Ain't nothin' gonna happen you ain't already seen." He turned to Kessler. "Kess, clear 'em out, would you?"

Kessler turned on the crowd. "Let's move it the fuck outta here, assholes, or we'll fuckin' move it for ya!"

As the crowd started to disperse, Matt again told Cody, "I'm going in after him." He started for the entrance.

"Brenner."

Matt turned around and saw the revolver in Cody's right hand. He stared into the black bore of the .38 Smith and Wesson and felt his throat tighten.

"I don't aim to hurt you none," Cody said slowly, "but by God I'll stop you from goin' on in there."

Matt's voice was unsteady. "You found the other boy inside. They were together. That means Josh is in there somewhere. I'm going to find him."

Cody raised the revolver, aiming it squarely at Matt's chest. "That's an abandoned mine, friend. Fulla holes, loose rocks, lotsa dangerous shit. We almost lost a man gettin' the one boy out. We ain't gonna lose no more."

"If my son's in there, I'm bringing him out."

Cody stared at him. "Whatever's happened is happened. Won't do him much good for his Daddy to get hurt, too."

Matt took a deep breath to control his rage. "What's to stop me from coming back later?"

Cody nodded at Kessler, who stood off to one side, thumbs hooked through his belt, glaring at Matt. "For one thing, Deputy Kessler here's gonna watch this place for the rest of the night. For another . . ." Cody's eyes hardened, " . . . if you don't leave agreeable-like right now, I'll arrest you and put you in protective custody for your own good."

Matt looked at Cody with contempt. "You plan on walking away and leaving him in there?"

"We'll look for him." Cody lowered the revolver. "And we'll find him. One way or th'other, we'll find him." Cody replaced the revolver in his holster.

Robin moved up beside Matt, her eyes frightened. "You can't just leave him. He's alone! He's scared!" Her voice caught.

"I said we'll find him." Cody moved his hard eyes from Robin to Matt, then back again. "He never should of went in there in the first place. Goddamn sign over there ain't up just for decoration." Cody gestured irritably at the warning sign with its flaked yellow lettering. "Parents watch out for their kids like they're supposed to—"

Robin lifted her tear-streaked face. "You . . . bastard!" She broke into wracking, convulsive sobs.

Cody adjusted his Stetson. "Now," he said softly to Matt, "whyn't you just take her on home. And take yourself right along with her."

Matt looked up at him. "Fuck you, Cody."

Kessler moved forward. "You shut your—"

Matt turned to him. "And fuck you, too, sonny boy."

Kessler reached for his gun, but a look from Cody stopped him.

Cody stared at Matt. "You just pushed your luck right to the limit there, friend. Push it one inch further, and I ain't takin' no more responsibility for nothin'."

Matt said nothing. Cody stared at him for several seconds longer, then turned and walked slowly to his black-and-white patrol car. Matt put his arm around Robin. She was still sobbing brokenly as they started for the Mercedes. Kessler spit viciously on the ground.

Robin collapsed helplessly in the front seat. "We can't just l-leave him," she sobbed.

"Try and get some rest," he murmured, taking from the glove compartment a small flashlight and something else.

"Matt . . ." Robin's voice grew sharp with alarm. "Matt, what are you doing? Is that the gun?"

"It just looks like it," he whispered, tucking the snub-nosed .38 into his waistband behind his back.

She leaned forward in the seat. "Matt!"

He closed the car door, then walked back to where Deputy Floyd Kessler was standing officious guard like a Roman Centurion. The crowd had disappeared, mostly tourists, some locals, drawn by the promise of cheap thrills at the end of a dull day. The last stragglers were starting up their cars, backing out onto the main road and driving away, as Matt approached Kessler.

Kessler turned at the sound of footsteps. "Don't know when to quit, do you, asshole?"

"I want to talk," Matt said.

Kessler's brow contracted in an ugly scowl. "You had your chance to talk. Now get the fuck outta here."

Kessler turned his back on him. Matt glanced around quickly to make sure there were no witnesses, then he drew the snub-nosed .38, lifted it high in the air, and brought the barrel down hard on the back of Kessler's head.

In the movies when you do something like that, the guy keels over, out cold. But Matt hit Kessler right through his Stetson, and it cushioned the blow. The hat flipped off, and Kessler stumbled forward, grabbing at his head with both hands.

"Fuckin' shit!" he groaned, then staggered around and saw Matt. "Son of a bitch!"

Panic gripped Matt. He did not want to shoot Kessler, but he had already hit him. Kessler went for his own gun, fumbling at the holster, reflexes dulled by pain. Matt swallowed hard and hit him again, right on top of his now unprotected head.

Kessler roared with pain. He charged Matt, butting him in the stomach with his aching head. The blow carried both men to the ground. Kessler grabbed Matt's head, groping for the eyes with his thumbs. Matt hit him again with the gun barrel, then once again.

With each new blow Kessler seemed to lose momentum, like a battery-operated toy running down. Matt raised the gun again. Kessler gave a deep sigh and collapsed on top of him.

Matt pushed the slack body to one side, then got to his feet. His legs were shaking, and two fingers were numb from having got caught between the gun and Kessler's skull. A thin trickle of blood spilled from Kessler's hairline down the right side of his cheek.

The .38 still in his hand, Matt turned and headed for the mine entrance. Once inside, he noticed the smell—dark and moldy—and beneath it, like an unburied corpse, the stomach-wrenching death stench he had smelled before, in the forest the night of the accident, and beside Mirror Lake when Geza Todor first appeared. Fear prickled his scalp. Why in God's name did Josh come in here?

He swept the flashlight beam over petrified piles of bat guano, across walls and ceiling. He noted that they took advantage of a natural cavern entrance, just adding the basics and calling it a mine. The underlying stench worsened with every step. Matt saw Kyle Danforth's ruined face and body again, floating before him in the cave darkness like a vision from Hell. He gripped the flashlight hard, the gun even harder. If the tunnel in that basement runs all the way into this mine, he reasoned, then whatever lives in here . . . He did not finish the thought. It seemed absurd, childish.

When he heard the sounds, he almost fired the gun.

Something was moving across the mine floor in total cave darkness, heading straight for him.

Matt turned the light on the sounds.

Nothing.

"Who's there?" he called out, his question returning to him again and again as the echo faded into silence.

The sounds started again, moving closer. Matt tasted fear in his mouth. He raised the revolver, pointing it at the slowly approaching sounds. He thumbed back the hammer, as his heart thudded against his chest, and the hand that held the gun began to shake.

He scanned the darkness rapidly with the flashlight beam—rock wall, guano pile, stalactite, rock shards, rusted metal railing.

Something touched his arm.

He cried out and whipped the light in that direction.

The face was dirty, but with a distant, dreamy look to it. The mouth was hanging open and the eyes vacant, as though he had fallen asleep under bright moonlight in an enchanted hollow. He was nude. Scratches on his exposed skin looked as if he had stumbled and fallen, rolling some great distance down a steep, rock-covered slope but somehow, miraculously surviving.

"Josh . . ." Matt whispered, his voice hesitant.

"Joshua!" He took him in his arms.

Joshua moved his vacant eyes up to his father's face, and in a flat, quiet voice, said, "I'm back."

26

Revenge

Robin awoke with a cry, her body bathed in sweat.

In the dream she was stretched out spread-eagled on the ground, hands and feet lashed to stakes, while the hideous creatures from Gordon McLeish's painting swarmed over her nude body, clawing at her breasts and stomach with their hooked talons and MacLeish himself, hands and feet amputated, eyes gouged out, stood over them, urging them on, waving his bloody stumps in the air. When he opened his mouth in a chillling laugh, blood and intestines spilled out of it, splattering down onto Robin's nude body.

"Christ!" She sat up in bed and ran her fingers through her tangled, sweaty hair, shuddering violently at the still vivid images of the nightmare.

Then she remembered.

She was wearing a long nightgown, clinging damply to her body. She was in the second-floor bedroom of Kemmering House. It was early morning. She could see daylight through the closed curtains and hear birds singing. Joshua was back with them. Her baby was safe.

"Josh?" Her voice cracked with sleep and fear.

She turned around in the large, empty bed.

He was sitting in a chair by the wall, staring at her with his brown eyes, eyes that seemed dreamy and wandering yet sharply focused.

"Honey, you shouldn't be up yet." She got out of bed and came over to him. "Can't you sleep any more?"

"I'm not tired." His voice was quiet, without rhythm or inflection.

"Oh, baby . . ." Robin embraced him, holding him close to her. "Where's Daddy and Katie?" She kissed the top of his head.

"Downstairs. Getting the car ready."

Tears came to Robin's eyes. She blinked at them as she rocked Joshua in her arms. We're leaving, she told herself, as if it were the most wonderful thing that could ever happen. Dear God, we're finally leaving and that's all that matters now.

Outside, in the Kemmering House driveway, Katie lifted a small suitcase several inches off the ground. She gritted her teeth with the effort, then let it crash back down onto the gravel. "I can't lift it up, Daddy," she called to him as he came down the stone steps at the front of the house, a suitcase in each hand. "It's too heavy."

"Don't worry about it, Katie." Matt unlocked the Mercedes' trunk. "You can help with the pillows."

"I'll go get 'em." Katie turned and started running for the stone steps.

"Katie!" Matt called out sharply, and she stopped. "Stay outside. I'll bring things out to you."

Katie frowned. "I wanta help."

"You're helping plenty."

He was taking no chances. It was broad daylight. Everything seemed safe now, but he had spent most of last night uncomfortably awake, sitting in a straight-backed chair, staring at the locked door of the second-floor bedroom, .38 revolver in hand, while his family slept in the large double bed behind him. While Robin and Katie slept, he remembered darkly. Whenever he turned from the door to glance at them, to make sure they were all right, Joshua was wide awake, lying there staring at him with the fixed, vacant expression that had been in his eyes ever since he emerged from the darkness of the mine shaft. It was no damn good, and Matt knew it. Something had happened to him down there. Joshua said he just got lost, separated from Kyle, and was trying to find his way out when he saw the flashlight beam in the distance. But Matt knew there was more to it than that.

Later, he told himself, as he arranged fishing poles and jackets in the trunk. The main thing now is to get out of here before anything else happens.

"I'll go get my Star Wars dolls," Katie cried, turning toward the house.

"I'll get them. You stay here." Matt did not want her wandering around the house by herself, just in case something had crawled up from the basement and was hiding somewhere in an empty room. He swallowed hard.

Lack of sleep's got you jumpy, he thought, but it was not that. He saw Kyle Danforth's horribly mutilated body outlined by the flashing red ambulance light, and Geza Todor's cold face, the glass eye glittering like a piece of ice. Matt swore under his breath as he picked up a sleeping bag. He still did not know what was going on in Black Cavern. Now he would leave without ever knowing, and that made him angry. He hated quitting—leaving jobs undone, problems unsolved—but he knew now what kind of people were behind this and what they were capable of. That made him scared for his family. Very scared.

Katie sat on the Mercedes' rear fender, swinging her feet above the gravel. "It'll take a long time to carry all my dolls out here."

"Then we'll just move the car a little closer to the house. Upsy daisy." He lifted Katie off the fender and carried her around to the front seat. He got in behind the wheel and turned on the ignition.

Nothing happened.

"Start up the car, Daddy." Katie was drumming her fingers on the dashboard. "Turn on the car and let's gooooo!"

Matt frowned and turned the key in the ignition again.

Nothing.

"What's wrong, Daddy? Why won't it start?"

Matt got out and raised the hood. It did not take long to figure it out. Someone had pulled the distributor cap. Son of a fucking bitch! he thought, the fury starting to build within him. He had been worried that Cody might come by last night with a trumped-up arrest charge for what happened to Kessler and had counted himself lucky that the night passed without incident, but it had only seemed that way. They came by all right. He should have kept one eye on the bedroom door and another on the goddamn car.

Yanking the distributor cap like that was a nice touch. The run-down gas station at the edge of town with its three old-fashioned red pumps was not likely to carry spare Mercedes parts. He could always order one from down in the valley, if they wanted to hang around for a few more days.

Matt slammed down the hood.

Katie stuck her head out the door. "What's wrong with the car, Daddy? Is it out of gas?"

"No."

"Is it sick?"

"It's fine. I just have to go get something for it. Come on."

He took her hand and they walked back to the house. Robin met them at the door.

Her smile was radiant. "You've almost got us packed." She kissed him. "You're an angel."

"I helped," Katie announced proudly.

Robin bent down and kissed her. "Then you're an angel, too."

"Someone pulled the distributor cap," Matt said. "We're not going anywhere until I find another one."

"Jesus Christ . . ." The anger and disappointment showed in her face. "It's like someone doesn't want us to leave."

Saying it out loud somehow made it worse, and the brightness of the day seemed to dim slightly. Kemmering House had never looked more dark or ominous, brooding over them like a malignant spirit from some other, lost place in time. Robin shuddered and pulled Katie close to her.

"We're leaving anyway," Matt said, "whether someone wants us to or not. But first I've got to go into town and find us a new distributor cap."

"Into town?" Robin looked up at him. "Matt, that's not safe."

"Nothing's safe anymore."

Her mouth twitched. "Then you better take that . . . the gun." She did not like guns.

"You're keeping it."

"Matt, no!"

"Look." He stared hard at her. "After what happened yesterday between you and Kessler, and after my run-in with him last night . . . If he stops by here, I want you to have it. And be ready to use it."

"Matt!"

His eyes narrowed. "We're not playing games, Robin. You saw what they did to Roy Danforth's son."

Robin shuddered again and hugged Katie tight.

"Mom," Katie objected, "you're squishin' me."

"Keep your eye on everybody inside the house," Matt continued. "No wandering off into separate rooms. If anybody comes to the door, answer it with the gun in your hand." He hesitated. "And if you hear anything from the basement . . ."

Robin shut her eyes. "Don't even say that!"

"There's no point pretending it didn't happen."

"All right." She nodded wearily. "All right, fine. How long will you be gone?"

"Not one second longer than it takes to find a distributor cap." Matt glanced inside the living room. "Where's Josh?"

Robin turned around. "He was in the kitchen."

Joshua stood in the middle of the living room,

staring up at the animal heads lining the walls. His own head was tilted back, mouth open, hands folded almost as if in prayer. The look on his face was one of reverent fascination.

"Joshua." Robin stepped into the living room, holding Katie by one hand. "Why aren't you eating?"

Joshua turned slowly and stared at them with his empty brown eyes. "I'm not hungry."

Matt trudged along the road into town. He tried to make himself march briskly, but the sleepless night was beginning to take its toll. He had knocked on the door of the caretaker's cottage to see if Mrs. Wilkens could give him a lift into town in her ancient Rambler, but there was no sign of her or the car—or Prather. The sun filtering down through the pine boughs was beginning to get hot and Matt wiped the sweat from his brow. He did not know just what he expected to find in town when he got there. Maybe there was a clever old mechanic who could rig up something to serve as a temporary distributor cap, anything to get them out of this hellhole and back.

The roar of the truck engine shattered the still morning air. Matt could not see the truck, but the sound of its engine was moving down the road toward him. He remembered Kessler's muddy pickup and his dark, small eyes full of hate. It was just how Kessler would do it—a lonely stretch of road, no witnesses, no one to hear the gunshot. Then over to Kemmering House to take care of Robin.

In the distance, the truck shifted gears.

Blind, unreasoning fear grabbed hold of Matt. He glanced desperately at the pine woods on either side of the road. It was no good. The trees were widely spaced, the ground between them fairly level. Kessler would just turn off the road and come after him. If he tried to run, Kessler would use his gun. Matt wiped at his forehead again. There had to be someplace to hide—a boulder, a deep ditch—but Kessler had planned this very carefully, working out all the details while the short, red-faced doctor sewed stitches into his head. Kessler could afford to be patient and thorough. He would find him.

Matt suddenly stopped, glancing from the road to the pine trees and back again. Fuck it, he thought. He had picked a fight with these people. There was no running from it now. If Kessler killed him, he killed him, but Matt wasn't going to die on his knees, begging for mercy. He took a deep, steady breath and turned to face the oncoming truck.

It was visible now, barreling down the road toward him.

But it was not Kessler's truck.

A thick cloud of dust trailed out behind the black Ford Bronco. Matt squinted to see the driver, but reflections of bright sun and blue sky flashed off the windshield, obscuring whoever sat behind the wheel. When it was almost on top of him, the Bronco came to a jarring stop. While it was still rocking on its springs, the driver's door opened.

Roy Danforth climbed out.

Shit, Matt thought tiredly, I still get to fight today and might get killed. You don't underestimate the passion of a grief-stricken parent. Matt knew that.

Roy Danforth was still visibly shaken. His face looked pale and drained, his eyes red, but it was not the face of a grieving parent. There was a grimness to his red eyes, a crazy determination in the set of his pudgy lips that sent a chill up Matt's spine. This was a man who had come to avenge a terrible wrong, to settle a score and put things right—permanently.

"Matt . . ." Danforth's voice wavered. He cleared his throat, then reached out quickly.

Matt jumped back, instinctively protecting himself, but the hand was empty. It trembled slightly in the bright sunlight.

"Matt," Danforth tried again, "I'm sorry . . . about last night and what I said. I was out of my head. It's not true . . . what I said about your boy . . ."

"Forget it." Matt took the extended hand.

Danforth nodded, red eyes glistening. "Thanks, Matt. I really mean it. Thanks."

"Forget it." Matt hesitated, then asked the question anyway. "How's Kyle?"

Danforth took a deep breath. "Kyle's . . . They took him away in that goddamn ambulance down to the valley hospital."

"Who's 'they'?"

"Cody and that asshole doctor, what's-his-name, the one that hit me with the knockout drops."

Matt thought of the last patient sent down to the valley hospital—the boy who survived the wreck, but not the ambulance ride.

Before Matt could say anything, Roy Danforth cut him off. "I was on my way over to your place." He stopped, frowned. "So what the hell you doin' out walkin'?"

Matt told him.

Danforth nodded slowly, staring off into space, then turned suddenly to Matt. "Look, I'll make a deal with you, okay? I do you a favor, you do me a favor . . . a big favor. I take you into town. Find your car part. Hell, we don't find it, I drive you and the family back to L.A. No charge. But you . . ." The fierce determination came back into his red eyes again, gathering force like a storm cloud on the horizon. "You help me get even with these fucking bastards. For what they did to my boy."

Compassion pierced Matt's heart, but he knew, with the cold, selfish logic of survival, that revenge was not his responsibility. Not this time. His job was getting his family out of Black Cavern today—getting them out by car if he could find the distributor cap, by foot if he could not, but above all, getting them out and away from the nameless horror that crawled out of darkness and struck without warning at accident victims and defenseless children.

Danforth, taking Matt's silence for rejection, seized his shoulders and shook him roughly. "Matt, you got to help me. I know who they are, Matt, but I can't take 'em on by myself."

Matt knew what he should say, but instead he asked, "Who did it?"

Danforth's red eyes darkened with hatred. "Some sonofabitch foreigner. Can't even pronounce the fuckin' name. Somethin' Tordor. Some goddamn thing like that."

The shock of hearing Geza Todor's name registered on Matt's face. "How do you know?"

Danforth released his grip on Matt's shoulders. "That shithead Cody . . . I come outta the dope and find Kyle gone, so I ask Cody who did it. Who fuckin' did it to him?" Beads of sweat stood out on Danforth's fat face. "And Cody pussy-asses around this way and that and says somethin' about possible suspects and mentions this Tordor prick. And I ask Cody, why him? And Cody says, well, he can't exactly discuss it.'' Danforth paused, and for a moment something like a grim smile passed over his face. ''But I made him discuss it.''

Matt almost felt sorry for Buck Cody then. Roy Danforth was fat, ordinary and harmless, but an irrational horror had come without warning into his life, changing him terribly, leaving him no longer ordinary, no longer rational, and potentially very dangerous.

''Cody said this Torodor prick's the one who found the bikes.'' Danforth's eyes turned sharply focused and shrewd. ''How the fuck did he know where they were? Shari gets worried when the boys don't come back on time like they promised and she tells me go look for 'em. So I bust my hump drivin' all over the fuckin' place and don't find 'em. But this Torodor prick walks into Cody's office and tells him casual-like about these two bikes parked up by that old mine. So how the hell did he know?''

Matt saw the glass eye glittering in that cruel face, and a shudder passed through him. Everything he feared about Geza Todor was coming true.

''You gotta help me, Matt.'' Danforth seized his shoulders again. ''He lives up there,'' Danforth said, pointing to a steep ridge hazy in the distance, ''with some fuckin' cunt, Annabella somethin' or other. Two fucked-up whackos. Bastard's supposed to be over seven foot tall. Seven foot! Jumpin' Jesus Christ, Matt, I can't take him by myself! You gotta help me.''

What he had to do, Matt knew, was find the distributor cap and get his family out of Black

Cavern, but what about the others? Once he got his own family away from here, they would be safe, but the abominations would continue.

Matt remembered how Adriana Velotti had hovered over Joshua in the Grizzly Bar, trying to win his confidence, trying to seduce him. His anger swelled as he wondered how many more victims there would be before they were through. He could always do the "right thing" and alert the authorities the minute he got back to L.A. But what good would it do? If someone took him seriously enough to send an investigating team up to isolated Black Cavern, and if they were lucky enough to catch Todor and Velotti red-handed, or find evidence that would stand up in court . . . what then? There'd be a trial, with sympathetic media coverage for the distinguished Professor Todor and the lovely, photogenic Miss Velotti, then appearances on *Today* and *Good Morning America,* a cover of *People,* a publishing contract, probably an acquittal, or at the very worst, a sentence of ten to fifteen years with parole in two to five. Back outside, "rehabilitated," they'd be ready to resume useful roles in society.

And the abominations would begin again.

Matt turned to the desperate, unhappy man in front of him, tears trickling down his fat, bearded cheeks.

He said to him, "Let's go pay the professor a visit."

27

Disciple

The hunger came back suddenly to Joshua.

And with it came the memories, dim and distant, the stuff of dreams. But they were not dreams. They had happened. They had happened to him.

First came the dark, then the screaming, Kyle's screams and his own. The face of the demon—gaping mouth and bloody fangs. Foul, choking breath, hot and damp against his forehead. White eyes burning into his own. And the hands like claws grabbing hold of him. His own screams shattering into endless echoes, coming back at him out of the darkness as he screamed until his throat ached, until his voice went and a raw, tortured bleating was all that was left. Kyle's screams fading in the distance and the sound of clawed feet scraping over rough stone as they carried him deeper into the bowels of the cavern, his face pressed tight against the matted, evil-smelling hair of the demon's body.

Then, suddenly, light—not much of it, pale, blue-filtered—but enough to see dimly, to guess at shapes and motion. They tore at his clothes, ripping at them with their claws. He screamed again, but his hoarse voice only groaned, like a crippled foghorn in a blue mist. Then he was naked like they were, without their covering of coarse, rank body hair. They crowded close about him, staring at him with their white burning eyes.

I should be scared, he remembered thinking. They had him underground, in the dark, away from everyone. But the only thing that registered clearly on his stunned brain was the fact that he was alive. They had him, finally, but he was alive.

Then they brought him the Life. The *Pragha.*

It came in a clay cup that looked like a small bowl. It was warm and acrid, the smell piercing his nostrils. A demon held it out to him, dark, hairy arms extended. The creature snarled at him. Terrified of what might happen if he refused, Joshua drank.

It was only after the second swallow that he realized he was drinking blood.

He gagged violently and spit it out of his mouth. The demons fell upon him, pinning back his arms, forcing his mouth open, making him drink from the cup. As the blood flowed down his throat, he heard the slow, distorted chanting of inhuman voices.

" . . . Pragha . . ."

" . . . Pragha . . ."

" . . . Pragha . . ."

The *Pragha.* The Life.

As they forced it down his throat, it no longer made him sick. It tasted warm, rich, powerful. It mixed with his own blood, giving him strength and power he had never known, giving him courage and endurance, giving him Life. *Pragha.*

Next they brought the meat. Blood was the soul of *Pragha,* meat the body. Hands like claws raised the bloody slab of meat before him. He turned his head and closed his eyes. And with his eyes closed, he heard—inside his head.

You are mine . . . I have called you and you have come.

My Pragha is your Pragha.

My chosen one . . . my son.

Joshua opened his eyes and cried out. The demon before him dwarfed the others in size and hideousness. The lesser ones cowered in the presence of the huge creature, bowing before it, raising their hands in obeisance. And as Joshua looked into that monstrous face with its burning white eyes, he knew.

This was the one—the one who had stared at him the night of the accident, seeking him out in the darkness of the forest, the one who had called to him *you are mine* in the terrible basement of Kemmering House, the one who had lured him into the depths of this abandoned mine.

At the great demon's side crouched a withered, sickly creature that scampered about on all fours, cackling obscenely as it grinned at Joshua. Its long white hair and beard were encrusted with filth. It did not look like the other demons. Its eyes did not burn. Its body was hairless and weak. It might once have been a man.

The great demon took the bloody slab of meat and forced Joshua to eat. The other demons crowded closer but kept their distance, awed by the sacredness of the ceremony. Joshua was on his knees, hands held behind his back. The great demon gave him food. The chanting rose again, rumbling like distant thunder, until it filled the cavern, echoing through the darkness.

" . . . *Pragha* . . ."

" . . . *Pragha* . . ."

" . . . *Pragha* . . ."

It tasted rich and good. He chewed fiercely at it as the blood trickled down his chin and dripped onto his naked chest and belly. It was Life. *Pragha.* Becoming part of him. The blood his blood. The flesh his flesh. The strength his strength.

"Pragha," he whispered, eyes closed, mouth full of blood and flesh. *"Pragha!"*

When he opened his eyes he saw the human hand that he was eating. The ring on the third finger was inscribed with the name KYLE.

Joshua spit out the partially chewed flesh, his stomach contracting painfully. When he saw what he had vomited out upon the stone floor, he gagged and vomited again.

The withered, hairless creature cackled gleefully, waving its emaciated arms and legs as it scuttled across the cavern floor like an ancient, evil spider.

"It's all right," said a human voice beside him. Father McKerry, naked, blood running from his mouth down onto his chest and arms, placed a hand on Joshua's shoulder. "Your first taste of the Life has overwhelmed you. Its glory has humbled you. This is normal." His voice was warm, friendly, reassuring. "This will pass. The Life will become part of you. It will become your true nourishment. It will give you . . . Life. *Pragha."* The priest smiled, his teeth stained with blood, clotted with flesh. *"Pragha!"*

The dream world vanished, leaving Joshua alone with his hunger.

He was lying on his bed in the small downstairs bedroom. When he had refused to eat any breakfast, his Mom made him lie down while his Dad went out to look for the car part.

He got out of bed and opened the door to the living room. Voices drifted out from the kitchen—his Mom and Katie.

He could hear them clearly, every word they said. He could hear everything clearly now, and he could see better, especially in the dark. Before his Dad came down into the cavern, he was starting to see more and more in the darkness like the shape of rocks, their color and texture. When his Dad shined the flashlight into his eyes, it hurt. It was all part of the Life. You will still be able to see in the daylight, Father McKerry had explained, but gradually, you will begin to see things in their true forms only in darkness.

He looked up at the mounted animal heads lining the living room walls, the grizzly bear towering beside the front door and the eagle descending from above.

The Gods of the Hunt.

Within him, the hunger burned.

He closed the door to the small bedroom and quickly took off his clothes. They felt stiff and scratchy, unnatural, like wearing sheets of cardboard. When he was naked, he unlocked the double windows and climbed outside. He dropped to the ground, crouching in the grass on all fours. The bright sunlight hurt his eyes and felt hot and hateful on his body, as if it meant him harm, but the grass and the earth smelled good in his nostrils. He inhaled deeply. The clean mountain breeze carried other scents, the smell of living things, the smell of Life. *Pragha.*

He began to run. Crouching low to the ground, and moving quickly across the meadow that surrounded Kemmering House, he could hear the rushing of the mountain stream as it coursed through the meadow, water spilling over rocks and swirling into eddies. He could hear the wind in the trees of the forest.

And the sounds of the Gods in motion.

The animals were Gods. The world was filled with Gods—small Gods like the tiny butterflies that hovered over the meadow grass, and mighty Gods like the grizzly bear rising above the living room. The Gods were the source of all power, rich in *Pragha.* To become like the Gods you had to partake of their *Pragha* and consume the Gods within yourself.

Joshua heard a shrill burst of bird song. He stopped running. Ahead of him three cardinals stood lightly on the ground. One fluttered into the air, flying around the other two in widening circles. Joshua moved forward slowly, quietly, his arms extended to seize the Gods, to capture their *Pragha* and assuage his burning hunger. He was almost upon them when the other two birds took flight, slipping easily past his grasping hands. He bent over to pick up a rock, but the birds were winging their way across the meadow, becoming part of the sunlight and the sky.

The hunger burned, and anger darkened Joshus's face. He threw down the rock, watching bitterly as it bounced on the ground and rolled a short way before coming to rest.

He saw them then.

Not far from where he stood, inside a tiny bower of meadow grass, a mother cottontail rabbit nursed four babies. Joshua advanced carefully, scarcely daring to breathe. The wind rustled the grass. The mother rabbit twitched her nose, her eyes half-closed in the bright, warm sunshine. Joshua picked up the discarded rock. Suddenly the mother rabbit's ears stiffened as Joshua raised the rock. Her eyes opened wide, staring straight at the intruder. Joshua ran forward as she bolted, upsetting the four nursing babies. The younger rabbits scrambled after her as she bounded into the cover of tall meadow grass, but one of the smaller rabbits lagged behind the other three.

Joshua hurled the rock. It landed on the back of the struggling baby rabbit, crushing it to the ground. A small, sharp cry escaped from the wounded animal, and the frantic mother dashed out from the grass. The baby rabbit tried to crawl forward, its back broken. Joshua rushed in to pick up the injured rabbit. The mother rabbit hesitated, then darted back into the meadow grass.

The wounded baby rabbit kicked and struggled in its agony. The tiny claws scratched at Joshua's wrists. He carried it over to a large, flat rock. He lifted the injured animal high above his head, then brought it down hard, dashing its brains out against the rock. The struggling form lay still, hanging limp from his hand.

"*Pragha,*" he whispered, as the smell of fresh blood reached his nostrils.

He ran back across the meadow to Kemmering

House, his heart beating triumphantly, the kill held close in one hand. He had been favored in his hunting. He would now honor the Gods of the Hunt.

He crawled back in through the open windows and moved toward the bedroom door, blood from the killed rabbit dripping onto the floor. In the middle of the living room he knelt down before the Gods of the Hunt, bowing low, the dead animal held out to them on extended arms.

"Pragha," he murmured, the word rumbling deep in his throat like a growl. *"Pragha!"*

The kitchen door opened and Robin walked in.

At first the scene before her did not even register—Joshua naked, kneeling on the hardwood floor, bowing before the stuffed grizzly bear, holding up a twisted, bloody piece of fur, his hands and arms flecked with blood.

Then he brought the dead rabbit to his mouth and began tearing chunks of flesh and fur from its body with his teeth.

Robin started screaming.

28

Dark Angel

The town through which Matt Brenner and Roy Danforth drove was almost deserted.

"A fuckin' ghost town." Danforth slammed on the brakes to avoid hitting a fat old dog waddling slowly across an intersection. "Everything's closed up." He stepped on the gas again, and the Bronco lurched forward. "Went by that bar earlier to make a phone call, okay? Check at the hospital . . ." Danforth's voice wavered. "See how . . . things are. But the goddamn bar's locked up tighter'n a fuckin' bank vault."

As they turned a sharp corner, Matt could see that the Grizzly Bar was in fact closed, as was Hank's Hardware. The doctor's office where Kyle Danforth had been taken the night before was closed. Neither Buck Cody's black-and-white nor Floyd Kessler's pickup was parked in front of the

Summit County Sheriff's Office. The windows were closed, the blinds drawn.

All of Black Cavern lay silent, withdrawn.

They turned onto High Ridge Road, an aptly-named ribbon of dirt that wound up Overlook Creek, rising on the far side of town opposite the Paso Perdido Ridge. The Bronco's gears whined as it climbed High Ridge Road. Looking back, Matt could see Caiyallah Lodge outlined atop Paso Perdido. Up ahead, perched on Overlook, sat a large, three-story house with a pseudo-rustic, log cabin look to it. Framed by jagged boulders and thick pines, it seemed forbidding, inaccessible.

Danforth shook his head in bewilderment. "Road's one fuckin' ballbuster. Grinds the shit outta your transmission." He turned to Matt. "What kinda asshole wants to live way the hell up here?"

"Someone," Matt answered, "with something to hide."

They parked on top of the ridge, a good distance from the house. Next to it, but screened by pines and invisible from the road below, was the weathered blue van that Matt remembered from the Mission San Miguel lot yesterday afternoon. They got out of the Bronco and walked toward the house, gravel crunching underfoot.

Matt knocked at the heavy front door.

No one answered.

A cold wind whipped across Overlook Crest, and Danforth pulled his jacket collar closer. "You think maybe we should've brought somethin'?" he asked in a low voice. "You know, for protection."

"We're here to talk," Matt said, knocking harder on the closed door.

The sound reverberated throughout the house, but there was no response. Matt moved over to a window. He raised himself on his toes and looked in. The interior of the front room was dark, despite a broad patch of sunlight that fell from the window across the hardwood floor. A fire burned in the grate. The room was crowded with dark objects impossible to make out clearly in the dim half-light. Nothing moved.

"Jesus," Danforth said over Matt's shoulder. "Goddamn gloomy, ain't it?"

"You don't go off and leave a fire burning like that," Matt said, then went back and knocked on the front door again, loud enough this time to rattle it in its frame.

Again, no answer.

Matt put his hand on the brass doorknob. It turned. The door opened inward, rusted hinges squeaking.

"Maybe we should've drug Cody along after all," Danforth whispered, peering uncertainly into the darkness.

"Cody doesn't want to help us," Matt said, pushing the door the rest of the way open, "and we don't want his help."

"Matt . . ." Danforth hesitated at the thresh-hold. "What if this whole thing's some kinda trap?"

Matt looked back over his shoulder. "Then it's a damn good one. They didn't even know we were coming." He stepped inside.

Once his eyes adjusted to the dim light, Matt could see what the dark objects were—primitive masks, ceremonial spears, wooden shields, stone axes. A human skull stared at him with glittering rubies instead of eyes. War masks grimaced fiercely, mouths distorted, eyes narrowed, glaring down at him through the flickering half-light. Small statues of heads and pointed horns struck grotesque poses.

Matt Brenner drew in his breath at the sight of one statue with savage fangs in a snarling dog-like mouth, curved horns jutting from a shaggy head and clawed hands reaching out into the darkness. Firelight threw an expanded shadow of the statue's head onto the far wall, exaggerating its curved horns until they seemed to fill that side of the room.

On a table by itself squatted a headless statue of a naked woman, grossly fat, all drooping breasts and gaping vulva, legs and arms lost in the folds of stone flesh.

"Jesus H. Christ," muttered Roy Danforth, his forehead damp with sweat. "What in the fuck is all this shit?"

"A little home museum of primitive art," Matt said, then added, "with just a slight emphasis on the diabolic."

"No shit," Danforth agreed. "Hey!" He pointed. "Look!"

A shrunken human head sat under a glass dome. Its eyes had been preserved somehow. It seemed to stare out from its glass cage with a dark, implacable hatred. A look of almost supernatural cunning gave it the appearance of something not quite human, something that, if given the chance to escape its glass prison, could be deadly.

"Holy shit," Roy Danforth murmured.

Matt felt the skin crawl at the back of his neck. He looked away from the shriveled, staring head and saw the tape recorder.

It was a standard reel-to-reel, sitting on a low cocktail table in front of the fireplace. Matt moved toward it.

" . . . fuckin' haunted house," Danforth was saying. "Just charge five bucks a head and you could clear a fuckin' bundle."

The tape recorder was stopped in the middle of a reel. Matt bent over and switched it on.

The sound burst from the speakers with startling fidelity. Roy Danforth stopped talking and turned to the sound. It was loud, hollow, reverberating, as though recorded in an echo chamber. A chorus of voices, harsh and guttural, chanted in the background. In the foreground, high-pitched, quivering, terrified, was a boy's voice.

" . . . me go! Goddamn shitheads!" A sharp cry of pain. "Ow! Motherfuckers! Let me go!"

"Kyle!" Danforth rushed over to the tape recorder and hovered over it, hands trembling, face pale. "That's my boy!" He pointed excitedly. "That's Kyle!"

" . . . go, goddamn you!" A shriek of pain, followed by a broken whimper. "Please . . . Please don't do that again . . . Josh! Help! Help me!"

"Let him go!" Joshua's voice screamed from the speakers.

Matt's gut turned cold.

"Let him—" Joshua's voice was muffled suddenly.

The chanting rose in the background, swelling like thunder before a storm.

"Please . . ." Kyle was sobbing now. "Please! Help me! Somebody! Dadeeeeee. . . help meeee."

Kyle's voice rose sharply to a high-pitched,

shattering scream.

Roy Danforth turned and grabbed Matt by the shoulders. His face was ravaged by the same helpless terror and anger Matt had seen the night before.

"They're hurting him, Matt." Danforth's voice was wild, almost incoherent. "The motherfuckers are hurting him!"

Kyle Danforth's hideous screams rose and fell unevenly. The chanting grew louder, swelling until it echoed loudly in the darkened room.

" . . . *Pragha . . .*"

" . . . *Pragha . . .*"

" . . . *Pragha . . .*"

The word rumbled like a death knell. Roy Danforth hung onto Matt's shoulders, sobbing brokenly. Matt stared down at the slowly revolving reels of tape, the piercing shrieks of the tortured boy and the obscene, guttural chanting burning like fire into his brain.

"No!" Danforth turned and seized the tape recorder. He lifted it over his head, the incessant chanting and the screams of his son still echoing from its speakers.

"Roy, don't!" Matt tried to stop him.

With a strangled cry, Danforth hurled the tape recorder into the fireplace. The machine crashed against the grate. One of the logs fell off and bounced onto the hearth, sparks flying up into the air. The tape caught fire in a sudden flash. The smell of burning wire and plastic filled the room. Batteries exploded, throwing flames out from the fireplace. Matt protected his eyes, but Roy Danforth stood staring into the inferno, tears running down his face, fists clenched trembling in impotent rage.

"Bastards!" he sobbed, his voice broken.

Matt turned away and looked out at the dark shadows, the monstrous statues. An air of sinister unreality made it easy to imagine the statues mocking Roy Danforth's pain, their shadows shifting in the darkness.

One of the shadows really did move.

It loomed up suddenly, blotting out part of the light.

Something stood in front of the window.

Matt whirled around, expecting to see Geza Todor, but he was not prepared for what he did see.

A cry of fear and revulsion escaped him. Adriana Velotti stood before the window. She was naked, her white body perfect, the paleness of her skin set off by large dark nipples, erect with passion. Thick blood trickled down from her open mouth across her breasts and belly into her dark pubic hair.

Roy Danforth turned at Matt's cry, his fat face drawn, mouth slack. "Who are you?" He blinked his eyes at Adriana Velotti, uncomprehending, like an idiot child staring into the sun.

She kept her eyes on Matt Brenner. "I'm sorry it had to be like this, Matt." More blood spilled from her mouth, and a chunk of something that looked like meat. "But here we are, together at last."

Roy Danforth stumbled forward, his upper lip quivering. "Who the fuckin' hell are you?"

She turned to him. "I am the Life." She smiled, her white teeth stained with blood. "I am the *Pragha.*"

Roy Danforth's glazed eyes suddenly came into sharp focus. "You're one of *them,*" he murmured. Then he shrieked at her, "You hurt my boy!"

"Stay away from her, Roy!" Matt warned.

Roy Danforth hurled himself at Adriana Velotti, his hands reaching out for her white throat. She stood immobile, waiting, until he was almost upon her. Then she turned and kicked out at his right leg with a speed that blurred motion. The knee cap shattered, and Danforth fell forward with a gasp of pain, grabbing at his broken knee. She brought her right hand down hard on the left side of his neck. The impact snapped his head to one side with such force that his right eyeball popped out of its socket, dangling by an optic nerve. Danforth's neck broke with a sharp, clearly audible crack, and he fell heavily to the hardwood floor, knocking over one of the spears. It clattered onto the floor beside his motionless body. A thick stream of blood oozed sluggishly from his left nostril. His head lay twisted on the floor, mouth open, staring at the fireplace. Reflected firelight danced in his one open eye, making it seem still alive, while the other eye dangled from its socket like a broken spring.

Adriana Velotti knelt down beside Roy Danforth's corpse. She lifted his head and shoulders from the floor, cradling them in her arms, then she bit deep into his fat neck with her strong white teeth, pulling lose a large chunk of flesh and fat with a soft, tearing sound. Blood from his severed jugular vein sprayed over her naked body like water from a burst pipe. She chewed the flesh savagely, gobbets falling from her mouth as she leaned forward hungrily to drink from the fountain of spurting blood.

The killing of Roy Danforth happened so quickly

that Matt Brenner stood watching it like a stunned trauma victim.

But when Adriana Velotti began to cannibalize the corpse, he moved. He lifted one of the small demonic statues from its pedestal. The statue was amazingly heavy, and he staggered under its weight. Walking with difficulty, he carried the statue across the room and dropped it squarely on top of her naked, blood-spattered body.

She heard him and turned before the statue hit, taking much of the impact on her shoulder as she rolled out from under the weight. With an animal howl of pain and rage, she sprang to her feet. Her shoulder was lacerated, running with blood.

Matt jumped back, but not far enough. She hit him with a kick to the chest. Weakened as she was, it did not deliver killing impact, but it still hit him hard enough to knock him back across the room. He crashed into a display of spears and masks, slamming his head against the wall so hard he almost lost consciousness. He staggered forward, then slipped and fell in front of the fireplace.

As he turned over onto his back, head throbbing, blinking up at the oak-beamed ceiling, he was dimly aware of Adriana Velotti standing above him. The expression in her eyes was deadly, but there was a vulnerability to her face, a childlike look of hurt and disappointment—and physical pain. He had injured her badly with the statue. She held the wounded, bleeding shoulder higher than the other. Her entire right breast was darkening rapidly with ugly blotches of broken veins. Pain showed in the rigid set of her jaw, the stiffness of her movements.

"It could have been good for us, Matt," she whispered, staring at him with hatred in her eyes and pain on her face. "We could have become as one."

He tried to move, to lift himself up, but could not. In despair, he let his arms flop down beside him on the floor. An outstretched hand touched something—hard, wooden and long—the shaft of a spear. That's what it has to be, he thought, but he did not grab for it, or even glance in that direction. He kept staring up at Adriana Velotti, naked, hurt, beautiful, with a look of mourning on her blood-stained face and deadly fury in her dark eyes.

" . . . can still be as one," she whispered, barely audible above the crackling flames of the fireplace. "I will partake of you and you will become part of me. Forever." The dark eyes glistened, and she flashed a blood-stained smile. "Your life will become part of my life. Your *Pragha* one with mine."

She bent down toward him slowly, mouth open, eyes closed in ecstasy, a lover approaching her beloved.

Matt glanced at the hard wooden object lying within reach of his right hand. It was the handle of a primitive battle ax, the edge of the stone blade honed to a fine, cutting sharpness. Matt Brenner had not hit many people in his life, certainly never with the intention of killing them, but he knew that he was going to pick up the stone ax now and hit Adriana Velotti with it hard enough to kill her. If he did not, she would kill him, the same way she killed Roy Danforth. He would have only one chance, one very brief moment before she realized what was happening. Win or lose, it would all be over in a matter of seconds.

Please don't let me lose, Matt pleaded, reaching for the ax.

Adriana Velotti opened her mouth wide. Bits of human flesh were lodged between her teeth and the stench of stale, half-digested blood issued from her open mouth.

Matt swung the ax with a speed and force that twisted his arm in its socket. Her instincts sharp as a hunted animal's, she turned her head the moment she felt him move. She was fast, very fast, but not fast enough.

The stone blade sank into the side of her skull like a spoon into pudding. As she jerked away violently, the ax buried deep in her head, she smashed Matt across the face with the back of her hand. His head bounced on the floor, blood bursting from both nostrils, but there was no real force to the blow. Adriana Velotti was dying.

She struggled to her feet, clutching at the ax handle with both hands. She pulled on it, and a hoarse shriek broke from her throat. She pulled again at the stone blade embedded in her skull. It tore loose, blood oozing thickly from the open wound. Bits of grayish brain tissue dribbled down the side of her face.

She staggered forward, then fell facedown onto the burning logs in the fireplace. She screamed as the flames scorched her face. With an almost superhuman effort she managed to turn over and lift herself up on one arm, her hair on fire, then she collapsed backward onto the burning logs and lay still. Her dark hair crackled like dry brush. Her pale skin turned red, then black, then began to shrivel like scorched paper. Her eyes boiled up out of their sockets until they burst, ocular fluid hissing onto the flames.

The smell of burning flesh made Matt gag. He tried to get up and drag her out of the fire, but sharp pain tore through his chest and back, paralyzing him.

He tried again, crawling on his belly toward the fireplace.

He heard it then.

The heavy, irregular tread of someone coming clumsily down the stairs from the floor above, hesitating on each step, as if unsure of what the next might bring.

Matt made a final, desperate effort to get to his feet, open the door and reach the safety of Roy Danforth's Bronco, but he could not even rise to a partial sitting position. He fell back heavily onto the hardwood floor and lay there, waiting for whatever was coming down the stairs.

29

Punishment Room

The walls of Kemmering House seemed to be closing in on Robin.

They were moving down on top of her, even as she watched them, threatening to lock her in, suffocate her. This is crazy, she told herself. The walls aren't moving! But she knew they were, and she had to get out of there before the walls crushed her and Katie and Joshua.

Joshua!

The images came back to her, vivid and sickening. Tears trickled down her cheeks again, her whole body shaking with sobs as she leaned over the kitchen sink, arms trembling. She forgot about the moving walls.

She remembered wrenching the disgusting, half-eaten rabbit away from Joshua. He had actually fought her for it, growling at her like some dirty small dog defending a bone. She struck him on the side of the head. Her hand still felt numb from the blow, since she had hit him hard enough to knock him down onto the floor. Her stomach lurched as she remembered carrying the filthy, bloody rabbit corpse, holding it by one ear, its intestines dangling out where Joshua had bitten into the stomach and ripped open the guts. She had carried it from the living room through the kitchen and out the back door, fighting with nausea the whole way, trying not even to look at the damn thing but still smelling its freshly-killed rankness, then threw it into the trash bin, some of the blood spattering her hand.

Then dragging Joshua as he struggled and fought her—he once actually had struck out at her—and she could still feel the bruise swelling on the side of her leg. After washing his mouth out with Ivory Liquid, she flushed the hateful pieces of bloody flesh and fur down the disposal. Then shaking him by the shoulders until his head rolled back and forth, she asked him why.

"I was hungry," he answered, his voice flat, eyes empty.

She got food out of the refrigerator and ordered him to eat, but he would not eat. She tried to force him, stuffing it into his mouth the way she had when he was an infant in a high chair. When he spit it out, she threw down the fork and screamed at him again, her own nerves shattered.

"It's different." He looked up at her with his round, empty eyes. "It's not . . . Life."

At that moment Katie came into the room, glanced from her brother to her mother, and asked what was wrong.

Robin's head snapped up. "Get out of here."

"Is Joshua sick?" Katie took a hesitant step forward.

"Get out of here!"

Katie retreated, face fallen, eyes frightened.

Christ, I shouldn't have yelled at her, Robin thought, turning on the kitchen faucet and rinsing the tears from her cheeks and swollen eyelids. She was only asking an honest question. Robin turned off the faucet and it dripped slowly into the sink. What if he really is sick? The word *schizophrenia* pierced her mind like an obscene whisper.

"What did they do to him?" she wondered aloud, her voice hoarse. "What did they do?"

Sick fear gripped her heart. She kept staring at the dripping faucet, because she knew if she stared at the walls they might start moving again. We've got to get help for him, she reasoned calmly. But how? Matt was still out looking for the damn car part, and when they finally got the Mercedes running again, it would be a long, tense drive back to Los Angeles. Robin did not know if Joshua could make that drive. There was something in his empty eyes that frightened her—something dark, barely controlled, waiting for the right moment, when all four of them were cramped together.

Robin knew there was a very real danger and she had to do something about it, had to get him to a doctor.

She remembered the short, red-faced man at the abandoned mine last night. He was like certain other doctors she had known—quiet and sullen, as if he resented disease and accidents and the people afflicted by them—but he was a doctor. She remembered him giving the injection to Roy

Danforth, and how the fat, bearded man had calmed down almost immediately, the rage dropping from him like a bad dream. He can help Joshua, she told herself. He can help us get him back home.

Robin started up the stairs to the second floor, reaching into her shorts pocket for the key to the master bedroom. It was heavy, old-fashioned, with a loop at the top and large teeth at the end of a long shaft. The metal felt cold and oily to the touch. Sunlight from the high living room window slanted down onto the stairs at an odd angle, making them seem to tip slightly to one side. Robin grasped the bannister hard as she remembered dragging Joshua up those stairs, his empty eyes staring at her while she locked him into the master bedroom. The windows in there were sealed shut, and it was a long way to the ground. He could not get out, not easily anyway.

Her heart was pounding as she reached the top of the stairs, blood throbbing in her ears. She put the heavy key in the lock and turned it. The door to the master bedroom creaked open, revealing a silent room darkened by drawn curtains.

Joshua was naked once again, crouched on the window sill, scratching at the glass, trying to get out.

"Joshua!" She rushed over to him. "Get down from there!"

He turned and snarled at her, his eyes dark and feral. Robin drew back in horror, as if some animal in her son's shape had appeared before her. Then the fury took hold. She grabbed Joshua by the shoulders and pulled him from the window sill. He fell heavily to the floor, crying out in pain. He lay there for several seconds, then rose to a hunched sitting position, tears running down his cheeks.

Robin's heart swelled and her own eyes filled with tears. "Oh, baby . . ."

She knelt down and put her arms around her son, drawing him close to her. When she reached out to touch his face, he bit her, hard, on the fleshy edge of her right hand. His strong teeth bore down on flesh and muscle.

Robin screamed and tried to tear her hand loose, but Joshua would not let go. She slapped him hard on the right side of his face. The thud of flesh striking flesh echoed like a gunshot in the darkened room. Robin stumbled to her feet, holding her hand. No blood was drawn, but the teeth marks stood out like red welts. Joshua scrabbled away into a corner like a naked spider. He sat there staring at her out of eyes void of everything except darkness.

The tears came again to Robin's own eyes. "Josh . . ." She choked, swallowing hard. "Baby, I'm so sorry . . . . You'll get better." Her face ached, and tears spilled down her cheeks. "I promise," she whispered.

Joshua broke suddenly for the door, scrabbling across the hardwood floor on all fours. Robin beat him by a few yards. She slammed the door, put the key to the lock and turned it shut, just as Joshua hit it from the other side. The door rattled in its frame, the doorknob twisting back and forth as he turned it frantically. He hammered against the door, a snarl of rage breaking from his small throat.

Robin stepped back into the hallway, breathing heavily, terrified eyes on the locked bedroom door as it shuddered under Joshua's assault. And as she stood there, in her mind's eye she saw the basement door trembling under the impact of the creature on the stairs, the growls echoing from the other side as the barred door buckled against its splintered frame. But this is my son, her mind screamed, not some demon from hell!

But they had done something to her son, had changed him.

Robin put a fist to her mouth and wept.

"Will Joshua have to go to the hospital?" Katie asked quietly, her eyes grave, body tensed for another explosion as she stood in the hallway watching her mother.

Robin bent over and gathered her daughter in her arms. "Oh, Katie . . ." She held her close, rocking her gently. "Everything's going to be okay. Really it is."

"Are we gonna take him to the 'mergency room?"

Robin sobbed loudly and shook her head. "He just needs to rest."

Katie eyed the door, which shuddered as Joshua hit it again. "He doesn't sound very tired."

Robin stepped back, holding her daughter at arm's length. She studied the serious blue eyes that made the small child's face seem suddenly adult and responsible.

"Katie . . ." Robin smoothed her daughter's blond locks. "Mommy's got to go get someone to come take a look at Joshua, and since Daddy's not back yet—"

"Joshua's really sick, isn't he?"

"—you've got to be a big girl and take care of things while I'm gone. Here." Robin placed the heavy, old-fashioned key in Katie's small hand. "This unlocks the bedroom door. You keep it till I get back."

Katie glanced at the key, then looked up at her mother. "I don't wanta stay here by myself."

"There's nothing to worry about." There's everything to worry about, Robin thought, fear piercing her like a sharp knife, but I've got to get help for him. "Daddy'll be back in just a little while."

"I don't wanta stay here alone," Katie said.

"You won't be alone." Robin hugged her tight, trying not to think about Joshua growling like an animal behind the locked bedroom door or the thing in the basement. "You'll be taking care of your brother while I'm gone. And it won't be for long. Daddy'll—"

"Can I get Joshua a soda if he asks for one?"

"No!" Robin's head snapped up, her hands on Katie's shoulders. "Look at me." She lifted Katie's chin. "Don't open that door. Not unless there's a fire or an earthquake or something really serious. Understand?"

Katie nodded slowly, eyes wide with fear. "I understand."

Outside Robin knocked on the door to Mrs. Wilkens' cottage, but no one answered. She looked around in back. There was no sign of Mrs. Wilkens' car. Robin was a good half-mile up the road to town before she remembered the bikes. They had carried them back down from the Kemmering Mine in the Mercedes' trunk with the idea of returning them to Shari Danforth. Robin unlocked the trunk. By the light of day, both bikes looked sadly abused, but one of the bikes was still serviceable. It would get her to a doctor's office sooner than she could make it on foot.

The bike wobbled badly at first as she put it in motion. Then, as the automatic balancing sense came back to her, the vehicle's unsteady progress leveled out. Please let the doctor be there, she prayed, pushing hard on the pedals, her lungs pumping fast.

Downstairs, Katie looked up from her Star Wars dolls and eyed the malevolent animal heads on the wall with growing uneasiness. They're starin' at me, she thought, a chill creeping up her back. They know I'm here all by myself except for Joshua in the upstairs bedroom. And the monster in the basement—the bogeyman! she thought, uneasiness turning suddenly into sheer terror.

She was trying very hard not to think about the bogeyman crawling around down there in that dark and horrible basement when she heard Joshua, calling to her.

His voice was muffled by the locked bedroom door, but it carried clearly across the second-floor hallway and down the stairs into the living room.

"Katie . . ."

Katie ascended the stairs slowly. When she reached the second floor, she walked over and leaned her head against the bedroom door.

"What?"

"Open the door."

"No." She felt the key in her jeans pocket, all cold and slick like that old wrench she found in the garage one winter. "Mommy said I'm not s'posed to."

There was silence on the other side.

"If you open the door . . ." Joshua's voice dropped so low Katie had to press her ear flat against the crack in the door to hear him. " . . . I'll tell you what really happened last night in the caves."

Katie drew the heavy key out of her pocket and stared at it. The temptation was great. Joshua had not told her anything about that night. He told Mommy and Daddy some made-up story about getting lost and walking around in the dark, and they believed it even though you could tell it wasn't true, just the way parents always do. But something had happened to him, something weird enough to make him take off all his clothes and try to eat a dead rabbit. Katie wanted very much to know what that something was.

"Okay," she said at last, fitting the heavy key into the lock. "But you've got to promise not to tell Mommy."

30

The People of the Dark

The heavy footsteps halted at the bottom of the stairs.

Matt reached out for the stone ax, its sharp edge still wet with blood. Agonizing pain knifed up his spine, and he shut his eyes, wincing at the terrible pain.

When he opened them again he saw the dark shape standing in the doorway. It stepped into the room. The large bald head and cadaverous features were as Matt remembered, except for the open slashes oozing blood and the deep gouge down one side of his neck.

Matt reached again for the stone ax. Geza Todor lumbered forward suddenly, leaned over, blood from his wounds flowing down his arm, dripping off the ends of his fingers onto the floor. He picked up the ax. Todor glanced at Adriana Velotti, still smoldering in the fireplace, the stench of her burned flesh filling the room. Then he looked at Roy Danforth lying sprawled across the floor, one eye dangling from its socket.

Todor turned back to the ax, examining it carefully before asking, "Did you strike her with this?"

Matt said nothing. Fear made him mute.

Todor continued to study the ax. "This is a valuable piece. I am glad it suffered no damage." His voice was low, his accent marked. "It was given me by the chieftain of a New Guinea cannibal tribe. Used to behead captured enemy warriors before eating them. Fascinating, no?"

Todor turned and limped over to a far corner of the room. He replaced the ax in a wooden rack containing similiar weapons, then he came back to where Matt lay and leaned forward. Matt flinched as the bloody figure bent over him. Todor lifted him from the hardwood floor as effortlessly as a child might a rag doll and carried him over to a brown leather couch. Then he lowered his own bulk into an armchair facing him. He took out a handkerchief and wiped at the blood on his face.

"Why," Matt asked, as he drew a painful breath, "are you helping me like this?"

"Because, my friend, I owe you a great debt." Todor took the handkerchief from his lacerated face, the cloth wet with blood. "I owe you . . . my life."

Matt understood then what must have happened upstairs. "But she was working for you."

"Yes." Todor nodded slowly. "For almost five years now. I thought I knew her very well, but that is always the great human error, no? To think we know another well simply because we have known her long."

Matt thought of the almost unbridgeable gap that had opened between himself and Robin, but he said nothing.

"She dreamed the ancient dream," Todor continued, glancing at the charred corpse in the fireplace.

Matt frowned. "What are you talking about?"

Todor turned back to him, the glass eye shimmering in the firelight. "The dream of eternal life."

Matt's eyes narrowed. "Stop talking in riddles."

Todor smiled. "You are right, my friend. I talk in riddles." The smile turned into a hard, cold stare. "But no more. Now we talk the truth."

Todor leaned forward. "As a man of science, I am of course a realist, but I have seen things, my friend, that confound reality as we know it. I have seen realities more terrible than any horrors we can conjure in our darkest dreams." Todor straightened abruptly, a distant look in his living eye. "That is why I came to this place—to this Black Cavern, so well named. To learn the truth about the *k'tsa hulai nagrom.*"

A dim light switched on in the back of Matt's head. The People of the Dark. Flesheaters of Black Cavern. He smiled in disbelief, then he saw the guide shining her flashlight down on the flayed human head and the disbelief stuck in his throat.

"A primitive legend," Todor continued, "but how did we learn of it? The Caiyallahs were simple, semi-nomadic people. They spent their summers up here in the mountains, hunting game and gathering wild fruits and nuts. During the snowy winter months, they moved down into the great Central Valley. They left no written records. The Caiyallahs reported their tales of the *k'tsa hulai nagrom* to the Spanish missionaries, who duly recorded the information, then dismissed it, of course, as superstitious heathen nonsense."

"You're saying it's not?" Matt raised his eyebrows. "You think these flesh-eating People of the Dark actually existed?"

Geza Todor leaned forward. "The *k'tsa hulai nagrom* are not the only eaters of human flesh whose legends haunt these mountains. You are familiar, of course, with the tragic incident at Donner Pass?"

Matt nodded. Just last fall he had helped Joshua with a history report on the notorious Donner Party, the group of early California settlers who survived a terrible winter snowbound in the Sierras by eating the flesh of their dead companions.

"Does it not strike you as odd," Todor asked, "that this relatively isolated incident of pioneer cannibalism occurred in these same mountains where, in earlier times, man-eating creatures were rumored to have existed?"

Matt smiled skeptically. "The Donner Party wasn't attacked by flesh-eating ghouls. This People of the Dark bullshit is just . . . coincidence."

"Coincidence!" snapped Todor. "In my science, anthropology, there are no coincidences. There are only patterns. Some converge. Some do not."

"They have some pretty reliable accounts of what happened to the Donner Party," Matt pointed out.

"Reliable!" Todor turned on him, a fierce light

in his one good eye. "Babblings from human scarecrows who wandered half-crazed out of the mountains. Wild tales of horrible suffering and human depravity. Reliable accounts indeed!" Todor leaned forward in his leather chair. "What if the terror came from outside? What if the hapless members of the Donner Party did not cannibalize each other in their extremity? What if, instead, they were attacked and devoured by . . . ghouls, as you call them? The *k'tsa hulai nagrom,* foraging for food in the dead of a desperate winter. What then?"

"Then," Todor continued, answering his own question, "our patterns finally converge." He brought his hands together slowly until the tips of the fingers touched, forming an arch through which his glass eye glimmered like an idol in a shrine.

Matt realized then that he was alone in an isolated mountain cabin, miles from help, the air heavy with the stench of a burned corpse, while a madman spoke seriously of flesh-eating ghouls. He wished he had the stone ax again.

"But what, you ask, are these patterns?" Todor leaned back comfortably in his chair. His voice assumed the level tone of someone lecturing a freshman anthropology class. "In 1856, in the Neander Valley in Germany, not far from the city of Dusseldorf, a man named Johann Karl Fuhlrott discovered in a cave the bones of a very primitive creature. This creature lived anywhere from 50,000 to perhaps as much as 100,000 years ago. The creature was something like a man, but very much unlike any man or woman living today.

"Fuhlrott named the creature after the area where it was found. Neander Valley Man—or, in

German, Neanderthal. Perhaps the most well-known of prehistoric proto-men, he appears in cartoons and cheap movies as a brutish, low-browed savage with protruding eye ridges and a receding chin, slouching forward as he walks, carrying a crude club in one hand, the other entangled in the hair of his woman as he drags her home."

"How do we know what they really looked like?"

"We don't. What have we to go on? Some broken bones? Stone tools? We make an educated guess, but it's only a guess. Perhaps we are wrong." That strange light began to glow in Todor's living eye again. "Perhaps we are wrong about a great many things concerning Homo neanderthalensis."

Todor paused long enough for Matt to become aware of the mountain wind moaning down the open chimney flue, fanning the flames that still flickered beside the corpse of Adriana Velotti. "Perhaps we are most wrong," Todor continued, "when we assume that Neanderthal man disappeared from the face of the earth some 35,000 years ago. Vanished completely, like the rabbit in a magician's hat."

"Killed off by a more advanced form of man," Matt said. "Wiped out by us. Our ancestors. Homo sapiens."

Todor nodded. "Yes. The low, savage form of proto-man is destroyed, utterly eradicated from the face of the earth by ourselves. Rational man conquers beast man. A good story, no?" Todor smiled a dark, mocking smile. "There is only one problem with the story. It may not be true. Neanderthal man survived some of the most severe climactic conditions this planet has ever seen. During the Ice Age, when giant glaciers covered most of what is now Northern Europe, Neanderthal man lived in Central Europe. We think he accomplished this amazing feat with the help of fire, but he could not take his fire with him when he went out hunting food. We think he dressed in animal hides, but how long would you or I survive in sub-zero temperatures, my friend, wrapped only in rancid, uncured animal hides? Yet Neanderthal man not only survived these terrible conditions, he flourished. He was the primary, perhaps the only, form of human, or near-human, life in Ice Age Europe.

"And yet, when the glaciers retreat and the Ice Age finally comes to an end, what happens to this hardy, amazing creature? He is destroyed by a more advanced race of man, or even more strange, he simply disappears. As if the survivors of the Ice Age found life too boring when the weather got warm, and decided to say *adieu.*"

"The men who killed off the Neanderthals," Matt asked, "had more effective weapons, didn't they?"

"More effective weapons." Todor repeated the words with scorn. "In what way? Sharper arrows? Stronger bows?" He shook his head. "There is no reason to think that a powerful, well-adapted creature like the Neanderthal would have been destroyed that way. There is even less reason to assume that he simply withered and died, like a delicate flower." The terrible intensity in Todor's voice made Matt shift uncomfortably on the leather couch. "There is every reason, then, to conclude that the Neanderthal race did not become extinct 35,000 years ago, but survived into historical times. Even, in isolated instances, into our own time.''

Matt thought about it, then said, ''Bullshit.''

''The theory displeases you?''

''If Neanderthals were still around, we'd know about it.''

''How?''

''*National Geographic.* Reports of local sightings.''

''There have been sightings of unknown manlike creatures. The Abominable Snowman. Bigfoot. We ignore such things.''

''Those are tall tales.''

''How would we tell the difference?''

''You're the expert. All I know is we'd know.''

''There are now creatures proved to exist,'' Todor said, ''that were formerly dismissed as tall tales. The gorilla, for one. The okapi, for another. Occasionally a fisherman's net will yield a 'living fossil'—a member of a fish species assumed to have died out millions of years ago.'' Todor paused. ''By comparison, the survival of a higher life form like Homo neanderthalensis over a mere 35,000 years seems very probable indeed.''

''But if this is true . . .'' Matt began, then stopped. It's bullshit, he told himself. Then he saw again the deformed, bloody footprints on the basement stairs, the flayed head on the cavern floor.

He tried again. ''If this is true, then there's a group of cavemen who somehow survived the Ice Age—''

''Not precisely,'' Todor interrupted. ''We have good reason to suspect that Homo neanderthalensis has an average life span far exceeding our own, but the present group consists of descendents of the Ice Age dwellers."

"These things . . ." Matt hesitated, " . . . they're cannibals."

"Neanderthal man was certainly a cannibal," Todor agreed. "We know that much from our excavations of his prehistoric campsites. There is a tendency today to regard him as an occasional cannibal, a cannibal only out of necessity, but this may be mere romantic sentiment on our part." The glass eye glittered in the firelight. "It may be even more sentimental to regard them as our ancestors, however distant. We like to think that Homo neanderthalensis was a type of proto-man, a near human, because it fits better that way." Todor's one living eye narrowed. "It is most disturbing to consider that a nonhuman species resembling man may have preceded us on this planet, may still survive today."

Matt asked, "How did they wind up here?"

Todor shrugged. "Great migrations were common among pehistoric peoples. Isolated groups of Asiatic nomads crossed a land bridge from Siberia to Alaska to become the American Indians. The Neanderthal creatures might have come that way or by primitive rafts across the Atlantic."

"What about the ones who stayed in Europe? Didn't someone notice them?"

A brooding intensity came over Todor. "Have you never wondered if there might be some basis in fact for the European legends of werewolves, vampires and other unpleasant night stalkers? Most anthropologists dismiss such things as mere projections of a fear of the dark and the unknown, but even a projection has to be projected onto something." Todor leaned forward. "What would a Neanderthal creature look like, crawling through a dark forest? Pressing its horrible face up against the window of a peasant's cottage on a stormy night? A werewolf? A demon? The Devil himself?''

Matt thought of Joshua's and Katie's monster in the basement, of Robin's photograph of the thing that had crouched in the woods watching Katie. He said nothing.

''And if we consider the Neanderthal diet of human flesh,'' Todor continued, ''then we have a terrifying monster indeed. The tales of ogres snatching infants from cradles, of werewolves devouring hapless travelers beneath the full moon, suddenly begin to seem less like childish fantasies and more like distorted recollections of grim and terrible realities.''

A burning log popped, and Matt jumped, startled.

''We do not know for certain,'' Todor went on, ''but we can be fairly sure that to anyone who saw it, the Neanderthal would seem a true monster—hideous, savage, inhuman. Not at all the 'early form of man' so lovingly described by my anthropological colleagues.''

The pale light outside the window was fading and the whole world seemed to be slipping permanently into blackness. The shadows of the demonic statues wavered in the room's firelight. It all came back to Matt, rushing in on him—the missing body at the accident, the tale of Prather Wilkens' ghastly disfigurement, Katie's bear-like monster in the woods, Walter Selwyn's mysterious disappearance in quest of his lost daughter, Kyle Danforth's horribly mutilated body, the dark horror that came after Robin and

Joshua and Katie in the basement.

Matt looked up at Todor. "You knew about these . . . things. Why didn't you warn the rest of us?"

Todor smiled bleakly. "I tried to warn you, my friend. I was not entirely successful."

"You could've gone to Cody . . ." Even as he said it, Matt understood. "He's part of this, isn't he?"

"Yes . . . and no. The town of Black Cavern is a kind of secondary community, providing protection and nourishment for the . . ." Todor shrugged. "Why not use your word? Ghouls. Night stalkers who eat human flesh. It makes more sense than Neanderthal men. They no longer have anything to do with the Neander Valley, and they are not, as we use the term, men."

"Why haven't the people of Black Cavern gone in with guns and put an end to it?"

Todor shook his head. "My friend, you do not understand. These creatures, these ghouls, primitive as they are and without even the rudiments of our simplest technology, nevertheless possess powers such as we can only dream of. Their eyes, which glow with such eerie pallor, are immensely keen instruments of night sight, like infrared telescopic lenses. They can detect things at night, or in cave darkness, invisible to you and me. They move with the speed of panthers. Their energy is seemingly inexhaustible. Their sense of smell is as keen as that of the great hunting beasts, able to scent prey miles away. Their endurance is remarkable. They are mammals, creatures of flesh and blood. They can be wounded, as you or I, but they are difficult to kill."

Todor paused. "You can see, perhaps, why ordinary persons might regard these creatures as supernatural, as immortal, why the wretched citizens of Black Cavern continue to dwell among such monsters and do them reverence." Todor glanced at the fireplace and its smoldering corpse. "Why my late assistant betrayed—"

"No," Matt interrupted. "I don't see that. Whatever paranormal physical powers these things have, they can't just transfer them to—"

"Of course not, but their religious ceremonies involve the ritual eating of flesh and the drinking of blood. They think their powers come from the human substances they consume. And their powers, as I say, are persuasive."

"But how would Adriana Velotti . . . how would anybody find out what these things believe? They have a language?"

"Certain ceremonies can be communicated quite effectively without any words at all."

Matt blinked in confusion. "These things invite outsiders—"

"Not precisely." Todor hesitated. "The ghouls, for all their strengths, have one critical weakness. They are a highly specialized form of animal. The long fangs and claws are necessary hunting and eating tools. The profuse body hair is a legacy of Ice Age survival without the benefit of central heating. Because of their high degree of specialization, or perhaps because of their very long life spans, they do not reproduce easily or abundantly."

"They don't mate?" Matt asked, slightly nauseated at the thought of two semihuman monsters coupling in cave darkness like something out of Hieronymus Bosch.

''No, that is not the problem. They manage the sexual act itself with considerable vitality. The problem lies in actual reproduction. There is a great male-female imbalance in the present ghoul population, at least the one here in Black Cavern—something on the order of ten males for every female—and the few females do not give birth often or easily. So the solution . . .'' Todor paused. ''The solution is found in the same human community that provides their food source.''

''They mate with human beings?'' Matt asked, horrified.

Todor nodded. ''Sometimes. They select a human, most often a young boy, to mate with one of their own females. From what I have been able to determine, this method is usually the most successful. It results in stronger offspring. The issue of human females tend to be weak and die young.''

''How do you know this?''

''I have found, among other things, the remains of infant ghouls in bone piles deep inside the caverns.''

''They eat their own young?'' The revulsion showed plainly on Matt's face.

Todor shrugged. ''They are not human, my friend. It is not the same for them as it would be for us. To them, eating the flesh and drinking the blood of another being is a divine as well as nutritive act. Their word for blood, *Pragha,* is also their word for soul and life.''

A shock went through Matt as he heard the

word again. The guttural chanting from the tape of Kyle Danforth's torture seemed to echo inside his head. *Pragha . . . Pragha . . .*

"To drink another's *Pragha,*" Todor continued, "is to possess his soul, to make his life part of yours. All life, to these creatures, is an endless chain of eating and being eaten. The way to immortality is the constant ingestion of more and more *Pragha* into your own body."

Matt swallowed. "The young boys. How do they . . ."

"Select them? Instincts, my friend, unknown to you or me. A dark kinship between savage and civilized, ghoul and—"

"No!" Beads of sweat stood out on Matt's forehead. "What I mean is . . . how do they make them eat—"

"The flesh and blood of other human beings?" Todor spoke quietly, his words falling like stones in the darkened room. "By initiation. A rite of passage wherein the young boy becomes a member of the ghoul community. They give him flesh to eat and blood to drink. *Pragha rahim karak.* The Feeding. They teach him to partake of the *Pragha,* to make it part of him. And he becomes, in the process, one of them."

He won't eat anything, Robin had almost screamed it at him. Matt remembered the tears in her eyes, the tightness around her mouth.

Matt looked up at Todor. "My son . . ." His voice was hoarse. "My boy, Joshua. He got lost in the Kemmering Mine. In the caverns. All night. He was with another boy . . . Roy's son." Matt avoided looking at Danforth's corpse. "My boy wasn't hurt. But he's . . . he's changed. He won't eat anything anymore. Says he isn't hungry."

Todor stared at Matt, the glass eye cold and hard. "This is serious, my friend. We must—"

The howling cut him off.

It rose like a death wail from a distant chorus of inhuman voices. It swelled up from the town below and echoed against the mountains underneath the night sky. The unearthly sound seemed to freeze the blood in Matt's veins, paralyzing him. Even Todor's cold, impassive face flinched suddenly in the grip of fear.

"It has begun." Todor rose to his feet.

The howling echoed through the night air like the winds of death.

"We must move quickly." Todor took a deep breath. "Even now, we may be too late."

III: The Feeding

31

Darkness Falls

The streets of Black Cavern were empty.

Unreal, Robin thought, resting on her bicycle. Like a deserted movie set.

A cold wind from the mountains whistled down the empty main street of town, driving stray leaves and scraps of paper before it. Old-fashioned signs hanging above storefronts creaked painfully in the wind.

Nothing else moved.

Shivering, Robin pulled her thin jacket close. Daylight was fading slowly, turning the sky behind the mountains a pale, glowing magenta. Anxiety pierced Robin's heart. She glanced around the empty streets. Where was everybody? She had counted on asking directions to the doctor's office, but now there was no one to ask. The town was deserted, except for the wind.

She made her way around the town square, leaning hard on the bicycle pedals. It did not hurt so much now. At first she had thought her legs were coming off. Her calf muscles had burned, but then she got used to it, somewhat. She winced as a cramp dug deep into her right leg. The bicycle moved past the buildings lining the town square.

Glancing down a narrow alley between the Grizzly Bar and Hank's Hardware, Robin saw a small, white-frame house with green shutters and a white picket fence. A sign hung above the front door, creaking in the cold wind, barely legible in the fading daylight: Dr. Garret Krebs, M.D. Family Practice. Surgery. VISA. MasterCard. American Express.

Robin parked her bike against the white picket fence and mounted a short flight of steps to the front door with its stained glass panel. She pressed the old-fashioned doorbell and could hear it ringing distantly in the back of the house. No footsteps came to the door. She rang again. A strong gust of wind caught at her jacket. She shivered and started to turn away.

The door opened. "Yes?"

The voice sounded hoarse and rusty, as if it had not been used in a long time. Since no lights were on inside the house, Robin saw only a dark shape standing in the doorway.

She felt a chill crawl up her spine and lodge firmly at the base of her neck. "Dr. Krebs? I was looking for him."

"Dr. Krebs," grated the voice, "is not here. He is at the Mission."

Robin could feel hot breath against her face and smell something that made her stomach flip slowly over. She asked, "How do I get there?"

The dark shape seemed to lift its head, still indistinguishable, toward the pale magenta sky. "The road from here leads up to the ridge and the Mission."

"Thanks." Robin backed down the front steps, eyes on the dark shape standing in the doorway, her nostrils clotted with stench.

Her hands and legs trembled as she got on the bike and pedaled away from the white-frame house. She glanced back over her shoulder. The door was still open.

The howling began before she got very far up the winding road to Paso Perdido Ridge. Coyotes, she thought, goddamn dirty coyotes. She hated them—filthy animals, scavengers, sometimes even dangerous to children. But it was hard going on the road to Mission San Miguel and she had no time to worry about coyotes. Her lungs burned, and her leg muscles ached. The bicycle began to wobble. Sweat rolled down her face as she gasped for breath.

The child's BMX she was riding had a headlight, but it did not help much. The beam seemed pitifully narrow as it cut through the gathering darkness. She could see a thin slice of blacktop, and occasionally, when the road twisted suddenly, a stand of pine trees or a cracked rock face. Cold wind blew down from the mountainside. She shivered.

The howling grew louder.

It did not sound like coyotes any longer. There was a fierceness to it, a blood-hungry savagery that scavengers did not possess, and there were too many of them. Coyotes, she knew, sometimes traveled in packs, but this was no pack. The howling seemed to be coming from everywhere, piercing the darkness—dozens of separate cries, maybe even hundreds.

Something darted across the road in front of her. She gasped and hit the brakes. The bike threatened to veer out of control, but she managed to stabilize it. She could not see what had crossed her path, but it was something dark, fairly large, moving fast. She became aware of other dark shapes, running through the trees beside the road and tracking her as she struggled up the steep grade. *It's your imagination,* she told herself.

The road took a sharp turn to the left and started down an incline. The bike picked up speed, wheels rattling over rough blacktop. Wind speed increased, whipping the thin jacket against her back as she leaned out over the handlebars, trying to steady the bike.

The dark things in the trees increased their own speed. She thought she could see them now and hear them, crashing through the undergrowth, and howling as they gave chase. Her heart started shuddering. She turned to peer into the darkness beyond the narrow shoulder.

Then she glanced back at the road, just in time to see the black-and-white patrol car with its blinking red turret light parked sideways across the middle of the blacktop before she ran into it.

She jumped on the brakes and the BMX swerved into a long, sideways skid. She closed her eyes, bracing herself for the shattering collision of flesh against metal. With a sharp squeal of burning rubber, the bike slid to a full stop, inches from the parked patrol car.

Buck Cody, she thought wearily, *I'm even glad*

to see you. She got off the bike, every nerve in her body trembling with shock and fear.

A lanky figure stepped out from behind the patrol car. The dark metal of a holstered Smith and Wesson glinted under the flashing red light. A heavy white bandage covered his hatless head. When he recognized Robin, he grinned broadly, strong white teeth glistening against greasy, pock-marked skin.

"Well," Deputy Sheriff Floyd Kessler hissed softly, "if it ain't little Miss Rich Bitch, all by her lonesome self."

32

Flesheater

Robin stood and stared at Kessler, the patrol car's turret light flashing red, his greasy skin pitted like the dark side of the moon.

"You keep away from me," Robin warned, her voice terrified. "I mean it!"

Kessler's lip curled. "You and me, sweet thing, we got us a score to settle." He took a menacing step toward her.

"No!" Robin backed off, fists clenched in front of her.

Kessler threw back his bandaged head and laughed.

Then he rushed her.

Robin screamed, shutting her eyes and turning her head.

Kessler jolted to a full stop. His head snapped back and his mouth fell open. His arms jerked outward. Blood burst from his open mouth, warm flecks spattering Robin's face. He wavered like that for several seconds, rocking gently back and forth, arms held out sideways at a crazy, lopsided angle, then he pitched forward. Robin could hear the bones in his face break as he hit the blacktop. He lay there, facedown, arms sprawled beside him. She saw the jagged gash that had split open the back of his bandaged skull and the ax that had done the job, its sharp blade dripping blood.

Robin gasped to scream again, then recognized the pale hair and cold, gray eyes of the axman. Her scream collapsed into a frightened whimper. Gordon MacLeish stood beside the patrol car, his handsome features harsh under the pulsing red light, powerful hands gripping the bloody ax. He moved toward her. Robin stumbled back, eyes wide with terror. MacLeish raised the ax and threw it down. It clattered onto the blacktop with an echoing clang.

Robin's blood started pounding at her temples, and she had trouble breathing. Get out of here, her mind screamed. Run! But she was too exhausted to run, too terrified to speak.

MacLeish stared at her. "I'm glad to see you safe, Robin." His deep voice was quiet, gentle. "I didn't expect to see you again."

She stiffened. "About your jeep," she began, backing away as she spoke. "I didn't mean to steal it, and I didn't want to hurt you. But when you grabbed hold of the door hand—"

MacLeish cut her off. "The past is another world. We can't return there. Why make excuses for it? Now is all that matters." He held out a hand to her. "Let me be your friend, Robin.

Now."

A burst of howling echoed down the cold night wind.

"We must hurry." MacLeish looked up the winding mountain road. "They have our scent." He raised his hand. "Come."

Robin shook her head. "I've got to go to the Mission to find Dr. Krebs."

"It's not safe there now," MacLeish said. "Krebs has . . . gone below." He held out his hand. "Come with me. I'll take you back to your place."

"You're one of them," Robin whispered. "You draw them."

"I draw many things," he answered calmly. "I'm an observer of life in all its shades, dark as well as light." His handsome bearded face grew somber. "I draw a disaster at sea—sharks attacking a helpless woman. Does this make me a murderer?" He glanced with contempt at Kessler's corpse. "Or a rapist, like our late friend?"

"You murdered him," Robin said.

"Are you sorry? Would you wish him back to life?"

"No!" Robin cried, horrified at the thought of Kessler coming back to life, blood leaking from his split skull, broken bones shifting in his pockmarked face as he leered at her, dead eyes rolling slowly down from the top of his head.

The howling came again, sharp on the night wind, closer than before.

"Come." MacLeish opened the passenger door to his Cherokee, parked in the shadows behind Kessler's patrol car. "They travel fast on the scent of fresh blood."

Robin sickened at the thought. Trembling, she got into the Cherokee.

If we were truly one, MacLeish told himself, one soul, one *Pragha,* we would drink his blood and feed upon his flesh together, turning his weakness into our strength, his death into our life. But there will be time for that. He lifted his head toward the distant howling, the cold night wind blowing back his blond hair, pale moonlight glinting in his hard gray eyes. After the Master has taken her, all eternity will be ours.

They drove to Kemmering House in silence, through the dead, deserted streets of Black Cavern, down High Street to Black Cavern Road, out toward the cutoff. Robin sat on the far side of the Cherokee's front seat, one hand on the door handle, ready to throw open the unlocked door. She glanced nervously away from the road and over to MacLeish, then back to the road again, rushing up at her endlessly from beyond the headlights. MacLeish still affected her, but this time the emotion was fear, not desire, a fear that somewhere beneath Gordon MacLeish's calm, handsome exterior there lurked the ravening monster of his paintings, deadly and waiting.

The Cherokee pulled into the gravel driveway of Kemmering House. No lights were on. The tall, dark windows reflected pale moonlight like the glazed eyes of a corpse.

"Christ!" Robin exploded, kicking open the passenger door and jumping out onto the gravel. "Why aren't the fucking lights on?"

Before Gordon MacLeish could answer or get out, she was running, across the gravel and up the stone steps, two at a time.

"Josh!" She screamed into the dark living room, her voice echoing off the walls. "Katie!" She fumbled for the light switch, and the living room lights came on. The stuffed grizzly loomed up out of the darkness. The animal heads on the walls stared down at her, a malicious look in their flat, black eyes.

"Joshua!" She ran across to the kitchen. "Katie!" She pushed open the door and found the light switch. "Where the hell are you?"

The kitchen was empty.

She rushed back through the living room, her heart pushing its way up into her throat, like an animal trying to escape. She dashed up the stairs, two at a time, gasping for breath, her hand on the railing, squeaking against lacquered wood.

"Joshua!" Her voice rasped, hurting her throat. "Katie!" She reached the top of the stairs, chest heaving, lungs on fire. "Answer me!"

She remembered then: the key. She had left Joshua locked in the bedroom, and she had left Katie with the key.

She stopped.

The bedroom door was open.

"Josh?" Robin moved forward slowly, her stomach cramping with fear. "Katie . . ."

The bedroom was dark. The only light in the hallway came up from the living room downstairs, filtering through the balustrade in stripes and shadows. The bedroom door had not been forced. It had been opened by someone with a key. Robin stopped in front of the black doorway.

She heard it then—a sucking sound, like an animal at a stream, but muffled. The sound stopped abruptly. Robin stood staring into the dark doorway.

''Who's there?'' she called out.

Nothing.

Then the growl rolled ominously out of the darkness.

Pain burned in Robin's chest, and for one blinding instant she knew she was going to die, standing there in the dark hallway, hands clutching at her chest, mouth open, eyes staring straight ahead and seeing nothing.

But she did not die.

She pushed forward into the dark bedroom and clawed at the light switch, her fingernails grating noisily across the wallpaper.

The light came on.

At first the brilliance blinded her, exploding before her eyes like a second sun. She could see only fragments—lace curtains, brass headboard, flowered wallpaper, huge blossoms, long vines twisting and turning and curling like snakes, overturned bedside table, shattered glass vase.

And the bodies.

Joshua, naked, was bending over Katie, who was lying on her back on the floor. Joshua seemed to be giving her mouth-to-mouth resuscitation. Jesus, she's unconscious, Robin thought immediately. She fell and hit her head and got knocked out. Joshua was on his hands and knees, bent over her, his face covering hers.

''Joshua. . .'' Robin moved forward. ''Honey . . .''

He lifted his head.

The eyes were unchanged, except that now they were darker than before, staring out at her, like the animal heads on the wall.

Blood spilled down from his mouth and onto his naked chest. Katie's throat lay torn open, gouged out, muscles exposed. Blood still pumped sluggishly from the gaping wound, forming a pool around her head, already starting to congeal, turning from bright red to a dull rust brown.

Like that girl in the accident, Robin thought distantly, seeing again the halo of black blood around the head of the girl with the severed leg, lying there by the side of the road. And for a moment she thought she was back at the accident, everything dyed bright, nauseous orange by the flames from the burning Toyota, the greasy smell of roasting human flesh heavy in her nostrils. It's that other girl, she heard a loud voice say inside her head, because this one is dead and it has to be her. Or Walter Selwyn's daughter, because she's dead, too.

But this one was her own daughter.

Joshua swallowed. Raw chunks of his sister's flesh fell from his mouth, dribbling down to the end of his chin. He caught them with his fingers and stuffed them back into his mouth.

A dying sound rose from Robin's throat.

Then she went after him.

Joshua jumped back fast, but not fast enough. Robin grabbed hold of his right leg. He snarled at her and kicked out hard with his left foot. It caught her on the side of her face. Enraged, she seized his shoulders, yanking him to a sitting position. She hit him hard across the face with her open palm, right to left. Then back again, left to right. Joshua squealed in protest, blood spilling from his nose.

Robin rushed over to where Katie lay motionless on the hardwood floor. She shook her, searching frantically for any sign of life, but it was like shaking a rag doll. She crushed her dead daughter to her breast, an animal wail of loss breaking from her throat. Katie's head hung back limply from her shoulders, blood trickling down through her blond hair and onto the floor.

Joshua wiped the blood from his own nostrils and started to move. Robin dropped Katie and hurtled across the floor to him on her hands and knees.

"You!" She grabbed his face and twisted it toward her. "What did you do to her?" She brought her own face in close to his, her eyes mad, nostrils flaring.

He opened his mouth wide and Robin could see the blood and pieces of flesh stuck in his back teeth. Her stomach heaved, and she swallowed hard to keep back the vomit.

Joshua bit her, sinking his teeth into her right cheek. Robin yelped in pain. His teeth cut through her flesh. She shoved him away violently, a small strip of her skin torn off in his teeth. He clawed a her arms with his short fingernails. She grabbed a handful of his hair and smashed his face down onto the hardwood floor. He screamed horribly. She lifted his head and brought it down again, smothering his screams.

"You shut up!" she shrieked at him, the blood glistening down her torn cheek. "You shut up and lie there or I'll fucking kill you!" She shook him savagely. "I brought you into this world, and I'll take you out of it, by Christ!"

Robin staggered to her feet, pulling him up with her. He struggled feebly, blood leaking from his nose. She dragged him across the bedroom floor and out into the hallway, his legs trailing behind him like broken sticks. She pulled him into the bathroom and groped for the light switch. Bright light bounced off white walls. Robin saw her own reflection in the bathroom mirror and almost screamed. Her hair was tangled, matted with blood. Blood was spattered across her shirt and oozed from her torn cheek. Jesus save me, she prayed weakly. Make this all a nightmare. Then Joshua started to struggle again in her grip. She remembered Katie lying dead in the next room, her sightless, staring eyes. . .

She turned from the mirror, threw back the toilet seat and pushed Joshua down onto his knees in front of the open bowl, leaning his head out over the water.

"Spit it out," she hissed in his ear. "Open your mouth and spit it out!"

Joshua crouched over the bowl, blood from his nose dripping down into the water. His sobs came in a ragged, choking rhythm.

"Spit it out!" she screamed in his ear.

Joshua began to howl like an animal.

Robin gripped the back of his neck with her right hand, digging into the sternocleidomastoid muscles. She shoved her left hand down his throat, depressing his tongue with her fingers to make him gag. Joshua's howl turned into a strangled, wretching sound. He beat blindly at the hand wedged down his throat. Then he vomited.

It welled up in a warm rush over Robin's hand, splattering down into the water and over the sides of the bowl onto the bathroom tile. The blood came up a dark, rust-colored liquid, almost black, lumpy with pieces of shriveled, grayish-white stuff that looked nothing like human flesh. My own daughter's flesh, Robin thought abstractly, as if observing a scientific experiment.

Then her own mouth filled with vomit.

She stumbled back, still holding Joshua's head

out over the toilet bowl, and threw up into the bathroom sink. Her throat and stomach contracted violently, and tears came to her eyes. She had eaten almost nothing for the past 12 hours, but the sight and smell of her own vomit made her throw up again. She fumbled at the faucet, turned on the cold water and bathed her face. She let the chill water pour over her, numbing her, taking away the heat and the horror.

She became aware of Joshua clawing at the hand that still held the back of his neck. She shut off the water and flushed the toilet. The blood and flesh whirled away down a dark vortex. My own daughter's blood, she thought again, and her stomach cramped so hard she cried out, but there was nothing left inside to vomit up—except the pain. She looked down blankly at Joshua reaching back to claw at her restraining arm.

She yanked him to his feet, spinning him around to face her. "Why?" she screamed at him, her voice cracking. "Why?"

Joshua stared back at her, blood crusted around both nostrils, chin sticky with vomit. His eyes were expressionless as ever, now slightly glazed with pain.

"Why did you do it?" She shook him violently. "Answer me!"

Joshua mumbled something.

"What?" She brought her face in to his.

"Hungry," he whispered, the stench of blood and vomit filling her nostrils.

She struck him across the face, hard as she could. He squealed in pain, as more blood spilled from the crusted nostrils.

"Don't lie to me, damn you," she screamed into his face. "I don't want to hear that shit! Tell me why you did it!"

Joshua trembled in her grip. His eyes no longer expressionless; they were wide with terror.

"Answer me!"

"*Pragha,*" he whimpered, his voice weak, trembling.

"I said I don't want to hear that shit!" Robin screamed. "I want to know why—"

The arms grabbed her suddenly from behind.

She cried out in shock and tried to break free, but the arms that held her were powerful. As she struggled, she caught a glimpse in the gilded bathroom mirror of a handsome, bearded face and cold, gray eyes.

"Let go of me!" She twisted around.

But Gordon MacLeish was not looking at her. His hard gray eyes stared at Joshua. Several long seconds passed before Joshua realized that he was no longer restrained. He started to run, then stopped and looked up at MacLeish.

MacLeish nodded solemnly to him. "Go. Take your *Pragha.*"

Joshua scampered across the bathroom floor and out into the hallway, his naked limbs blurring with the speed of motion.

Robin gasped in disbelief, twisting around again to glare at MacLeish, her face tight with fury. "What the hell are you doing?" She threw herself forward with all her strength, only to be brought up short by MacLeish's powerful arms. "Let me go!"

Suddenly she was moving out from the bathroom and into the hallway, but MacLeish was moving her. Robin cried in rage as she saw Joshua dragging Katie's corpse out of the bedroom and across the hall toward the stairs, blood from her gouged throat leaving a wide smear behind the corpse, like moisture from a janitor's mop. Joshua pulled her down the stairs to the living room, dragging her by the feet, her head thumping against each step with a soft, hollow thud. Robin screamed at him until her voice broke, but he did not stop. When he reached the bottom of the stairs, Joshua began to drag Katie toward the center of the living room.

As MacLeish forced her down the stairs, his strong arms pushing her forward and holding her up at the same time, Robin twisted around to shout at him, "Why? You said you weren't one of them! Why are you doing this?"

MacLeish said nothing. He looked beyond her, at Joshua in the center of the living room. Joshua lifted Katie's corpse up off the floor with difficulty. Moving awkwardly, he draped her across his naked shoulders like a dead beast of prey, his shoulders sagging beneath her weight.

MacLeish nodded his approval from the bottom of the stairs. "Take your *Pragha* before the Master, as He has commanded. *Go.*"

Joshua seemed to bow slightly, the weight of his dead sister making him stoop like a hunchbacked dwarf.

"Joshua!" Robin cried, straining forward in MacLeish's grip. "Baby . . ." She choked on a sob. "Don't listen to him, honey. Josh, baby . . . Mommy loves you . . ." Robin's voice broke again. Tears trickled into her torn cheek, making it burn. "Listen to *me,* baby . . . don't listen to *him!*"

Joshua seemed to hesitate for an instant. Something flickered in his dead eyes like a spark catching fire in the darkness but only for an instant. Then it was gone. He turned around, carrying his sister's corpse to the double front doors. He opened one of them and disappeared into the night.

"Joshuaaaaa!" Robin strained forward until her arms ached in MacLeish's grip. Then her heart seemed to burst. Her head drooped, and she began to sob in great, shattering gasps.

MacLeish released her. She fell forward onto her hands and knees and stayed there, head bowed, sobbing incessantly. When she finally lifted her head, she saw through a blur of tears MacLeish standing in front of the open door, straight and tall, looking out onto the darkness like a guardian at the Gate of Hell. Her despair and rage gave way suddenly to hatred, a hatred more dark and overpowering than any she had ever known before. It burned into her soul, a passion so fierce she must quench it or die.

That was when she remembered the gun, the one Matt had left with her. *I want you to have it,* he told her, *and be ready to use it.* She was ready. She got to her feet, still sobbing. Gordon MacLeish stared out the open door into the darkness. She had hidden the gun in a kitchen cabinet, behind a bowl, higher than Joshua or Katie could reach. *Katie,* she thought, and almost fell to her knees again, but the hatred sustained her and drove her on.

She found the revolver. It was heavy in her hand, the black metal cold and oily. She had never fired it before, never even aimed it. Her heart started pounding.

She stepped cautiously out into the living room, afraid that she would find him gone—or waiting for her, ready to take the gun away. He was still standing in front of the open door, his blond hair and beard outlined against the darkness, his powerful body motionless, like a statue poised before eternity. He's so beautiful, Robin thought for a fleeting instant, then the hatred surged forth again. She raised the revolver in front of her, gripping the handle clumsily with both hands. The gun wavered in front of her, bobbing up and down. She took a deep breath to steady her trembling hands and pulled the trigger, but it would not move. She again pulled hard on the trigger, the barrel aimed at MacLeish's broad back.

The shot exploded inside the living room, the recoil kicking against her hands. Her ears felt as if someone had plugged them with sealing wax. She could hear nothing except the ringing inside her head and the echo of her own despair. Shit, I missed!

MacLeish pivoted, a stunned look on his face. Robin pulled the trigger again, and a red blotch appeared suddenly on his right thigh. MacLeish's mouth opened slowly, but no sound came out. He reached for his thigh in slow motion. The red blotch started to expand rapidly, bulging outward like an instant tumor. It burst, and blood splattered down his jeans leg and onto the hardwood floor. More blood started to spray from his thigh. MacLeish stumbled forward, one arm reaching out limply toward her. She shot him again. This time the bullet took him in the chest, knocking him backwards, arms flying up above his head. His knees buckled and he crashed to the floor, blood still spurting from the thigh wound.

Robin staggered toward him, the gun held out

away from her with both hands like a deadly animal. MacLeish opened his mouth again and worked his lips slowly, as if trying to say her name. She shot him in the face. The bullet hit him above the left eyebrow, shattering the frontal lobe and taking off the top of his head. Robin fired point-blank into his face again. The bullet hit him on the upper lip, collapsing his mouth into a gaping, bloody hole.

She felt the footsteps at the front door before she heard them.

She turned, the gun held out in front of her. She pulled the trigger, again and again, the cylinder revolving with short, sharp clicks, the hammer pulling back and falling.

But the gun was empty.

33

Holocaust

Geza Todor's worn-out van jolted over the rough dirt road to Kemmering House.

"Can't we step on it?" Matt demanded.

"Not without risking an accident." Todor glanced over at him. "These creatures, as you know, are drawn to blood."

A chill went through Matt as he remembered Joshua's vision the fateful night of the wreck. Joshua . . . Tears filled his eyes, blurring the dark road ahead.

"Besides," Todor continued, "if we were to have an accident now, with those explosives in back . . ."

Matt frowned. "We should have left that shit at Hank's Hardware where you found—"

The gunshots sounded then.

Sharp blasts, followed by a crackling reverberation as the aftershocks rolled through the dark forest like distant thunder. Two more shots rang out.

"What is it?" Matt's face tightened.

The dirt road turned hard right. The van followed, lurching wildly on worn-out shocks. Kemmering House loomed ahead, dark and forbidding, crouched in the open meadow like a malignant night creature. A lighted window and the open front doors glowed against its blackness.

A final shot rang out, coming unmistakably from within.

Todor turned into the circular gravel driveway.

Matt threw open the passenger door and jumped out.

"Stop!" Todor grabbed for him.

Matt ran toward the open front doors, leaped up the stone steps and burst into the living room, heart racing. Gordon MacLeish's corpse lay sprawled across the hardwood floor, blood flowing from the gunshot wounds in thick, jagged lines. Ghouls, he thought, staring at the shattered head, the burst thigh, blood still pulsing from the severed femoral artery. He looked up and saw Robin aiming the .38 Special straight at him, gripping it with both hands, pulling the trigger repeatedly as the hammer clicked again and again on an empty chamber.

"Robin . . ." Matt's arms dropped to his sides.

An ugly gash oozed blood down her right cheek, and scratches streaked both arms. She kept pulling the trigger of the empty gun again and again.

Matt walked toward her with slow steps, reached up, grasped the .38 by its snub-nosed barrel and pulled it gently but firmly out of her grip. She staggered back, both hands rising to her open mouth as if to stifle a scream. Then she did scream—a long, despairing wail—and toppled forward. Matt caught her before she fell. He held her in his arms, kissing her torn cheek, his lips salty with the taste of fresh blood.

"I'm sorry," he whispered. "Sorry about everything." He rocked her for several more seconds, cradling her close to his chest, then asked, "Are the kids okay?"

She tore free from his embrace and shoved him away from her, hands flat against his chest, with a violence that startled him. She stood there staring at him, a deadly look in her eyes.

He tried to move toward her, but she backed off. "Has anything happened to them? Robin!"

As his wife stared at him with those deadly eyes, Matt Brenner had the unsettling but certain feeling that if she could find more bullets for the .38 Special, she would shoot him dead as that unidentified lump of meat bleeding on the floor.

Outside, Geza Todor unloaded supplies quickly from the back of his van. He heard no more shots after Matt entered the house. Whatever had caused the shooting was gone now—or dead. Lucky for that young fool, he thought wearily, placing the dynamite sticks with care into a metal tool box. He'll get himself killed and take me with him, he thought, but then Todor remembered that he was alive now only because Matt Brenner had interrupted Adriana Velotti's plans. A pain flared in Todor's heart, momentarily eclipsing even the throbbing of his infected wounds. Admit it, old fool, he reproached himself sharply, you loved her. You did not simply admire her; you *adored* her. He gave a deep sigh, remembering her soft white skin and brilliant dark eyes, the youthful excitement she brought to any new project. Then he forced Adriana Velotti's painful memory from his mind, dislodging her hold upon his heart. For the time being, anyway, he reflected sadly, but she'll come back to you, old fool, in the lonely hours of the night. She's not done with you yet.

Todor loaded ropes, flashlights, shotgun shells, pickaxes, knives, matches and other essentials into two medium-size backpacks. In his own pack he placed the metal toolbox with the dynamite and also put in an item he had not taken from the dark shelves of Hank's—a large wooden mask, grotesquely carved, like a technicolor devil's head under the pale moonlight. He carried the backpacks and two shotguns up the stone steps into Kemmering House, closing the open door behind him and locking it securely.

Turning, he saw Matt Brenner and his wife standing still and staring at each other like two statues in an empty museum. Pine logs crackled in the marble fireplace. Matt's face was pale and haggard, as though someone had opened him up and drained out all the energy and hope, leaving the used-up body standing there like an empty oil can. His wife stared at her husband with the disoriented gaze of a trauma victim. He saw Gordon MacLeish's bloody corpse and the wound on Robin's cheek and thought he began to understand some of it.

Then Matt told him the rest.

"This is bad," Todor muttered. "Very bad."

Robin turned suddenly. "But what are we going to do? Nothing will bring my babies back!"

She burst into tears. Matt tried to comfort her,

but she twisted away.

There was steel in Todor's voice. "We are going, Mrs. Brenner, into the basement—"

She looked up in horrified alarm. "No!"

"—and from there into the tunnel that leads to the abandoned Kemmering Mine." Todor stared at her. "The only place we can hope to find your son . . . alive."

Matt glanced at the barred basement door.

The howling came again, closer now, much closer, as if ghouls were closing in on Kemmering House from out of the night, drawn by the smell of blood and fear.

"No," Robin whispered, hugging herself tight to keep from shuddering.

Todor looked out the living room window into the dark night. "They are coming for us. We must distract them."

"How?" Matt asked. "With what?"

Todor's glass eye glittered fiercely. "Fire. Their eyes are extremely sensitive to light." He turned his hard gaze on Robin. "Mrs. Brenner, you are familiar with the inventory of the kitchen shelves. What do we have that will burn?"

Robin shook her head, confused. "I don't . . . unless . . . oil? Cooking oil?"

Todor nodded. "Precisely."

Matt and Robin carried out several gallon jugs of cooking oil from the kitchen. Robin splashed oil across the floor and over the furniture, while Matt doused the heavy curtains, the walls and the animal heads mounted on the wall. Todor covered the enormous stuffed grizzly bear, using his superior height to coat the monster from head to foot. Then, using a poker, he dragged two burning logs from the fireplace and rolled them across the floor toward the oil slicks. The oil burst into flames with a soft *phhhuuuummmph!* Fire raced up the curtains. Armchairs blazed. Animal heads flamed into torches. The eagle above the front doors became a phoenix, its wings burning brightly. The stuffed grizzly caught fire, flames tracing its massive hind legs and leaping across the broad chest, up to its extended forelegs and heavy paws. The huge head was on fire, smoke issuing from its gaping jaws like dragon's breath.

"The bear is their god," Todor explained, "the source of their own strength. Their *Pragha.* Fire is also a god, a lesser one. Now, to their eyes, the lesser god has mated with the greater, producing an almost inconceivably powerful god, a being of ultimate strength and terror."

The howling outside turned abruptly into a confused, fearful wailing. Claws scratched at the living room window, and glass shattered. A gray, scaly claw groped through a ragged hole in the window. Robin screamed and grabbed onto Matt, burying her face in his shoulder.

"They want to see, do they?" Todor muttered, his glass eye reflecting the flames of the burning bear. "Very well. We shall let them see!"

He unlocked the double front doors and threw them open.

Outside were dark shapes, barely discernible against the black night sky. Glowing points of light winked shut in pain as the creatures massed before Kemmering House stared in awe and horror at the mating of the Great Dark God with The Sun That Feeds on Trees. The wailing of the ghouls became an eerie, semi-human keening. Their gods, and the world they ruled, seemed to be coming to an end in an agony of painful, blinding light.

Todor scanned the walls and ceiling beams. "The structure itself is catching fire. That will hold them off." He glanced at the wailing ghouls outside the open front doors. "For a while, at least. But we must hurry. We must descend the basement stairs."

He turned to the barred door. "We must enter the tunnel."

34

Underworld

Inside the tunnel, beneath the flames of Kemmering House, they made good progress. At first, using flashlights to check the terrain ahead, they moved quickly down long, lightless corridors with level dirt surfaces and only an occasional sharp turn. Then the descent began in earnest. Gradually at first, the floor dropped with the smoothness of a slanted loading ramp, then more abruptly, the surface underfoot became suddenly uneven and treacherous. Large boulders blocked the way. Corridors became twisting mazes. The trio started to descend sideways, like mountain climbers, hands braced for support, legs straddled. Todor distributed pickaxes, then ropes. Flashlights became difficult to hold while climbing and were exchanged for spelunkers' helmets with head lamps.

Their progress slowed down to a tedious crawl.

"Shit!" Matt lost his footing once again, scrambling for leverage on a steep slope. "How the hell did Old Man Kemmering ever use this tunnel?" His voice echoed in the underground darkness.

Todor looked up, breathing heavily. "Marius Kemmering did not build this passageway for his own amusement. He built it for them."

A silence followed that seemed to deepen the darkness of the tunnel.

Finally Matt asked, "How do you know?"

"Because Marius Kemmering left a journal." Todor's words fell heavily in the darkness. "I learned about this from Father McKerry. He let it slip accidentally, then denied it. The late Miss Velotti, under my orders, used all her considerable charms to obtain the journal for me. I read it." Todor's wounded face hardened under the dim light from the helmet lamps. "It was . . . unpleasant reading. I knew then what I was dealing with. Before, I had harbored suspicions, but now I knew." He looked up at Matt. "That is why I tried to frighten you that day beside the lake, scare you into leaving, make you flee an ancient horror that, even then, was watching you and your children."

Robin gasped.

Matt did not look at his wife. "But if Kemmering knew what was attacking his men . . ." Matt stopped in confusion. "Then why did he lead them down—"

"He didn't," Todor explained. "That was just a local legend to cover up the fact of his disappearance."

"Disappearance?" Matt frowned. "How—"

"No one knows. The last entry in his journal reads: *I go into the Dark. I become the Pragha. It is His Will. God have mercy on my soul. I can not fight His Will.*"

Matt moistened his lips. "Ghouls get him?"

"No one knows."

"Bullshit! What do you think happened?" Matt stared at Todor. "You think he became one of them, don't you?"

"No one knows. But there were rumors, yes."

They continued their descent. The steepness grew worse, the way more treacherous. They lost their footing often. Robin, slipping on loose gravel, fell and began to tumble down the steep incline. Todor caught her at the last possible moment. After she recovered, they went on. The descent became agonizingly slow and perilous, each step threatening to plunge them into darkness and death.

And then, without any warning, it was over.

They found themselves on level ground in a large, high-ceilinged cavern room. Stalagmites of all shapes and sizes jutted upwards from the cold stone floor. From the darkness ahead came the faint sound of falling water.

"We are now in the caverns themselves," Todor said, his voice echoing off stone walls. "Be alert for hazards."

The sound of falling water grew louder. Chill dampness hung in the dark air. Todor swept their most powerful light over the cavern room. He picked out several small pools of water, steaming like underground spas. A large body of black water extended far into the darkness. Water dripped down from above onto the multicolored stalagmites rising from the cavern floor.

Todor aimed the light at one of the room's stone walls. Matt gasped in astonishment, and Robin clutched at his arm.

Painted directly on the cavern wall, 20 to 30 feet in height, were crude but compelling designs outlined in bright, glaring colors. An enormous grizzly bear covered one half of the wall, dwarfing by comparison even the stuffed giant at Kemmering House. On the other half of the wall a huge saber-toothed tiger crouched in ominous majesty, eyes burning bright, fangs smeared with blood.

"Incredible," Matt whispered, awestruck. "Who painted these damn things? Kemmering?"

"Hardly," Todor replied. "Marius Kemmering had no interest in art of any kind. His only passion was power."

"Then who . . ." Matt stopped, the realization coming home to him. "Impossible," he muttered.

"Not at all," Todor countered. "We have abundant evidence of Neanderthal art from the Franco-Cantabrian caves."

"But—" Matt started to object.

"But monsters can't create art?" Todor suggested.

Matt said nothing, his eyes moving slowly over the massive wall paintings. He pointed suddenly. "What's that?"

Todor's light fell on a painted figure with the body of a ghoul and the head of a saber-toothed tiger. The long arms were spread wide in a ritual gesture.

"Don't tell me that survived the Ice Age, too." Matt's scalp pricked at the thought of meeting one in cave darkness.

"The Master of the Animals," Todor explained. "Animals are gods, of course. The being who is part animal and part man is then the mediator between the two worlds of gods and men. A type of Messiah, if you will."

Matt remembered the blood-streaked Christ leering down from the chapel wall of Mission San Miguel. A shudder coursed through him. Then he noticed a smaller figure on the cave wall, a ghoul imitating the gesture of the Master of the Animals, some kind of spear grasped in its raised claw.

He pointed again. "What about that?"

"The Master of the Hunt. A type of shaman or priest. He allows himself to become possessed by the spirit of the Master of the Animals. Thus he is able to help the tribe's hunters find game."

"I thought you said they gave up on four-footed game a long while back."

"Tribal memories are even longer. These beasts on the wall for example." Todor pointed to a giant woolly mammoth, long tusks curved like mighty scimitars. "Some of them have been extinct for many thousands of years, and yet . . ."

Robin was not listening. She was not even looking. She walked away slowly from the two men, reliving in her mind the horror of the upstairs bedroom, playing it over and over again like a loop of movie film.

The underground waterfall seemed to echo her tortured thoughts, mocking her with constant, meaningless repetition. The pain swelled in her heart. It grew from a dull ache to a sharp, burning agony. She wanted to die, to lose herself in the darkness, to find a small, quiet place to lie down and die in. We all come out of the darkness, she reasoned slowly, and we all go back into the darkness when it's over.

The noise of falling water gradually became

distant, replaced by another sound inside her head—a throbbing, a low rumbling like a drum beating miles away. The drum beat again and again. It beat with a human voice, many voices repeating again and again.

". . . Pragha . . ."

". . . Pragha . . ."

Robin's skin crawled. The bloody images of Joshua and Katie faded suddenly, dissolving into darkness.

". . . Pragha . . ."

She was afraid.

She had wanted to die only moments before, but now she was terrified of death and darkness. The dark death had come for Katie, devouring her flesh, and the filthy, inhuman darkness had seized Joshua with its cold hands, destroying his soul.

"Matt?" she whispered, glancing around fearfully.

Her helmet lamp revealed only darkness—and in the darkness, strange shapes. Monstrous stalactites hung down like dragons' fangs, dripping with clotted venom. Huge fissures in the rough stone floor, gaping cracks in the very bowels of the earth itself, led down to dark horrors beyond human imagination. The panic began to rise in Robin's throat, gagging her. She was lost. Somehow she had wandered far away from where the two men stood discussing the wall paintings. She glanced around desperately, trying to find the way back. Her helmet lamp sliced erratically through the darkness, while somewhere ahead of her, echoing against stone walls, inhuman voices chanted endlessly.

". . . Pragha . . ."

". . . Pragha . . ."

". . . Pragha . . ."

She turned frantically back to the way she had come, but nothing looked familiar. She could not remember how she had got to where she was now. Her heart started hammering against her chest; breathing became difficult. The grisly specter of Kyle Danforth's body drifted across her consciousness along with images of the other victims.

She shut her eyes and put her hands to her head, squeezing it tight to halt the rush of mad, obscene images. Involuntarily, her eyes opened.

She noticed the light then.

It was more a glow than a light—dark orange like a distant fire on a beach at night or the flames of a burning car.

She stared at the faint orange glow pulsing from the darkness before her. She opened and shut her eyes several times, but the light did not vanish. She moved toward it. Gradually, the glow's intensity increased. She began to distinguish objects faintly by its light—huge stalagmites rising from the stone floor in front of her like a forest of diseased tree stumps, the narrowing stone walls of the corridor down which she advanced, the outsized boulders that blocked her path. And above all else, there was the gradual lowering of the dark stone ceiling until she found herself walking hunched forward like a crippled old woman, drawn irresistibly toward the strange, glowing light.

The glare from her helmet lamp seemed harsh, so she reached up and shut it off. She could see more clearly then—rock formations and the ever narrowing corridor.

And the source of the light.

The chanting was no longer distant. It rose and fell thunderously, like waves crashing against a rock-bound coast.

"... *Pragha* ..."

"... *Pragha* ..."

"... *Pragha* ..."

The opening stood directly ahead of her, small, about five feet in diameter, like a window cut from the dark stone of the thick cavern wall through which the orange light burned. She could smell the resinous smoke from the torches down below, miles below it seemed. She got down on her hands and knees, heart beating fiercely, mouth dry. She looked out the stone window.

Torches flared from a raised stone altar in the middle of an enormous cavern room. Smoke from the burning torches floated up into the darkness far above Robin's head. Surrounding the altar was a vast sea of . . . the monsters from Gordon MacLeish's paintings. The ghouls knelt facing the altar, chanting the two syllables over and over with one inhuman voice. Some of the more ardent worshippers bowed low to the floor, hideous faces pressed against cold stone. As Robin stared at the chanting figures far below she could see that not all of them were ghouls. Buck Cody's tanned naked body was wrinkled and sagging like the desiccated hide of an ancient lizard. Morton Gormley, manager of the Caiyallah Lodge, lay flat across the cavern floor in groveling obeisance.

They're all part of it, Robin realized with a stunned sense of horror. The old joke about a tourist trap surfaced in her mind, but it was not funny. The trap had caught Katie and Joshua. It had caught them all.

Behind the altar squatted a hideous stone idol, a crude representation of a female figure with huge pendulous breasts and a great gaping vulva. Beneath it, on the altar itself, crouched a thin, frail creature whose long white beard only partially covered a sickly pale body blemished with open sores. When the creature moved, it resembled nothing so much as a giant white spider. But Robin could see, even from that distance, that it had once been human.

Near the front of the altar were two smaller shapes. At first Robin thought they were severed parts of human bodies and she did not look closely at them. Then she happened to stare in that direction again.

She saw what they were.

"Joshua!" Robin's shriek carried over the chanting like a rifle shot. She rose quickly to her feet, cracking her head hard against the top of the stone cleft. Her mind reeled as she almost lost consciousness. She screamed again, over the pain and nausea, "Joshua!"

Some of the worshipping ghouls glanced fiercely around the large room, fangs bared. Father James McKerry rose to his feet, torchlight flashing off his thick plastic lenses. He looked about in confusion, searching for the source of the cries.

"Joshua!" Robin screamed again, beyond fear or pain.

She kept screaming his name. Her son looked up from where he knelt bowed over his sister's naked corpse. He saw the small figure in the distant cleft of the far wall, calling out to him, waving frantically, arms outstretched. His face gave no sign of recognition.

Robin did not hear her husband and Todor

calling for her as they rushed down the narrow stone corridor toward her.

"Joshua!" Her voice cracked pitifully.

The small figure on the altar looked away.

"Joshua!" Robin threw herself forward, hands reaching out into nothingness.

She toppled headfirst into the chamber below.

Iron claws seized her in midair and yanked her back onto the ledge, the torchlit chamber swaying dizzyingly beneath her. Malodorous breath hissed in her ear. Turning, she saw the ghoul's horrible face pressed close against her own, slaver drooling from sharp fangs, white eyes burning with primitive rage.

She could hear Matt calling to her, his shouts echoing in the distance.

Then cries and gunshots.

Then nothing.

35

Master of the Hunt

Consciousness returned to Matt Brenner in jagged pieces—suffocating stench, dead bodies, rotted meat turning to liquid in the dark. He gagged and tried to raise his head. Sharp claws dug into his flesh. A nightmare face glared down at him, long fangs bared. He shrank back, pressing flat against the cold stone floor. Four ghouls crouched over him, holding him down while incessant chanting rumbled in his ears. Suddenly, his guards lifted their deformed heads toward the center of the massive cavern room. Matt raised his own head and went numb with horror.

On a raised stone altar, surrounded by smoking torches, Joshua stood naked, eyes lost and empty. Beside him stood Father James McKerry, also naked, black-framed glasses contrasting absurdly with his flabby, pallid body. Off to one side, away from Joshua and the priest, Robin stood, naked like the rest, eyes wide with fear, tan skin glistening under torchlight. A ghoul crouched on either side of her. Huge claws gripped her arms. Burning white eyes lingered on her pale breasts and dark blond pubic hair. Matt cried out in alarm. But her captors were not intent on harming her. They were only guards, keeping her in a certain place, waiting for an appointed time.

Matt's panicked cry caught the attention of his own guards and they turned on him, snarling. A heavy claw shoved hard against his bare chest, slamming him onto the cavern floor. As sharp rocks cut into his back, Matt realized that he too was naked. His brain began to spin out of control. They had them all. Him. Robin. Joshua. Everyone. Except Todor. He had either escaped or been killed. Probably killed, Matt thought miserably.

The blackness of despair fell over him. For one hopeless moment he wanted only to bring the agony to an end. Then, from the stone altar, there came a scream of terror and revulsion. Matt's despair vanished. Robin screamed again, and he raised his head.

It towered above her and Joshua and Father McKerry, a shape of unimagined horror. The giant ghoul hunched forward, thick dark body hair streaked with white, taut muscles rippling under leathery gray skin. Fangs like tusks jutted out from a wet black-lipped mouth. White eyes burned, emitting a strange, mesmerizing radiance. It was hideous beyond description or belief, but there was power in the burning eyes. They commanded and you obeyed.

The creature hovered over Joshua like a guardian demon. One huge claw, large as a garden rake, rested lightly on the boy's naked shoulder with a proprietary, almost fatherly tenderness. The monster twisted its fanged mouth in a grimace that might have been intended as a smile.

Joshua had learned well. He knew what offerings pleased the Master.

In his thin boy's arms he balanced the naked, bloody corpse of his sister. Katie's mouth hung slack, her sightless eyes staring up at the dark cavern ceiling. Joshua's own eyes bore the distant, empty look that had marked them ever since he returned from the Kemmering Mine. His face was solemn as an acolyte's. Slowly he raised the corpse, arms trembling with the effort. He held it out before the assembled ghouls, swarming like scavenging rats beneath the stone altar.

Father McKerry pointed an outstretched arm. "*Pragha rahim karak!*" he shrieked, his voice carrying through the smoky darkness. "*Pragha!*"

With one vast, inhuman voice, like thunder rolling down an empty plain, all the ghouls echoed, "*Pragha!*"

"*Pragha!*" rumbled the Master, the word echoing from deep within its massive chest.

Joshua lifted his sister's corpse before the multitude. Claws reached up toward his burden.

The Master's white eyes blazed with a fierce, evil light.

"Joshua!"

Robin's cry cut through the chanting, and Joshua almost dropped the corpse. He turned awkwardly to his mother, naked on the altar next to him.

Other heads turned with his, and an angry snarling broke from the assembled ghouls.

"Listen to me," Robin was shouting, her voice hoarse but under control. "Joshua, put Katie down. Don't give her to them!"

His face lost its rigidity. It became that of a frightened boy, and for an instant, brief as a flash of light, a look of mingled fear and love appeared in his lifeless eyes. He took a step toward his mother.

The Master voiced displeasure, a roar bursting from its throat. Followed by a mental command, unspoken but heard as clearly as a shout. *You are mine! Obey me!* Robin heard it, her skin growing cold as the obscene thought penetrated her mind, digging into her soul with filthy, clawed fingers. No one had spoken, but she had heard it in her mind and saw it in Joshua's eyes, dark and distant once again.

He turned from her and gave his sister's corpse to the hungry multitude.

The howling ghouls tore at each other mindlessly, clawing to get at the dead flesh. Father McKerry lifted bloodstained hands in a solemn ritualistic gesture. The emaciated creature with the long white beard scuttled madly across the altar, spinning in circles like an albino spider in its death throes. Robin threw herself forward, only to be jerked back by the dark claws that held her arms. She screamed hysterically as she saw her daughter torn to pieces by ghouls fighting fiercely with one another for possession of a severed limb, a mouthful of bloody flesh.

Robin collapsed, her head dropping forward. She hung limply in her captors' grasp like a crucified criminal.

Matt watched in horror. Tears blinded him as he screamed his hatred, his impotent rage.

But it froze in his throat without a sound.

The Master, coarse hair flecked with blood, raised a huge clawful of bleeding flesh and brought it up to Joshua's lips. The naked boy knelt in the middle of the altar, eyes closed, mouth open. Father McKerry stood behind him, moving his arms slowly in elaborate gestures beneath wavering torchlight.

"Pragha rahim karak!" the priest shouted, his sharp voice rising above the feeding ghouls.

They stopped to watch, blood dripping from gorged mouths.

The Master put the torn flesh to Joshua's mouth. He ate of it, devouring and swallowing greedily.

"Pragha!" Joshua cried, ecstatic. *"Pragha!"*

"Pragha!" echoed the chorus of watching, hungry ghouls.

Matt finally found his voice. A throat-bursting scream tore loose from his chest. His guards turned on him, but he kept screaming. He did not fear death now. He welcomed it.

The Master turned toward the screams. A barked command echoed across the huge room. Matt's guards yanked him to his feet, dragging him through the loathsome, scrambling mass of feeding ghouls and humans who had become ghouls.

Past the blond tour guide, Katie's blood smeared across her tan arms and firm young breasts, her long blond hair streaked with more blood, her blue eyes bright with a fierce, unclean hunger. Past Hank, the hardware store owner, and the regulars at the Grizzly Bar all swarming like starving dogs beneath the altar, mouths open, straining for stray morsels. Past Violet Greenway, swaying rhythmically with the chanting, gorging crowd, her withered breasts swinging slowly back and forth.

The guards dragged Matt up onto the altar, cutting his shins on the sharp stone edge, and brought him naked before the Master.

The huge ghoul stared down at him, black-lipped face wrinkled into leathery gray folds, white eyes burning with primitive hate. The creature growled at Matt, exposing long fangs encrusted with flesh and blood.

Matt turned to his son. "Josh, we'll get you out of this! Josh . . . hear me?" Matt's voice caught. "Scout? . . ."

Joshua was still on his knees, eyes closed, body swaying gently to the renewed chanting of the massed ghouls.

"Joshua," Matt shouted at him, "I'm your father. Answer me!" He took a step forward, but his guards jerked back hard on his arms. "Answer me!"

Joshua opened his eyes and looked directly at his father. The eyes were dark and still and empty. Christ, there's nothing there, Matt thought. It's like looking into an empty grave. Something died inside Matt Brenner then. His only son was gone, and he knew it.

The Master placed a scaly claw on Joshua's head and stroked his hair approvingly. The hideous face leered over at Matt. *He is mine.* Matt heard it echoing inside his mind, cutting deep into his brain. *He is mine forever.*

The venom gathered in Matt's throat, and he spit it full into the Master's horrible, leering face.

The giant ghoul roared in fury and clawed at the

spittle dribbling down its gray skin. Matt's guards turned on him with bloodlust in their white eyes. He braced himself for the deathblow, but the Master barked sharply at his underlings. They dragged Matt over to where Robin still hung unconscious between her two guards.

"Robin!" Matt called out to her above the throbbing, endless chanting. *"Robin!"*

Her eyelids fluttered. She shook her head slowly, but nothing registered in her eyes. They stared at him, blank, unfocused.

"Robin, baby . . ." He leaned forward.

His guards yanked back on his arms, almost wrenching them from their sockets, and Matt cried out in pain. His feet slipped out from under him as they dragged him back, away from his wife. Then they stopped and repositioned him. One claw grabbed his head and twisted it violently, forcing him to stare straight at Robin hanging limply between the two ghouls.

Torches were brought closer for his benefit. The ghouls squinted painfully at the increased light. Matt's guards shifted uncomfortably, but did not loosen for an instant the pressure of their grip.

The Master shambled toward her.

Jutting out from below its knotted gray stomach, almost like a grotesque extra limb, the creature's huge phallus stood fully erect, gray and scaly, bursting with whatever inhuman blood coursed through its veins.

Holy fucking shit, Matt thought numbly. A hoarse cry rose in his throat, but the claws holding his head tightened. He could feel their razor-edge sharpness cutting into his skin. The iron grip on his arms cut off his circulation and the blocked blood began to throb painfully.

Robin was conscious again now, her screams horrible to hear. Pleading, she cringed as the monstrous phallus approached her. The guards threw her roughly down onto the altar, pinning her firmly against the coarse stone, their white eyes burning with a brutal, primordial lust. Robin screamed helplessly. Before, in the safety of her home in the Palisades, a world that now seemed as distant as another planet, she had once tried to imagine rape, envision its pain and horror, its degradation and crushing brutality. When she had lain beneath Gordon MacLeish and all the passion had disappeared suddenly, leaving only a mindless, rutting urgency in its place, as he hammered away at her like an idiot with a club of flesh, she had thought then that rape must be like that—disgusting, mechanical, meaningless.

But nothing, not the imagined violation or the hollowness of Gordon MacLeish's passion, was anything like the actual horror.

It was annihilation.

The Master entered her with one crude, violent thrust, growling deep in its throat like a jungle cat. And as the movement began, the pain tore through her in waves, each new one more terrible than the last. Even worse than the pain was the knowledge that her son was watching this, her desecration. She knew, in some obscure part of her mind not made mad by the thrusting, searing pain, that her husband was watching, too. But this was *his* fault. It was all his fault.

Slaver dripped down from the Master's fangs onto her bare breasts.

She had never hated Matt like this before—hated him for her pain and degradation, for killing her daughter, for making her son watch his mother's rape.

But Joshua was not watching. His eyes were dark and empty, as if they had turned inward and were observing something deep inside himself, something that still lived on secretly in a world of darkness and death.

Matt was watching. All he could do was watch, watch with the coolness of someone who has moved beyond pain and loss, suffering and rage. *They'll pay for it,* he promised himself. *Every last one will pay.*

The Master reached climax with a shuddering howl. Robin screamed soullessly as the icy semen ejaculated inside her, causing a pit of terrible cold to spread from her womb through her stomach and into her heart, chilling it and turning it to brittle ice. The feeding ghouls took up the howl of climax, their horrible voices echoing like the cries of the damned under the cavern's stone roof. Torchlight flickered over a chaos of monsters, howling in sexual frenzy, the blood of innocence staining their devouring mouths.

The Master of the Hunt withdrew from Robin's limp, unconscious body, the huge phallus still engorged, dripping blood and discharge. The creature turned slowly, deliberately toward Matt, huge claws raised, fangs bared.

Matt's guards thrust him forward, and he glanced at the burning torches. *If I can just take him with me,* he thought coldly, calculating his chances of grabbing a torch.

The Master of the Hunt reached out for him with a blood-stained, razor-tipped claw.

Then it suddenly recoiled in fear, hissing loudly, savage claw drawn back against its massive chest. The ecstatic howling of the ghouls before the altar broke into guttural shrieks of terror. The guards released Matt's arms, backing away from him, awe and horror on their inhuman faces.

Matt glanced over the enormous torchlit room, fear clutching at his own heart as he sought the cause of the ghoul's panic.

He saw it then.

The terrified ghouls fled howling before the appariation as it shambled toward the altar. It bore the head of a demon, the body of a naked man. The demon's head seemed to float above the body—lurid, glowing, unreal.

"The Master of the Animals!" Father McKerry cried out, his voice shattered by fear. "The God of Gods!"

Matt Brenner watched the terrible demon's head, harsh with violent colors—red, yellow, orange, black—as it drifted toward him, floating above the cowering ghouls. He had seen this before, but it was several long minutes before he remembered, and saw it again in his mind's eye. It had been hanging on the wall in the dark room that stank of death and burning flesh, surrounded by other grotesque masks and monstrous statues.

Matt stood open-mouthed in shock as Geza Todor climbed up onto the stone altar, his naked body scored with wounds, the primitive ceremonial mask completely obscuring his face.

Todor spoke rapidly in a low voice, muffled by the mask. "My guards . . . did not release me until . . ." The masked head nodded at Robin's unconscious body. "Afterwards . . . they let me go. The guns . . . destroyed. But this . . ." Todor slowly raised a stick of dynamite, clutched tight in his hand like a ceremonial wand. "With this I can distract their attention while you and your family . . ."

"Nobody's leaving," Matt muttered thickly. "I'm taking everything out with me." He glanced at the ghouls cowering before the altar. "Every last fucking one of them." He reached for the dynamite stick.

"Don't be a fool!" Todor jerked it back away from him. "Your wife needs your help . . . your son—"

A thin, high-pitched wailing cut him off and he and Matt turned toward the sound. Scrabbling across the stone altar like an enraged spider, the emaciated creature with the long white beard rushed toward them, dark eyes filled with hate. Its long filthy nails were chipped and broken, and it gave off a stench of disease and death, of open wounds and running sores.

"What is it?" Matt whispered in horror.

"That," Todor's muffled voice replied, "is Marius Kemmering—what's left of him."

Matt shook his head, stunned. "Impossible. . ."

"This is the immortality for which he sacrificed his wife, his children, his fortune . . . his humanity."

With a strangled cry Matt leaped forward and fell upon the diseased, mottled body. The wailing turned into a desperate shriek. Thin, spidery arms flailed at him, trying to reach his eyes, but Matt's hands found the creature's throat first. With one hand gripping the scrawny, filthy neck, he closed the other into a fist and brought it down hard into the face of the thing that had once been Marius Kemmering.

The cracking of brittle bones was clearly audible

as Matt's fist smashed into the wasted face. Blood spurted out onto his naked body. He pulled back his fist and brought it down again. He could feel the skeletal structure of the face giving way, turning into a yielding, gelatinous mass. The skull split open under repeated blows, brains oozing out along with blood. The thing went limp in Matt's grasp, but he kept on smashing at it, as if by utterly annihilating what had once been Marius Kemmering he could undo all the evil that Kemmering had caused.

There was no more skull left to batter, only a shapeless lump, when Matt stopped, gasping for breath, blood-soaked fist still raised above his head, bits of flesh and brain tissue splattered over his hair and face. With a mad animal cry, he raised the limp body to him and bit into the withered neck that had once supported Marius Kemmering's head. Growling with rage and hatred, Matt tore open the neck of the corpse, jerking fiercely on the stringy flesh like a dog pulling meat from a bone.

An iron hand seized him by the hair, yanking him back from the corpse. "Stop it!" Todor hissed. "Have you gone mad?"

"My God . . ." Matt whispered through blood-stained lips, looking up at Joshua, then at the Master of the Hunt, who stared back at him with burning white eyes that pierced to the very center of his soul.

The shock traveled through his whole body as Matt recognized the horrible ancestral kinship between himself and the savage People of the Dark.

One Life, he heard inside his head. *One Pragha.*

"It's a trick," Father McKerry cried out suddenly. "Don't you see? It's all a trick!"

The Master of the Hunt glanced uncertainly at the naked priest, then at Matt Brenner and the masked Geza Todor. A dull comprehension narrowed the creature's burning eyes.

"He's not the Master of the Animals," the priest screamed, pointing at Todor. *"Azgarok Pragha kh'asht'l na hr'adak!"*

From the ghouls surrounding the altar there rose a terrible howling that increased rapidly in volume and intensity until the altar itself seemed to tremble with rage.

The Master of the Hunt stared at the two hairless ones with the cold, white eyes of death.

Matt grabbed the dynamite stick from Todor, and with the same movement thrust the fuse into the wavering flame of a torch held by one of the guards. The Master snarled, monstrous claw raised to strike.

The fuse caught first.

It ignited with a sputtering, crackling hiss, throwing off sparks and smoke. The ghouls wailed in terror. Even the Master of the Hunt recoiled. Here, surely, was some new and dreadful anger from the God That Feeds on Trees. And the anger of a God is to be feared.

Matt held onto the stick until the burning fuse was almost at the gelegnite, then he threw it out into the cavern in a long, rising arc that carried it above the heads of the watching ghouls. There was a last sputter in the darkness at the far end of the huge chamber.

Then the explosion came.

A flash of intense light snapped in the darkness, followed by a roar so deafening it seemed to carry all other sounds before it. A shock wave rolled across the room. The cavern walls seemed to split apart, and loose rocks and heavy boulders rained down upon the shrieking ghouls. The chamber shook violently, as if in the grip of a killer earthquake.

Ghouls fell to the cavern floor, crouching low, foreheads pressed against cold stone to honor the Terrible White God and appease his wrath. Even the Master of the Hunt became a helpless, frightened animal, roaring madly as it glanced about, searching for protection from the anger of the God. Screams of agony punctuated the frenzied howling as huge boulders fell on the cowering ghouls, crushing them. A flying piece of stone caught one of the creatures in the head, splattering its brains across the altar. The dead ghoul crumpled to the altar floor, a burning torch rolling away from its lifeless hand.

Matt scooped up the torch and thrust it at Todor. "Here! Light it!" He nodded at the second dynamite stick clutched in Todor's left hand.

A tremendous crack sounded from the high ceiling of the cavern room. More loose rocks and fragments of the ruptured ceiling spilled down. Ghouls shrieked as heavy blocks of stone landed on them. One fell near the altar, tipping it slightly to one side.

"Get out of here," Todor snapped. "Take your wife. Your son. Leave!"

Matt looked at Robin's limp, unconscious body, and at Joshua, oblivious to the explosion and the chaos around him, his dark eyes staring intently into nothing.

Matt turned back to Todor, shaking his head slowly. "There's nothing left," he whispered.

"They're gone. All I can do now is avenge them." He thrust the torch at the fuse of the second stick.

Todor pulled the dynamite back from the flame, then reached up and tore the mask from his face. It was horrible to look upon. Matt sucked in his breath. Slashes made by ghouls' claws were thick with clotted blood, and the surrounding skin was a deep infected red. The glass eye was gone for good, jarred loose by the attack in the narrow stone corridor. Only a gaping black hole remained.

But Todor's one good eye, blazing almost as fiercely as a ghoul's, held Matt motionless with its intensity.

"Fool," Todor rasped at him, his deep voice trembling with rage. "Vain, arrogant fool! So secure in your false knowledge and yet so helpless, so dangerous in your crying ignorance. So deadly to those you claim to love!"

Todor stepped closer, his one eye burning into Matt's brain. "I tried once before to save you, to warn you, but you would not listen." Todor gasped for breath, his powerful frame shuddering. "Do not ignore my warning again!"

Matt saw once again, like a vision from a dream, the tall figure in black standing beside Mirror Lake, warning him to leave Black Cavern. Now Geza Todor was warning him again, trying to save his wife and son, even at the cost of sacrificing his own life here in the darkness beneath the earth. And Matt finally realized that he could have saved all of them himself so easily—if only he had tried to understand.

His eyes filled with scalding tears. He looked through them at his wife lying unconscious on the cold, rough stone of the altar and at his son, lost in the darkness, still waiting to be rescued from the horror that was Black Cavern.

He turned to Todor, choking on a sob as he saw the cruel wounds, the dark death that pressed hard on a strong, brave man.

The cavern ceiling split again with a sound like the Crack of Doom. As stones and broken fragments rained down into the room, ghouls howled in their death agonies. Huge stones crashed down onto the altar, tilting it violently sideways. Todor staggered and Matt fell to his knees.

He looked up at Todor, tears streaming down his face. "I'll go," he blurted out. "I'll go!"

36

Saved

The second explosion finished what the first had begun.

Matt was struggling up a long, low-ceilinged corridor that seemed to be ascending gradually toward the surface. His left hand gripped Joshua's right, hard enough to hurt the boy. Joshua said nothing. He stumbled along through the darkness and falling dust of the trembling corridor, his eyes blank, unseeing. Matt half-pulled, half-dragged the boy over broken rocks and fissures newly opened in the rough stone floor. With his other hand he steadied Robin's motionless nude body draped limply over his right shoulder. The extra weight slowed him down, pulling at his lungs and legs, but he kept moving forward, dragging Joshua, balancing Robin, his only thought escape.

The second explosion came then.

And the real cave-in began.

The corridor started collapsing in upon itself like a deflating inner tube, stones rattling down onto Matt's naked back. He knelt and covered Robin's body with his own, then reached out for Joshua and pulled him in underneath. The rain of loose stones intensified and through them he saw a faint glimmer of light ahead.

Another fucking torch, he thought, but then he realized that no torch could withstand the dust and rocks of the cave-in. The light was coming from somewhere else.

From the surface.

Matt moved. A heavy rock bounced off his shoulder, numbing it, and another struck the back of his neck. He almost lost consciousness. With a last, desperate effort of pure will, he staggered to his feet and dragged his wife and son through the downpour of falling stones, through the choking dust, the roar of the crumbling cavern thundering in his ears like the final destruction of civilization itself.

Until they came into the light.

They were inside a narrow fissure, about four feet wide, filled with loose rocks and debris and choking, strangling dust. They coughed, gasping for air. Outside in the corridor, the cave-in continued with a deafening roar, but inside the fissure they were safe. The light that had guided Matt to safety was barely visible now, a dim shaft filtering down through the fissure from some unknown opening hundreds of feet above. It would have been invisible to anyone not groping blindly in the eternal night of cave darkness.

Slowly, very slowly, like insects crawling across a heap of broken stones, they began to move toward the surface. Joshua, gripped firmly in Matt's left hand, climbed on his own, but Robin still had to be carried. Behind them the roar of the cave-in gradually subsided. Once the fissure trembled violently beneath them, and Matt's heart stopped as he waited for the narrow passageway to collapse on them. But the trembling passed, and they continued their slow, tedious climb to the surface.

The light grew stronger as they neared the top. Beams of sunlight lanced down into the darkness, and they could smell fresh air and hear the sound of the moving wind. The nearness of the surface gave new energy to weary limbs. Even Joshua seemed to climb faster. Robin stirred restlessly in Matt's grasp. He pushed forward, slipping on loose stones, his heart almost bursting with eagerness.

The way out was a narrow hole partially filled with rocks. Matt cleared them from below, one by one, his arms shaking with excitement. Joshua was the first one out. Then came Robin's unconscious body, pushed from below by Matt and pulled from above by Joshua. Then Matt himself reached the surface, shivering as the cold mountain wind blew over his naked body and squinting into brilliant sunlight that burned like a white fire in the dark blue morning sky.

Matt rested on his hands and knees, sucking in great lungsful of clear mountain air. Then he raised his cracking voice in a loud cry of triumph. "We're out," he shouted, his voice shattering into distant echoes. "We made it!"

"Right on," Joshua yelled, his voice bright, piercing, full of life.

Startled, Matt turned around and saw that his

son had returned to him.

The wind blew Joshua's reddish brown hair. His skin was pale, smears of drying blood bearing horrible witness to the hell through which he had passed down below, but his eyes were dark brown and alive, sparkling with a youthful joy and energy that brought tears flooding into Matt's own eyes.

"Josh . . ." Matt reached out hesitantly for his son. "Scout . . ."

"Dad!" Joshua threw himself into his father's arms. "Oh, Dad . . ." His voice broke off in a sob as he buried his head in his father's chest.

Matt held his son, the two of them motionless, as the cold mountain wind blew over them and the hot morning sun burned down with the fierce brightness of a primitive sun shining down on a naked hunter and his young son at the very beginning of time.

Matt lifted his tear-streaked face and looked over the harsh, rock-bound wilderness that surrounded them, the dark green of the forest blurred in the distance below like the indistinct hope of new life waiting to be born.

"Dad . . ." Joshua sobbed again, trembling in his father's arms. "Dad, I love you . . . I love you so much." He was crying helplessly now, the tears wet against Matt's chest.

"I love you too, Josh," Matt whispered. He had not said it often before. On a few occasions, he had said it when he hadn't meant it very much, but he meant it now. God, how I mean it, he thought, hugging his son close to him.

Suddenly Joshua pushed away from his father. He turned his back to him, naked shoulders trembling.

"Josh?" Matt moved toward him.

"No!" Joshua turned around, his face a mask of agony, tears running down his cheeks. "It's not the same anymore. You can't love me! I killed her!" He sobbed brokenly. "I killed Katie!"

Matt said quietly, "It wasn't your fault, scout."

"It *was* my fault. I killed her!"

"You didn't do it on—"

"I did too! I wanted to kill her!" He was screaming now, face red, eyes terrified. "I was hungry and I killed her and I ate her!"

Matt's heart contracted in his chest. "Joshua, it wasn't your fault."

"Whose fault was it?"

"Mine."

The simplicity of the answer stopped Joshua in mid-scream, and he stood there, mouth hanging open.

"The whole damn thing's my fault. All of it. If I'd listened to you . . . about what you saw that night . . ."

"You listened," Joshua said quietly.

"No." Matt shook his head. "If I'd really listened, I would've understood. If I'd listened to Katie or your Mom . . . or that man down there who died helping us get out." The tears came to Matt's eyes again, but somehow it was easier, admitting it like this to his son. It did not lessen the guilt, but it was easier. "It's my fault Katie's dead." His voice caught, and he swallowed. "My fault and nobody else's. Understand? It's important that you understand that, Josh."

Joshua looked up at his father, squinting against the bright sunlight.

"Do you understand?"

"Yeah," Joshua said, "I guess so."

"Good." Matt nodded slowly. "That's very good."

Joshua's face tightened with alarm. "Mom!" His voice quivered. "Mom!"

Robin crouched low on the rock ledge, arms hugged tight against her naked breasts, hair blowing coarsely in the wind, matted with blood. Her eyes, unfocused, glared out angrily at the hot, bright midmorning world.

"Mom, you okay?" Joshua started for her.

Matt pulled him back harshly. "Your Mom's not okay." His voice was unsteady. "But she's going to be okay. Understand?"

"Yes, sir." Joshua shrank back.

Matt Brenner walked slowly toward his wife. As he drew near, Robin backed away, keeping low to the ground, gravel scraping beneath her bare feet. He reached out for her. She jumped back, eyes flashing wildly, arms still clutched to her breasts.

"Robin . . ."

She said nothing, just crouched there, glaring at him.

A chill crawled up Matt's spine. What now? he wondered. Do I get him back just to lose her?

"Robin, baby . . ." He reached out and laid a gentle hand on her shoulder. Her flesh quivered at the touch, and she glared fiercely at him.

"It's going to be okay." He spoke softly, slowly. "Everything's going to be okay. What's happened is . . . over. I'm . . . sorry." He took a deep breath. "I'm very, very sorry. But it's . . . over. All gone. It won't ever come back again. Everything's going to be all right. I promise. Trust me."

Robin stared at him and said nothing.

"We have each other," Matt persisted. "We still have Josh. We can start again. It's not like we have nothing."

"Nothing," Robin repeated in a hoarse, broken voice. Her angry eyes softened slightly and began to fill with tears. "Nothing . . ."

"No!" He reached out and took her in his arms. "I love you!" He crushed her naked body against his until he could feel her heart beating like a muffled, distant drum. "I love you!"

The tears burned down his face as he held her under the primitive sun, but it was not like holding Joshua. There was no response, no returning of love. There was nothing. He hugged her even harder, his eyes shut tight, tears squeezing out beneath closed lids, so he would not have to look into her angry, unforgiving eyes as they stared at him.

Joshua, with the natural resilience of childhood, was recovering rapidly from his ordeal beneath the earth. He felt warm and happy in the bright sun. Even the wind felt good, cool instead of cold as it blew over him. The air was sharp and clear, and he could see for a million miles in every direction. The mountains towered above him, the green forests and meadows washing away from their feet. Snow capped the distant peaks. Fleecy white clouds drifted lazily across a deep blue sky. His Dad wasn't mad at him anymore, even after Katie . . .

The tears came again, rolling down his cheeks. He really missed Katie. She could be a real airhead, but he still missed her. And he knew, somehow, that he would always miss her. No matter how old he got or how far away these things might seem one day, some part of him, deep inside, would always miss her.

And that made him cry even harder.

When the crying stopped, he was still thinking about Katie. He wiped his nose, snuffling loudly. He noticed the different colored rocks at his feet—gray, white, reddish orange, black, speckled, like bits and pieces of broken dishes. He knew Katie would be interested in something like that. Probably start pickin' em up and stuffin' 'em in some ol' bag, he thought, and then it'd get too heavy and she'd make me carry it.

He began picking up rocks. Comparing colors, shapes and sizes, he discarded most of them, keeping only the perfect ones, the ones Katie would have wanted. He was moving across the rock ledge systematically when he noticed an especially interesting specimen. Shiny black, as though cut from dark glass, it was resting on top of a disorderly heap of stones. Joshua moved toward it quickly. He shifted the rocks he had already gathered to his left hand and reached out with his right, bending low over the rock pile.

His fingers curled around the shiny black stone, feeling its cold, flat smoothness.

As he started to lift it up, he saw the pile of stones shift slightly.

A huge malformed claw burst from beneath the stones, catching his own hand in a crushing, vice-like grip.

The Master of the Hunt rose from beneath the rubble like a corpse from a hastily dug grave. Half its face was torn away, exposing ligaments and muscles twitching in a bloody mass. One burning white eye remained in the shattered head, staring straight at Joshua.

You cannot escape me. You are mine!

Joshua opened his mouth and screamed. It rang out against the stone flank of the mountainside. Joshua tried to wrench his hand loose from the Master, but the wounded ghoul held on to it with a death grip.

When Matt saw the giant ghoul rising from the rock pile he thought, Impossible! The thing's fucking dead and buried under a thousand fucking tons of rock!

Then he heard Joshua screaming.

"No!" Matt roared in a frenzied, half-human voice.

He lunged forward like a drunken man, like a runner in a dream, arms flapping wildly, feet weighted with lead. The distance between himself and the ghoul seemed to stretch out into infinity, but still he kept running.

He was almost there when the monster turned.

Still holding Joshua in one huge claw, the creature struck out with the other so fast Matt did not see it move. He only felt the shock of impact that knocked him hurtling through the air. He crashed down on his back, scraping off skin as he flipped over backwards several times before coming to a stop. He started to get to his feet.

The pain hit him like a blowtorch flame. The huge claw had laid open his chest. Flayed skin hung in ribbons, and blood flowed over his stomach and down his legs. But he stumbled to his feet and lurched toward the ghoul. He knew he would not be conscious long, not losing blood like this.

He stopped to pick up a small boulder, about the size of a bowling ball but twice as heavy. He staggered forward with it. The giant ghoul had turned its attention back to Joshua. The creature tore a piece of red, shredded flesh from its own ruined face and held the dripping meat out to Joshua, who turned his head away, struggling vainly in the monster's grip. The ghoul pushed the bloody flesh against the boy's closed mouth.

With a half-mad bellow Matt brought the boulder down with all his strength against the back of the ghoul's skull.

There was the soft, sickening crunch of collapsing bone structure. The boulder bounced off the creature's head and rolled down its back to the rock ledge. A howl of rage burst from its throat. The monster released Joshua's hand from its grip and turned to Matt in a killing frenzy.

Matt was vaguely aware of Robin screaming behind him and Joshua shouting somewhere out in front, but all his attention was fixed on the narrow space separating himself from the wounded ghoul as they stood squared off, facing each other like primitive warriors in a single combat to the death.

Everything leads to this, Matt thought with a strange, numbed clarity.

The monster snarled, bloody slaver stringing from its gaping mouth. Several fangs had been shattered by falling rocks from the cave-in and by the long, half-blind crawl to the top, guided only by animal instinct and a dark, primordial hatred.

Matt's vision blurred suddenly, then cleared.

The monster raised its powerful arms, razor-sharp claws poised for attack. Matt steadied himself.

The ghoul howled in fury and clawed at the back of its neck like a man trying to swat a stinging hornet. Joshua had climbed up onto the monster's back and was hacking away at the crushed skull with the shiny black rock.

"Josh!" Matt screamed, his voice thick with horror. "No!"

Matt rushed in close to the giant ghoul, striking at its genitals with his bare hands. The monster brushed him away like a fly, and Matt fell hard on the rock ledge. The bright sun flashed red before his eyes.

You are mine! Obey me!

"I'm not yours!" Joshua cried, striking savagely at the back of the ghoul's skull with the sharp black rock. "I hate you!"

You are mine! Forever.

"I hate you!"

In a wild frenzy the monster whirled around and around like a dog tormented by wasps, grabbing for the boy at the back of its neck. One of the turns brought it perilously close to the edge of the rock ledge.

"Joshua!" Matt staggered to his feet. "Let go!"

The monster teetered on the edge, swaying dangerously, arms pinwheeling to regain its balance.

Robin rushed up beside Matt, her eyes wild with fear. "Joshua!" she shrieked hoarsely.

"Josh!" Matt screamed. "Jump!"

With a hideous cry of terror, the Master of the Hunt pitched backward and over the side of the rock ledge.

Matt leaped forward, clutching desperately for anything to hold on to, grabbing for his boy, his life.

"Joshua!" he howled deliriously.

He grabbed a handful of blood-splattered hair which ripped loose from the ghoul's shattered skull.

Joshua reached out toward his father, arms flailing helplessly.

Matt's own arms extended out over the abyss, grasping for his son.

"No!" Robin screamed madly. "No!"

They dropped into the chasm—the monstrous, deformed gray body, covered with blood, and the small, pale child's body clinging to its back.

Robin drew a rasping breath. "Noooo!"

As they fell, the two bodies disengaged from each other, dropping slowly, silently, like flowers into a stream.

Matt leaned out over the abyss. He closed his outstretched hand into a fist until the knuckles went white and the nails drew blood.

Robin fell to her knees, howling down into the chasm like an animal. "Joshuaaaaaaa!"

Only the echoes returned.

Epilogue: The Return

They came down from the mountain. Kemmering House had burned to the ground, the fire destroying the meadow up to the edge of the stream. The caretaker's cottage stood untouched. They found clothes and rags to bind Matt's wounds and the black cat Katie had found. Its fur and whiskers had been badly singed. It crouched in a corner of the cottage, back arched, hissing at them.

Gordon MacLeish's Cherokee was still parked in the circular gravel driveway, the keys hanging from the ignition.

They left Black Cavern. Matt Brenner spoke to his wife, but she did not answer. They drove in silence. He thought that if they could make it down to the valley in time, they would be all right. They could start over, make a new beginning. They could learn from the past. Then his chest started to burn and he stopped thinking about anything except driving the Cherokee safely down the steep mountain road to the valley below.

Robin was thinking of nothing, but deep inside, beyond the pain of her violation, the emptiness of her loss, she felt something. The stirring of new life. She knew it would continue to grow until it became full, finished Life. Then, when the appointed time came, it would reach out to enfold more Life, all Life, within its own Life.

She smiled.

And for the first time, in a long time, she was happy.